ASHLING

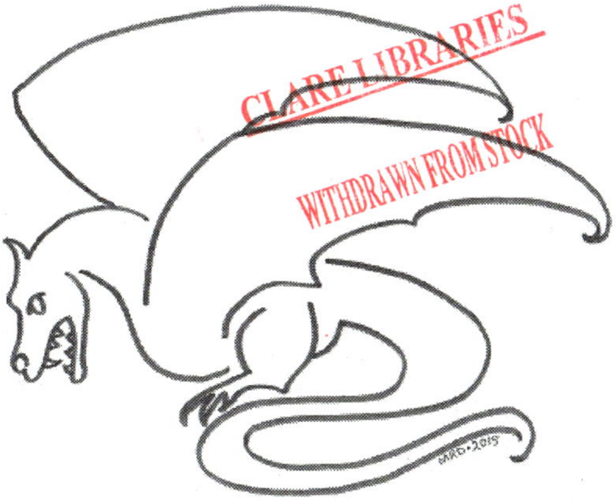

by MARY MACK™

Copyrights, Credits, & Disclaimers

This is a work of fiction in which fictional characters have fictional interactions with some real-life institutions and organizations. This story does not necessarily represent the views, traditions, opinions, beliefs, policies, or procedures of any public or private institution, organization, corporation, entity, or person, including the author.
Any resemblance to any person, alive or dead, is purely coincidental.

If you purchased this book without a cover, you should be aware that it was probably stolen. That's because the cover art is amazing and is without a doubt hanging in somebody's private collection.

Author Photo by Martin Dunne.
Edited and formatted by Mary DeSantis.
Maps and wyvern sketch by Mary DeSantis.
Cover design by http://**DeSantisDeSign**.squarespace.com
Art elements courtesy of DreamsTime, 1001Fonts, and Print Prefect Fonts Deluxe.
Printed by CreateSpace, a division of Amazon.com.

Library of Congress Control Number: 2017901640

School of Hard Knocks Publishing™
PO Box 402636, Hesperia,
California 92340-2636, U.S.A.

ISBN-13: 978-0692761168
ISBN-10: 0692761160

This story is dedicated to

THE

WORD

without whom nothing was made
that has been made.

Acknowledgements

I owe a debt of gratitude to my parents
—John and Teresa McCormack—
for teaching me my first words
and for shaping me right.

Thanks are due to my children
—Joy, Rea, Melchizedek, and Jemma—
for believing in this story,
providing honest and constructive feedback,
and encouraging me to write my dream.

I tip my hat to fellow members of the
High Desert branch of the California Writers Club
who critiqued my manuscript,
introduced me to self-publishing,
taught me about marketing,
urged me on,
and led by example.

Prologue

As I write this account of the Danaan Land War and the events that robbed our tribe of a homeland for the span of a generation, the bellicose sons of Milidh the Traveller are fighting tooth and nail over which clan rules the prettiest corner of Ir Land. Our planet is safe for the time being: the gods have been banished to Hades, Earth's crust has stopped heaving, and dragons are on the wane. But our young ones have lost sight of the tremendous sacrifices that ushered in this era of peace and plenty. Without a common enemy to unite them, they waste precious life in petty quarrel.

Few are left who remember those turbulent years when our tribe was almost annihilated. Perhaps my words will survive the entropy of time and serve to warn and guide those who follow—be they Human, Elf, or otherwise.

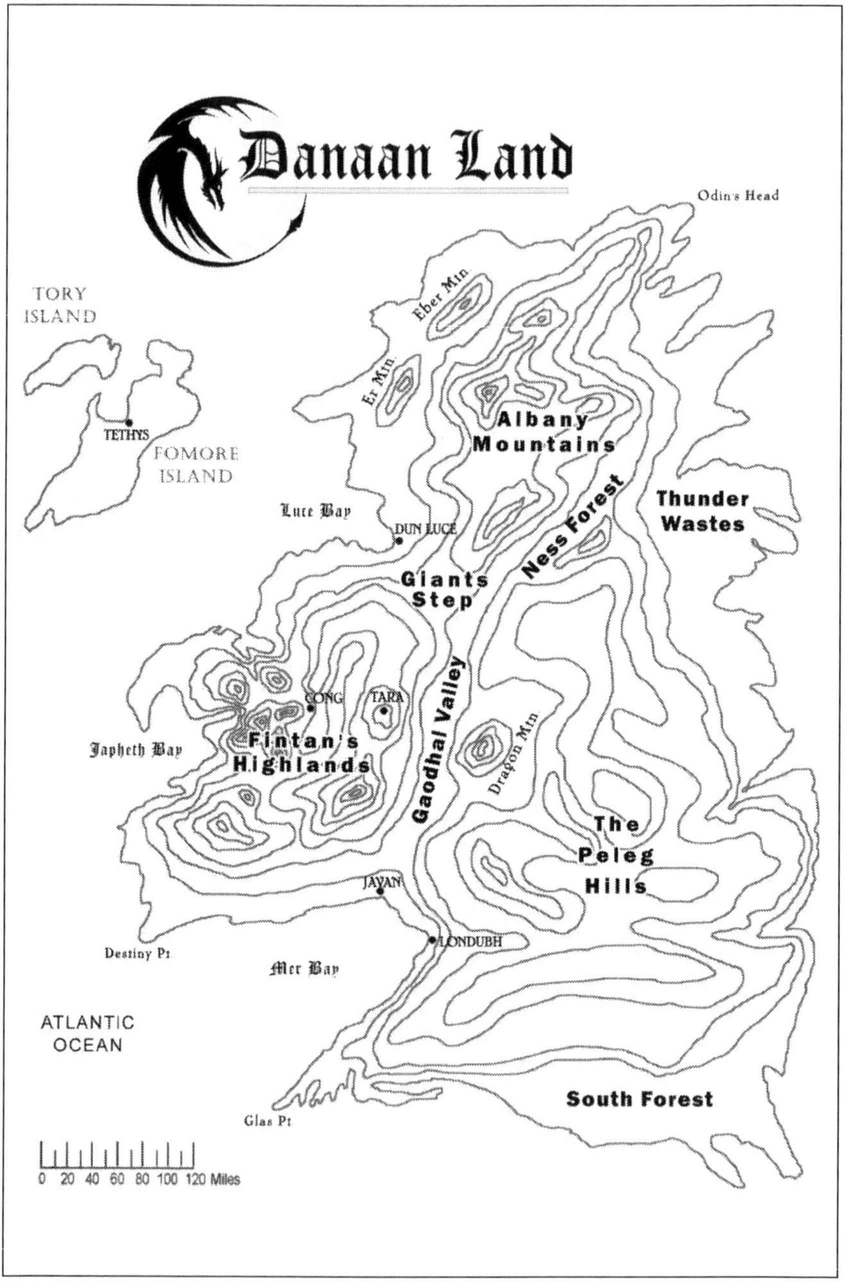

Map of Danaan Land

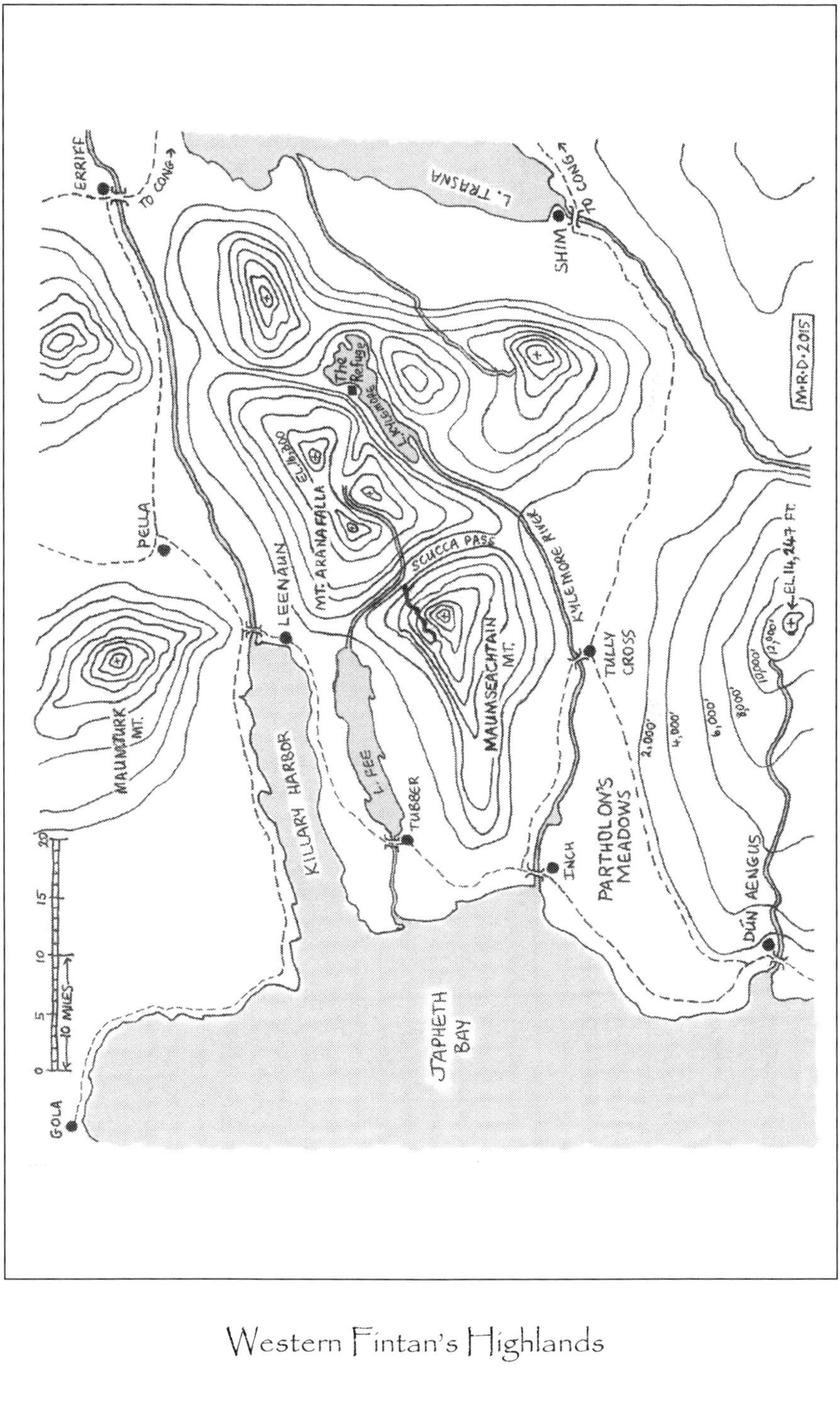

Western Fintan's Highlands

Chapter 1

"Yes, I am a woman. Don't hold that against me," I fumed at Coach Griffin while a pair of his alpha males tussled in the ring and splattered sweat around the steaming, stinking, Mixed Martial Arts dojo.

"Ashling, my dear girl," grated Griffin as he towered over my petite, five-foot frame. "It goes against my principles to partner you with a man."

"That's chauvinism talking, not principles," I retorted.

"Women don't get dragged around by their hair anymore," said Griffin, shaking his head with obvious regret. "Society demands that we treat you differently nowadays."

"By treating me 'differently' you are in effect discriminating against me," I pointed out, my voice approaching the shrill zone.

Griffin just stood there, gloating at me from behind stubbly jowls and bleached-out, missed-his-chance eyes. My skin crawled as Coach's goons scuttled into position behind me like a swarm of snickering beetles, ready to defend Griffin against the danger I presented. As they closed in I could smell the dried urine that stained Gary O'Grady's underwear, the sour cream odor from Frank Mangan's armpits, the petrol on Denny Coughlan's sneakers, and the cheap cologne and garlic that were Tony DeSoto's calling cards.

Coach's eyes flicked behind me briefly and I knew from his grin that O'Grady was putting on his effeminate act. He was probably tottering about on tiptoes as though wearing stilettos, tossing a non-existent mane of hair over his shoulder, swinging his hips, and splaying his fingers as though drying nail polish. At six foot seven and weighing eighteen stone, O'Grady thought he was too much of a He Man to ever be mistaken for anything but a man's man, yet his act was *very* good—too real to be far from the truth. While O'Grady preened behind my back, his mates got a good laugh out of my abasement.

I swung the gym bag off my shoulder and plonked it onto the floor. I was now irate.

"I'm trying to protect you," Griffin blundered ahead. "If I pit you against a man, you could get hurt."

"I can protect myself," I said in exasperation. "All you have to do is treat me equally."

The laughter behind me told me that O'Grady was illustrating my words as best he could. Meanwhile, Coach was tiring of the argument.

"Let me put it in financial terms: if I let you fight a man in my dojo, my insurance would be cancelled."

"So, you're actually protecting yourself," I translated.

"That's right," he said, thinking that he had finally put an end to the debate.

The focus of my outrage shifted to this new sin.

My eyebrows arched in disbelief as I switched tack.

"Is sexual discrimination *really* written into your insurance contract? 'Cos I know a civil rights lawyer—"

"It's not discrimination, little lady," snapped Griffin with angry sarcasm. "It's chivalry." He spat the word.

"Chivalry?" I yelled. "That's just a code word for femicide!"

Coach knit his brows. Clearly, he had never run across that word before. Sensing his hero's rapidly approaching demise under an avalanche of big words, O'Grady grabbed me from behind, pinned my arms to my sides, squeezed hard, and lifted me off the ground.

"I'll liberate her, Coach," said the big oaf.

His pals laughed hysterically... except O'Grady wasn't joking. The attack was unexpected and I was completely taken off guard, which was the only reason O'Grady was able to get so far with me. I struggled fiercely, which made all the lads laugh, but I was completely helpless in the grasp of the young giant. He tightened his arms around my chest like a cooper's apprentice, and my lungs started to compress. This close to him the smell of urine was overpowering. I didn't know which would make me pass out first—the lack of oxygen or the excess of ammonia.

My anger changed to panic and I'm ashamed to say that I began thrashing about in mindless desperation. I could not draw a breath. My cells began to close down in preparation for complete system failure. All my skills fled in the face of this fear. The sounds of the gym faded, replaced by dull pounding in my ears as my slowing heart tried to warn me of its distress. My face turned blue and my eyes bulged, and I faced death alone in the midst of that mob.

Then Coach tapped out for me and pulled the two of us apart. O'Grady dropped me in distaste and shoved me hard when my feet hit the floor. I staggered against Coach and braced myself against him for a split second; then I spun ferociously to dismantle O'Grady. I was still heaving for oxygen, but my face was wild like a cornered wolf. I hit that filthy, cowardly bully like a tornado, and ensured with my first kick that he would be speaking in a falsetto for a while… perhaps permanently.

O'Grady's pals jumped to his defense, but Griffin ordered us all to back down. The only thing that stopped me that evening was the years of strict discipline and unquestioning obedience to a Sensei's commands. I backed away and picked up my gym bag without taking my eyes off those louts. O'Grady was curled up on the floor, moaning, but the other three were oozing revenge. Coach Griffin pulled me away and forced me to walk with him to the door of the dojo.

The other gym activities were suspended and all eyes darted between me and the giant on the floor. The alphas inside the ring banished me with hoots of derision. My ears burned and my resentment burned hotter still.

Undeterred by what had just occurred, I made a final, frustrated appeal to Griffin.

"Coach, I need a tougher training regimen. How am I going to improve if I am not challenged beyond my skill level?"

"You're out of your league here, Ashling. You saw what just happened. Go on home, now, like a good girl. The Women's Workout is on Wednesday."

He opened the door and pushed me outside

without ceremony. Then he slammed the door shut behind me and I could hear a bolt sliding home on the other side. Several male voices raised a victorious cheer within.

I had relatively few goals in life, but the obstacles I encountered seemed disproportionately excruciating compared to the simplicity of my dreams. I mean, I didn't expect instant success, but any kind of progress would have been welcome. I had reached a plateau in my martial arts training and I needed a better challenge than the Women's Workout on Wednesdays. Coach Griffin's treatment of me in front of the entire gym was unwarranted.

Once again, I would have to go it alone.

Tears of anger, frustration, and humiliation filled my eyes and I wiped them away in annoyance; it wouldn't do to crack my façade of stoicism. When a curious passerby looked my way, I glared, snapped my teeth, and growled aloud. The poor woman averted her eyes and picked up the pace, and I felt a twinge of guilt; it hadn't been her fault and her curiosity was probably motivated by kindness; but I didn't need pity.

I threw the gym bag over my shoulder and strode diagonally across the busy street.

I never once looked back.

Chapter 2

Professor Carlyle was in rare form during his Ancient History of the British Isles lecture the following morning. He paced restlessly in front of the amphitheater full of students, alternately waving his battered copy of *Beowulf* in the air to punctuate a random point and then clutching it possessively to his argyle sweater. I waited in fascination for one of the loose pages to separate from its tenuous hold on the binding during one of the more violent shakings, but like the old professor, the book had a tenacity for life far stronger than its outward appearance suggested.

"There are striking similarities between the mythologies of our planet's varied cultures," the old boy was ranting. "Globally repeated themes imply a single source." He paused dramatically and clutched his bible to his chest with thin, white fingers while scouring the lecture hall for non-believers. His let out both his words and his suspended breath all in one go. "Allow yourselves to be disturbed by that."

Carlyle swapped his *Beowulf* for a stack of tests on his desk and handed them out to students in the front row. As they passed the tests back, the old man droned on, "Historians are detectives. We analyze evidence…"

Sitting in the second row, I shuffled through the pile until I recognized my epistle, and passed the stack back before noticing the big red 'D'. I gasped audibly, then blushed to the ears in a mixture of shame, anger, and shock.

A snooty girl who didn't have to work three jobs to put food on her table because she lived with Mummy and Daddy in a big house in Salthill and had her own car and her pick of boyfriends, leaned forward and berated me with a stage whisper, "Go back to your tent, Tinker!"

Her best-friend-cum-lackey seconded that emotion without any attempt at whispering, "Yeah, hit the road!"

A burst of laughter died quickly as Professor Carlyle bristled and shot the discriminators a warning glare. My blush deepened, but I set my jaw and tilted my chin.

Then the old man pointed at me. "Miss MacGillycuddy. My office. After class."

I looked at him in outrage. "That's unfair! I didn't say anything!"

He stared back sternly, blinking rapidly behind a pair of spectacles that reflected glare from the overhead lights.

I bit my lip, shoved the stupid test into my backpack, and scowled at the floor for the remainder of the class.

While Carlyle prepared tea for two in his cluttered, book-ridden office, I sat tensely on the wooden arm of a saggy leather armchair, hugging my backpack tightly and prepared to state my case.

"I studied hard for this test, Professor. I didn't deserve to fail."

"Your work exhibits a disdain for the past," he explained as the electric kettle came to a boil and snapped itself off. He poured water into two cups that were balanced precariously on the edge of a counter alongside sliding stacks of manila folders.

"Disdain?" I wasn't expecting this sort of feedback. I felt my whole face scrunch up in puzzlement.

"You are inflexible. Judgmental. I want you to explore the past with enthusiasm. With an open mind."

Oh, no. Here we go again, I thought. *The old man's 'look beyond what you see' lecture.* "I don't understand, sir. Facts are facts. I memorize them. Right? Isn't that what students do?"

Carlyle was spooning sugar into his cup and got carried away. "Yes, learn the facts. Then explore the possibilities," he said enthusiastically. I watched in amazement as six, seven, eight spoonfuls went in, one after the other.

"What possibilities?" I asked, more to distract him from the sugar than because I really cared. Big mistake. The old man launched into his favorite topic. But at least he stopped adding sugar. Now he swirled the spoon vigorously, creating a whirlpool inside his cup. The teabag string wrapped around the spoon until the teabag was reined in. I watched in awe as the edge of the vortex climbed higher and higher, but Carlyle was unaware. His eyes adopted a faraway look.

"Nobody alive today really knows what happened that far back in Ireland's past. We examine the clues from inside our tired old box, and we reach conclusions that may or may not be right." The tempest in the cup splashed over the rim and onto his thumb, and Carlyle looked down in surprise. He took out the spoon-and-teabag combo and threw it into the trashcan. No doubt he'd be searching for that spoon later, because it was silver and looked expensive. Probably part of a set that he had been gradually throwing away by accident over the years. He opened a mini fridge that was buried beneath a pile of books, and took out a carton of milk.

As he poured, I quizzed, "You mean you don't know what you're teaching us?"

That solicited a hearty laugh from Carlyle. "You've found me out! I'm a fraud. I haven't a bull's clue what happened prior to written records." He continued chuckling as he left the milk on the counter and put the cup of tea into the fridge.

"So, anything goes?" I asked.

The old man handed me the second cup, greatly satisfied with himself. "Your guess is as good as mine," he announced with a grin. He picked up the milk carton and drank from it. I winced. This was too much. If he habitually drank directly out of the milk carton, then the stuff he offered me was probably contaminated with old-man germs and God knows what else. I glanced into my cup, but it only contained boiling water. He hadn't even put a teabag into it! Unbelievable.

"So, if I invent an interesting story to fill in the blanks, I'll get an A?" I continued.

"Treat the evidence seriously. Assume that our ancestors were at least as smart as we are." He wiped milk from his lips with his shirt sleeve.

"So—make assumptions."

"No. Cast aside your presuppositions. Think outside the box."

"Pretend. Fabricate."

Carlyle was becoming increasingly animated. "Keep an open mind. Imagine."

"Imagine what?"

"What the world might have been like if the ancient myths and legends were actual historical accounts—not just fantasy or allegory."

"Wow," I said with complete disdain, but it was lost on the old man.

"Wow, exactly! We arrogantly believe that we are the pinnacle of evolution..." He held up the milk carton to illustrate. "...but we weren't there, so we don't know what it was like."

I sighed deeply, frowning at the patterned carpet. Carlyle suddenly noticed the milk carton in his hand and returned it to the fridge.

"Is there any way I can raise my grade, sir?"

Carlyle closed the fridge door. He had retrieved his cup of tea. "As a matter of fact, there is," he said with a happy smile. He walked to his desk, sipping his tea, and picked up his tattered copy of *Beowulf*. He held it high and gave it a shake.

I groaned, knowing full well what was coming next.

"An essay," he pronounced.

Chapter 3

While studying at the library the next day, I couldn't concentrate on my research. My meeting with SUSI Grants Awarding Authority the following week loomed ahead like the Spanish Inquisition. Just that week—a mere two months shy of graduating with a Bachelor of Arts in Ancient History—the Administration Office at the university had sent me a letter asking for written evidence of my birth.

Personnel in the various institutions I had been processed through down all the years had always accepted my physical presence as proof that I had, indeed, once been born; but not the soulless computer system at the National University of Ireland. There was a gap in the data and I would not receive my degree unless it was filled. The killer was that my SUSI grants depended upon my citizenship, and I was being called upon to verify my eligibility. I agonized over the forthcoming review. I'd had it tough in the past, but this situation raised the bar. Four years of hard work and study were about to be cancelled, and the future I had planned for myself was in real jeopardy. My dreams were evaporating before my eyes.

I had emails backing up in my inbox, sent by scholarship sponsors demanding to know if their investments were going to be realized. I had made employment commitments to my primary sponsor, pending my degree. They were all threatening me with legal action for absconding with their funds, and asking me how I intended to repay the money I had spent during my four years at NUI.

The inquest into my birth certificate had cut me adrift in a weird sea of disconnect. I belonged to neither the settled nor Travelling communities, but I was Irish and nobody could take that away from me—or so I thought. Now that my identity was in question it was as though my very presence on Earth was being erased.

Ever since childhood I had walked the fence between the Travellers and the settled. My father was a Traveller. Bangor Óg had been hired by a wealthy landowner because of his gift with problem horses, but was not considered good enough to associate with the boss's daughter. When she married Bangor for love, her father disowned her and ordered her out of his sight.

The Travelling People welcomed Debra into their tribe. After a few years had passed, Debra grew lonely for the settled ways and desired their child to grow up surrounded by the benefits of civilization. Out of love for his wife, Bangor Óg gave up the nomadic life he had been born to and settled in a town.

His tribe could not accept his rejection of the ancient ways, and no longer recognized him as one of their own. It was a violent separation: Bangor's best friends gave him a brutal going-away party that left him with broken bones and internal bleeding. The greatest tragedy was that Debra's tribe didn't want her back either.

I was only two years old at the time. Since schools didn't accept 'Tinkers', my mother taught me at home. I remember her sadness, her lack of belonging, and the sense of inferiority it wrought. But I also remember the rakish tilt of my father's cap and the way he walked proudly and knew his own worth. We had each other; it was the three of us against the world—and then both my parents were killed in a car crash when I was only seven. Things were rough for me after that and I had to toughen up to survive.

On my own and ostracized by both sides, I had neither traditions nor cultural ties to bind me. Free to choose my own direction in life, I always inclined towards the non-traditional. My passions were hang gliding, archery, sailing, fencing, and martial arts. There again I was thrown into a world of stereotype and discrimination, but I was well used to that challenge. I survived the bigotry and loneliness of my childhood and decided to brave a university education. By the time I was ready to graduate, fighting was part of living for me. I never knew a time when I could draw a breath on equal terms with another.

Perhaps it was my lack of place in the present that caused me to study the past. My courses at NUI Galway comforted me with the knowledge that the people of Ireland shared common beginnings. We are a nation formed of violence, invasions, and the constant intermingling of races, and I knew that I fit in there somewhere—a product of the turmoil of the past. Shared roots meant that I didn't need anyone's permission to belong.

Until now.

There was only one road to redemption: the computers would accept a Proof of Citizenship form in lieu of a birth certificate. It had to be filled out and signed by a civil servant who had personal knowledge of me since infancy. Well, that ruled out all the orphanages and foster homes I had shuttled between since I was seven. My only option was to take myself to the Travellers' Winter Camp to see if any of them remembered me.

Another student at my table kept stealing glances across the top of his textbook. I was staring at a spot on a shelf behind the idiot, and didn't even register his presence, but he caught my dreamy gaze and assumed that he was the cause of my sighs. When his sickly smile and adoring eyes solidified out of the fog of my distrait, I was mortified. I snapped back to the here and now and ducked back into my work. I could feel his eyes upon me for several more minutes.

"Fascinating, isn't it?" he ventured bravely.

I looked up quizzically. "What is?"

"Whatever you're studying."

"How would you know?"

"You are totally engrossed."

"Yeah, well, I'm monomaniacal, so that's no indicator of my interest in a subject."

"I'm researching the coat of arms of every branch of the House of Windsor."

"Yikes." I felt sorry for him.

"You're in my Ancient History of the British Isles class." He blushed at his audacity.

"Oh?" *Great. A stalker.*

"Yeah," he continued. "I... I'm doing my

dissertation on the British monarchy."

"Huh." I couldn't have been less interested, but he assumed my monosyllabic response meant I was shy, and he decided I needed social interaction.

"What's yours on?" he coaxed.

"Mythological Creatures as Allegory in Early Historical Accounts," I said with a challenging ring to my voice.

Jeepers! The way he reacted, you'd have thought I was planning to steal the Crown Jewels.

"Do… do… do you think you should?" he sputtered. "I mean, you… you know how Carlyle goes on about, 'We weren't there, so we don't know.'" He pushed his glasses higher up his nose in agitation. "He might fail you."

"I'm doing it *because* Carlyle is so idiotic about it. Besides, I've found tons of documentation to support my thesis."

"He only wants us to keep an open mind."

"Look," I said, getting heated up. "We have evidence that dinosaurs roamed the Earth. We have proof that humongous, bird-like pterodactyls once dominated the skies. What we *don't* have is fossil evidence of dragons, unicorns, griffins, centaurs, etcetera. Not even Carlyle's precious—and *very* creepy—grendels."

"Well, maybe you can swing it if you take that perspective. Yeah." He appeared to be analyzing the pros and cons inside his head. Then something occurred to him and he made a snuffle-snort noise that was supposed to be a chuckle.

"You know what's funny?" He waited for my answer, but I just gave him an off-putting frown. Only he wasn't put off in the slightest.

"Your surname is MacGillycuddy."

"So?" I said in a voice that would have been warning enough to a being of higher intelligence.

"Well, n-no. That's not funny, of… of course," he stammered. "B-but actually, someone way back in your family tree believed in dragons enough to incorporate one into the MacGillycuddy coat of arms." His shoulders shook in a lame attempt to control his nerdy laughter. He rummaged through the stacks of books in front of him and pulled out one titled *Irish Families,* by Edward MacLysaght. He flicked through the pages until he pounced on the one he wanted. Spinning the book around on the table top, he stood up and pushed the book towards me, tapping an illustration of a golden dragon on a red shield.

My heart lurched at the sight of it.

"That's a wyvern," he said. "A two-legged dragon. Wicked, eh?"

I couldn't respond. My blood was stirring at the cellular level. I was connecting in a visceral way with the image in front of me. I had never before seen my family coat of arms, and yet—somehow—I recognized it. The young man cleared his throat and I snapped out of my trance. I reached for the book. Dust sprinkled golden in the shaft of sunlight that warmed the red cloth binding of the old volume. The yellowed pages exuded must and cobwebs and wooden shelves.

"Did they fly?" I asked.

"Well, to quote Professor Carlyle, 'I wasn't there to see it myself'," he said, "but that's probably what the wings were for." Then he started off with that snorkeling laughter again.

I read the caption next to the picture and then took out my Smartphone. I selected the camera app and positioned the phone for a picture. I noticed him watching with what seemed to be a nervous air of possessiveness, so I asked, "Is this all right?"

"Verily, m'lady," he replied, bowing low. He meant it to be a grand gesture, but his arm swept a stack of books onto the floor, and he slammed his forehead onto the table with a loud crack.

I barely noticed the epic crash when the books hit the floor, so engrossed was I in examining the details of my golden dragon. If he needed any more proof that I was monomaniacal, there it was.

He picked up another stack of books and muttered something about reshelving them, then left in an awful hurry.

Chapter 4

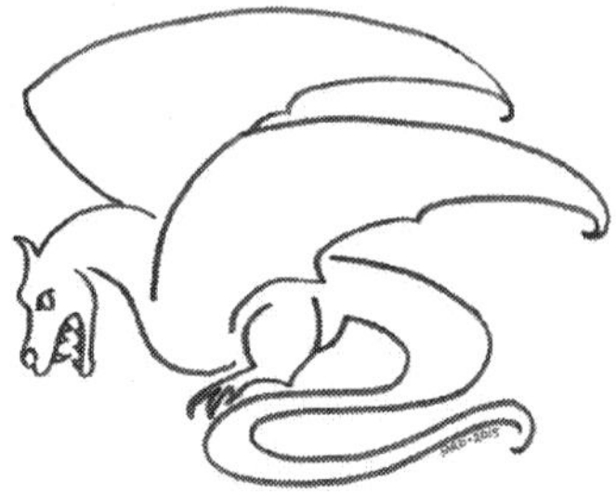

That afternoon I breezed into the flat I shared with Caroline Keane, art major extraordinaire. She was gathered in the living room with a bunch of her bible study friends, so I ignored them and betook myself to my room. I didn't mean to slam the door as hard as I did, but it felt really good. I could never stand the holier-than-thou way those biddies talked about me. I wasn't the biblical version of womanhood that they all strove to be. I wasn't meek or submissive. A woman should have higher goals in life than to be a good wife and mother. You wouldn't catch me dead searching for a man to provide my daily bread, and I certainly didn't believe that husbands should rule their wives. If there was a God, I had never seen him. I wasn't sitting around waiting for any deity to reveal my purpose in life. Anything I achieved in life was going to be through my own efforts—no God was going to get the credit. The only Holy Trinity I believed in was Me, Myself, and I.

Yeah, there was no love lost between me and Caroline's bible study group.

My room was large enough to swing a cat in. A

narrow bed was jammed up against one wall, sharing space with a walk-in wardrobe; the connecting wall sported a desk and chest of drawers; and the remaining wall space was taken up by a generous window, a floor-to-ceiling bookcase, a display of assorted weapons, and my folded hang-glider kit behind the door.

I set my laptop on the desk and plugged it in, then busied myself with searching online for women's self-defense videos. I found one hosted by a tiny slip of a woman named Primrose Prendergast, who taught me more in half an hour about extricating oneself from the death grip of a man twice one's size than Coach Griffin had taught me in two years of MMA training.

"At close quarters, a giant's skill won't harm you," said Ms. Prendergast on her video, "but his size and brute strength might. What you lack in size, you must make up for with technique." And she proceeded to trounce her six-foot-eight training partner.

When the bible thumpers were gone, Caroline tapped on my door. I was in the middle of an advanced kata with a Japanese bokken, putting the wooden training sword through a complex series of attack-and-defend movements.

"Just a moment!" I yelled. I finished my routine and brought my sword to rest. After performing the traditional bow, I returned the bokken to its wall mount above my recurve bow and quiver of arrows, before calling out to Caroline, "Enter only if you have streaks of paint on your earlobes and clay under your fingernails!"

Caroline came in and went straight over to my

mirror and studied her ears closely. "Oh, no!" she moaned, rubbing fiercely. "That's been there all day! I had oil painting this morning." Then she examined under her nails and looked at me with a new respect. "Lord, Ashling, you have excellent eyesight. How did you see all that while passing through the flat?"

"I didn't," I said smugly. "It's an example of my superior intellect, Sherlock Holmes style. I knew you had oil painting this morning and that you *adore* that cute French professor, Monsieur L'Amour—"

"Monsieur Laroche, silly," interrupted Caroline with a giggle. Her left hand unconsciously started pulling on her earlobe.

I pointed to her ear and exclaimed, "Aha!"

"What?" she asked, puzzled.

"Whenever you get nervous you pull your ears."

"No I don't." She put her hands behind her back. "Well, then, smarty pants. How did you know I had clay under my fingernails?"

"Elementary, my dear Caroline. Your last class today was sculpture. You had to rush home to prepare for your bible study and you probably didn't have any time to dig the clay out."

Caroline just shook her head and smiled. "The world needs more people like you, Ashling."

"Will you put that in writing? Better yet, why don't you come with me next week and testify before the SUSI Review Board?"

"What review board?"

"Look at this." I plopped into the desk chair and opened an email from the university's Administration Office. "I have to produce a birth cert by next week or the uni will cancel my degree. Because of that, the SUSI

Grants Authority wants an explanation." I pushed away from the desk and executed a few crazy spins in the swivel chair.

Caroline speed read the message and straightened with an angry gesture. "That's ridiculous! You've only got a few weeks to go. Why wait until now?"

"I don't have a birth cert."

"They knew that when you signed up—four years ago." Her voice sizzled with scorn.

"Their computer system has a data gap. They can't process my degree until I prove I exist."

I stood up, got a pair of nunchaku from a hook, and began a spirited kata. Caroline hopped up on the desk and tucked her knees under her chin to avoid getting clunked by my swinging nunchucks, even though that would never happen; I had complete control over my weapon at all times.

"Would they accept a photograph?" she asked.

Her humor was usually uplifting, but failed to raise a smile on this occasion.

"They want a number. Something official," I explained without pausing my nunchaku routine.

"But you were born on the side of the road," she mused, then quipped wittily, "Did you happen to get a license plate?"

"They'll accept a Proof of Citizenship form."

"Send that in, then."

"It must be filled out by a civil servant who has personal knowledge of me since birth."

"So—the foster care system?"

"I didn't enter that 'til I was seven."

"Oh, right."

"I suppose I could go to the King of the Tinkers."

"Is there really such a thing?"

"Well, they call themselves Travellers these days."

"Shouldn't *you*?"

"I'm not a Traveller anymore."

"How can you say that?"

"That choice was made for me. They cut my Dad off when he settled. There was a lot of bad feeling."

"So, tell me about the King of the Travellers." She emphasized the word Travellers for my benefit.

"He wins and retains his title through bare-knuckle fighting."

"You're kidding."

"Travellers are not like everybody else." I emphasized the word Travellers to show her I'd learned my lesson.

"But is he a civil servant?"

"He's not very civil at all."

"If his title is legit, he should serve your purpose."

"The Irish Traveller Movement claims him as their official leader."

"You don't sound impressed."

"Tall Peadar Ward was my father's best friend."

"But…"

I finished my kata and performed an elaborate curtsy in place of the traditional Japanese bow; then straightened up, grumbling, "He's no Prince Charming."

I hung up my nunchucks and began searching through my chest of drawers for a change of clothes. "I hate having to grovel to that lout," I told Caroline bitterly. "He's never worked a day in his life. I've slaved for this degree, and it galls me that I have to ask him for permission to graduate."

"This will all work out, Ashling. Nobody's insane

enough in this day and age to withhold your degree for lack of a birth certificate. It would be discriminatory. The Irish Traveller Movement would have a field day in court."

"Yeah, but I can't prove I'm a Tink—" Caroline glared at me. "—Traveller, unless Peadar Ward condescends to fill out this form."

"It's an unusual situation, to say the least."

"I don't exist."

"I could adopt you."

I laughed at that. "More paperwork to fill out!" I held up two different tops and Caroline pointed to one. I dumped the other one back and hip-checked the drawer.

"It's not fair," complained Caroline. "You've worked harder than anyone I know. The rest of us have the normal struggles of a working student, but you've had to contend with discrimination and social ostracism on top of all that. I wouldn't like to fight the giants you face every day, but you have handled yourself like a champion."

I couldn't answer. I was overcome by her words. To cover my uncharacteristic emotional reaction and regain my composure, I bent over and pulled up the quilt to search under my bed for a pair of shoes. Nobody had ever seen me cry, and it wasn't about to happen now.

Caroline's eyes were drawn to a box of canned food under the bed. She sighed and shook her head. "Are you still hoarding food?" she asked softly.

"Those are just emergency supplies," I answered defensively and snapped the quilt back into place.

"Okay," she said. "I understand."

Her attention riveted to a picture on my desk and I was glad of the diversion. "What's this?" she queried, moving a book aside and picking up the printout.

"That's my family coat of arms," I said. "I was going to ask if you could paint this dragon in gold on my hang glider." I pointed to the red glider that was taking up one corner of the room.

"Oh, that would look stunning! Yeah, I can do that, no problem."

I grinned with delight. A ray of sunlight was peeking through the clouds.

Chapter 5

"Hitchhiking isn't safe anymore in Ireland!" Caroline yelled after me when I left the next day. Maybe not, but I didn't have a car, it was too far to cycle, and buses don't run on Sundays.

I knew I would be picked up within minutes of sticking out my thumb. The scruff of the open road and countless campfires had been scrubbed off my skin years before, and my dark-red tresses were no longer wind-tangled. I styled my hair in a pixie cut that enhanced my elfin features and showcased my chocolate-colored eyes. My figure was petite and fine boned, yet generously curved where it mattered, so I quickly found a man to drive me far out of his way despite the lashing rain and the late hour.

When the Winter Camp was within walking distance, my lusty knight parked his dinky car and lunged for me across the gear stick, but a stiff-fingered jab to his eyes deflated any romantic plans he may have had. And when I slammed his head against the dashboard and his nose cartilage gave way, he was fully convinced of his mistake. But I chose to think of him in a good light and thanked him politely for chauffeuring me to my destination.

I got out of the car, but leaned back in for a final piece of advice. "You should be more careful," I admonished him. "Hitchhiking isn't safe anymore in Ireland."

If my errant knight's vision had not been clouded by tears and pain, he would have been glad I put paid to his unknightly plans, for the murky shapes of four riders now loomed through the sheeting rain. They were the outriders who patrolled the Winter Camp on their piebald steeds. Travellers live by time-honored rules of behavior and they would have taught my chauffeur a more memorable lesson than I for violating a woman's virtue.

I slammed the car door and started toward the lane that led into the mountains. The Traveller outriders pushed their horses into my path and I stopped. Squinting through the rain, I could make out several tall, long-haired, lanky youths with black plastic bags draped over their clothes. Their horses were not saddled. The only outward appearance of control over the beasts was a simple halter and reins combination made of rope.

"Where d'ya think you're going, *lackeen*?" asked one of the guards pleasantly enough.

"*Grālta,*" I answered demurely. "My business is with Tall Peadar Ward."

That surprised them. They didn't expect an outsider to know the Tinkers Cant. They muttered to one another in Gammon before addressing me again.

"And what business would that be?" pressed the youth in English.

"Oh! Mr. Ward, is it?" I asked, feigning surprise

and delight. "*Slum dorahōg*! What on Earth is the great King of the Travellers doing patrolling the *sridag* on a night like this?"

"I am not Peadar Ward," snapped the young man, and his friends glowered.

"Then don't invite yourself into his business."

He stiffened in anger and his eyes narrowed. "*Gadjes* have no business with Peadar Ward. *Crush* back into that tin can of a *lawk,* and *hie* back to your own *cradgie*."

At that very moment, my knight in the tin can regained his vision and turned the car around with a great splashing of mud. His car took off and disappeared around a bend. I turned and looked at the outriders with a smug expression that said, 'I can't leave now'.

"Makes no difference to me, ya brazen hussy. Go on, now! Off wi'cha!" shouted the angry rider.

"I claim the *Minceir* blood right to *toiree* with the king on a matter of great importance," I staunchly replied.

"And which *fean's* moniker do ya carry?" growled another rider.

"That of Bangor Óg na gCapall."

They regarded me in silence. This mention of the legendary horse trainer and healer carried great weight. I stood as patiently as did their horses. The rain danced staccato on the black plastic bags, the horses steamed and smelled of warm hay, and the lads and I exchanged mutual distrust.

Suddenly and simultaneously, without any outward sign of communication between them, the four riders kicked their horses. One spun and galloped up the lane, two surged to flank me, and the fourth reached an arm down to pull me up behind him.

The whole camp was out to see the *gadje* visitor. Fifty or more caravans dotted the meadow haphazardly, in no apparent order, though I knew each family was positioned according to rank and importance. In the center of this hodge-podge of tents and trailers, rubbish tips and clothes lines, stood the king's own caravan—a huge, modern affair that belied the apparent poverty of the man himself. The Travelling People lavished their wealth upon Peadar Ward as befitted a king.

I slid off the massive piebald stallion and regained *terra firma*. The rain crackled on the galvanized caravans like rashers thrown onto a hot pan. The people stood aside and opened a muddy path before me. The crowd was silent except for the crazed muttering of a wickedly wizened old woman wrapped in shawls, who trembled violently when I passed her.

I was ushered inside the king's chambers and instinctively recoiled from the smell. Boiled haddock and Beyoncé's latest *Eau de Quelque Chose* were powerful fumigants when combined. My reaction wasn't missed by the three scowling women who bedecked the interior like gaudy costume jewelry. Something about the way they perched on stools, waiting to strike, was so reminiscent of the witches of Macbeth that I furtively glanced around for their bubbling cauldron. I felt battered by their evil intentions.

Tall Peadar Ward was dressed in rags like a Traveller of old, despite his opulent surroundings and the modern conveniences inside his ultra-luxurious caravan. He glanced my way as though not expecting a visitor, and sighed with annoyance. He didn't turn off the television, however. He kept his feet up on a hassock and pretended to watch the telly.

"*Slum dorahōg*, Mr. Ward," I began hesitantly. "I am the daughter of Bangor Óg—"

"I know of no such *fean, byohr*," interrupted Ward, without taking his eyes off the television.

I was taken aback by his rudeness. I wasn't off to a good start. "He's dead, sir," I explained, knowing full well he already knew that. "He was killed in a car accident fifteen years ago."

I waited for him to engage me in conversation, but I couldn't compete with Sky TV. Well, I hadn't been kicked out yet, so I continued. "I've been studying history at NUI these past four years," I said, trying to sound confident and not at all desperate, "and I'll be getting my degree in June. But first I need to have this Proof of Citizenship form filled out."

Not a twinge of response from Ward. I paused for a polite interval… then plunged in again. "It must be filled out by someone in authority who can testify to my birth and who knows my family."

No response. I cleared my throat and plowed ahead, feeling the ice crackling beneath my trepidant feet. "Mr. Ward, I am here to ask you to fill out my Proof of Citizenship form so I can get my degree in June."

I hated that I needed his bloody signature. I had worked hard for my degree without a smidgen of help from anyone, and every bit of the credit was my own. Yet I had to grovel before this slovenly gobshite who had never worked a day in his life, and beg his permission to graduate.

Ward clicked off the television and got to his feet. He strode across the caravan until he was close enough to bless me with his stale, unwashed-Traveller smell. I backed up to the door and could retreat no further. He towered over me and pinned me in place with steely-grey eyes. One of the massive fists that had won him his crown in countless bare-knuckle brawls that spanned twenty years and the length and breadth of Ireland, was positioned threateningly in front of my face. A Churchill-cigar-sized finger jabbed the turned-up tip of my nose. Speaking slowly and heavily as to a brainless clod, Tall Peadar exhaled CO_2 into my airspace and I was able to identify at least four ingredients of his most recent meal.

"You are not a citizen of the Travellin' People," rasped the smoke-choked Galway brogue. "When your *gathra* chose to settle with the *gadje*s, he decided your citizenship for ya… *gradum*."

"But I was born *before* he settled!" My temper was rising with my bile.

"I know you not. You are not one of the *Lucht Siúil*. Be gone wi'cha."

So saying, Tall Peadar opened the door of his caravan and shoved me out into the rain. I heard his womenfolk cackling before the door shut off the sound. I stumbled awkwardly down the steps and felt a gentle hand on my elbow, balancing me. I turned and beheld the wrinkled, toothless smile of the crazy old woman who had trembled to see me earlier.

"Get out of my way!" I said. I was furious, but her gentle face suspended my warlike response. She returned my crazed expression with a winsome smile.

Her eyes glazed over and she began to rock in small, hypnotic circles. A stream of unintelligible words poured from her mouth in what sounded like a chant, or poetic recitation. It was very similar to the Old Shelta dialect which hadn't been spoken by the Travellers in several hundred years. My second-year project at NUI had been to compare the linguistic roots of Romani and Shelta, an ancient language that had been kept alive by the Travellers since pre-Celtic times. In this woman's monologue, I recognized the word *manyath,* meaning 'heaven', and the words for 'fly' and 'daughter'.

I tried to pull away from her, but her grasp was surprisingly strong. She held my arms firmly with both hands. A middle-aged woman sloshed up to us through the mud and scolded the old woman fiercely. She pried us apart and jolted the crone back to consciousness.

"What's she saying?" I asked.

"Nothing at all," said the middle-aged woman. "Come in out of the rain, Mam." But the old hag shrugged her daughter off. She grabbed my hands in hers and looked deep into my eyes. With a shocking sense of being exposed and vulnerable, our souls leaped to meet one another. There was a strong flame burning deep inside of her that threatened to consume my own spirit. She gloated at what she saw in me, as though a truth had been confirmed. She switched to a mixture of English and Gammon, the modern Shelta dialect.

"Fly!" whispered the old woman in a conspiratorial tone. "Fly, Daughter of Cain! Cross the heavens on your golden dragon. Sound the death knell for the enemies of our people. *Stafa tapa hu*!" She broke into peals of ancient laughter and a delicious shiver ran all over me. Goosebumps made the hair on my arms and scalp stand upright.

What the hell?

The old woman finally gave in to her daughter's will and allowed herself to be dragged away.

"My father's name is Bangor, not Cain," I called half-heartedly after them; but I was alone in the rain, and nobody heard.

The soothsayer's words reverberated inside me forever. Crazy as it sounds, I believe that her words vibrated their way into my DNA and established permanent residence there, as though they had wandered the Universe for eons in search of their origins, and found both their source and fulfillment in me.

From that day on, I was filled with restlessness; an insatiable thirst for something unknown to me.

Chapter 6

After my SUSI review the following week, I stormed into the flat like a murderous squall. Right away, Caroline knew something was terribly wrong. She turned away from her easel and propped her paintbrush on a palette.

"Ashling?" she asked. She wiped her hands on a rag and followed me into my bedroom.

I slammed my backpack onto the desk and collapsed into the swivel chair. Caroline stood in the doorway, waiting. Her kindness—and the fact that she was *there* for me when the rest of the world opposed me—brought me close to tears. I fought to keep my composure. After several deep breaths, I blurted out.

"Basically, if the Admissions Office denies my degree, all my scholarships and government grants will have to be refunded… *retroactively!* Not only that," I paused to swallow, "if I can't prove my citizenship, I will have to pay back all my tuition fees at the non-EU rate."

Caroline gasped and clapped a hand over her mouth. She came all the way in and sat on the bed, pulling nervously on one ear and staining it dreadfully.

"That's thirty-eight *thousand* euros, Caroline!" I fairly screamed. "Plus the entire cost of my student exchange in Romania last year. They mentioned things like breach of trust, fiduciary responsibility, failure to disclose, blah, blah, blah…" I kicked my feet savagely against the desk and spun the chair in dizzying circles.

"They can't blame you for not having a birth certificate!" she cried in outrage.

I stopped spinning and looked all around my tiny bedroom as though saying goodbye to everything. "They can and they do," I said with a sigh.

"What are you going to do about it?" she asked.

I didn't answer immediately. The enormity of my situation had me by the throat. What *could* I do? Then all of a sudden I pounced upon a plan of action that would bring peace to my soul and provide me with time to think. "I'm going hang gliding," I resolved. I sprang to my feet and pulled a long-sleeved neoprene shirt and a pair of yoga pants from a drawer.

"You know what I mean, Ashling," Caroline reprimanded. "What's the next step?"

I grinned at my only friend in the whole world and placed a reassuring hand on her shoulder. "I'll figure that out once I've loosed the fearful shackles of Earth's constraining gravity," I joked.

Caroline couldn't help but laugh. "Go on with you, then," she said. "If the answer is in the heavens, you'll not find it on Earth."

"Wow, Caroline!" I exclaimed in admiration. "That was really poetic."

"It was," she agreed enthusiastically as she made a beeline for her own room. "I must go write it down before I forget it. Professor Lundy will think I'm a literary genius!"

I was still chuckling as I closed the front door behind me. I shrugged into the straps of the folded hang glider, dumped my parachute pack into the bicycle basket, and pedaled down the path.

And that was the last time Caroline and I ever saw each other.

Chapter 7

Lough Corrib was laced with whitecaps under a stiff breeze. I climbed the steep path to a broad, sloping field on top of the lakeside cliff, carrying my folded glider and beginning to doubt my decision to leave home without my windbreaker suit. Those whitecaps made me shiver just looking at them.

I squeezed to the side of the narrow path to allow a group of fellow hang-gliding enthusiasts pass on their way down.

"Blue skies!" I greeted cheerfully.

"Uh, actually, there's a weather system rolling in. We're grounding ourselves," admonished the leader of the troupe.

"Those aren't clouds—they're cotton puffs," I scoffed.

"Your funeral," came the callous response. They passed one by one, each looking at me disapprovingly as though I was an irresponsible imbecile. I rolled my eyes and blew air through my lips in annoyance.

Up top, I unfolded my glider and assembled it despite an errant breeze that pried and tugged at my wings and lines. I paused to admire Caroline's artwork. A fierce-looking wyvern in full flight covered nearly every inch of the red cloth. She must have used a whole gallon of gold paint to complete it. My soul stirred along with the lifelike movements of the dragon's wings in the breeze.

Once strapped into the harness, I balanced the bar in my hands and raced down the slope toward the edge of the cliff. Hang glider aficionados are either very brave or very stupid; I have yet to figure out which I am; perhaps a combination of both. Whatever compulsion causes us to defy gravity and sanity, and trust blindly to fate, filled me to the brim that day. Adrenaline built within me, the wind thundered past my ears, danger surged through my veins, and my blood pounded as I charged straight toward the edge of the world.

There was a cessation of all feeling at that instant when I leaped out into space. Time stood still, my breathing seemed to stop, and there was a suspended moment of absolute silence until the glider checked my descent and reconnected me with the material world. I whooped with unmitigated joy, using an exhilarating cry I had developed over the years, which was peculiar to me alone. It was the exultant ululation of a war-crazed Amazonian combined with the roar of an angry tigress and trailing off with the keening shriek of an eagle. It was a primordial expression of my spirit.

My glider caught an energetic updraft and I soared across the lake.

The view was spectacular… almost otherworldly. Reflections of the piled clouds above me appeared as gigantic mountains in the lake below. My equilibrium was affected by the vision and I felt a dizzying sense that the world was topsy-turvy. Afraid I would become disoriented by the optical illusion, I closed my eyes and turned my face into the breeze. I glided high on the thermals rising from the lake water, at peace with myself and free from the world's problems.

Overhead, the multicolored clouds began forming into a vast, convoluted, tubular structure, like a gigantic worm casting.

Something shook my craft and my eyes shot open. Had I bumped into another glider or a bird? I was enshrouded in piling, puffy, pastel-colored clouds and cut off from the world beneath. I searched, but couldn't see another soul. It must have only been a thermal that jolted my glider. No big deal.

My perusal of the clouds gave me great delight. The billowing formation became a playground to me, and I tested my skill by maneuvering the glider around and between the convoluted heaps of pink and gold cotton. Just as I was beginning to lose altitude, I spied what appeared to be a gaping tunnel entrance in the enswathing cumulus formation, directly ahead and less than a hundred feet away. With a whoop of delight, I angled my glider and zoomed into the opening.

The insides of the cloud tunnel looked surprisingly solid, with corrugated ribbing similar to clothes dryer ducting. A multitude of cotton wisps swirled around me. The twisting tunnel seemed to go on indefinitely.

At first I was unconcerned, thinking it a game. My glider fit perfectly inside the tunnel and I reveled in guiding it skillfully around each curved bend.

But then I got an eerie feeling that all was not right. The tunnel was too uniform, too continuous. No way on Earth was this a natural cloud formation. I took a closer look around me, but as soon as my concentration eased up for an instant, my wingtip glanced off the tunnel wall and jolted the craft.

What the hell? Solid walls? I worked to steady the glider, now thoroughly worried. "That's not possible," I whispered. "I'm in a cloud!"

A check of the GPS unit strapped to the bar displayed rapidly changing coordinates as though I was zipping through different time zones at a breakneck pace. The latitudinal coordinates had shifted northward of my original position, but if the longitudinal readout was to be believed, I was flying westward at great speed, in the opposite direction of the Earth's rotation.

I knew I needed to get out of this… this magnetic vortex thing… and fast! Carefully this time, I gripped the bar firmly, braced my body in the harness, and deliberately tilted the glider sideways to test the cloud. The wingtip whacked into it harder than before and the concussion shuddered through the glider. It was a real fight to right it this time, and required all my skill. I'm not ashamed to admit that I finally felt real fear.

A moaning wind sprang up behind me, pushing me faster. My speed increased the further into the tunnel I ventured, yet I couldn't slow down and couldn't get out.

The variometer—mounted on the hand bar next to the GPS device—had zeroed out, showing neither climb nor fall, but its escalating beeps warned me of excessive speed. A recheck of my GPS unit showed it churning through numbers like an unstoppable slot machine.

Every ounce of my strength and skill was now focused on keeping the glider in the center of the tunnel and steering it around each bend.

In the meantime, the air in the tube had altered perceptibly. It was purer, more vital, and my body seemed to crave it. My breathing changed. I began gulping greedy lungfuls of air. The oxygen was sucked directly into my tissues and cells and bones, and was instantaneously absorbed. I felt myself growing immensely stronger and more alive and incredibly energetic with each electrical surge of pure air.

The oxygen raced through my lungs and bloodstream until every cell in my body was saturated. The effect of this was that the cells began to function with pinpoint precision, and cell growth was facilitated and even accelerated.

Inside my brain, synapses started firing and new neural connections were created at an incredible rate. I could now analyze my situation with intense clarity. The minute mental calculations required to keep my craft balanced and on course became easy as improved brain performance finetuned my nerve and muscle responses. It was easier for me to fly the glider and make course corrections despite my incredible speed.

My eyesight improved dramatically and I could see more details about my flight than ever before. The whirring dials on my different instruments were now readable, even though the numbers were moving faster than most human eyes can register.

My altimeter needle seemed to be broken. It was acting crazily, like a compass needle does when held next to an electrical appliance; swinging first one way and then the other. I had no way of knowing my altitude.

At this point, the variometer's beeps were a continuous wail.

Then something strange happened to my body that was nothing short of terrifying. My scalp began to tingle and crawl and writhe eerily as my hair pushed through the follicles in an incredible growth spurt. I shook my head to dislodge or alleviate whatever was slithering all over my head, but my movement made the glider wobble. I chose to hold the glider steady and tolerate whatever was happening to my scalp, although my every instinct screamed to get rid of the alien sensation. The further into the tunnel I traveled and the more of this strange air I inhaled, the longer my hair sprouted, until it whipped around my face, entwined my body, and streamed out behind me.

My leg and arm muscles swelled under the synthetic fabric of my neoprene sports attire. My extremities stretched out beyond the hems and cuffs, creating the optical illusion that my clothes were shrinking.

My fingernails also begin to grow, although at a slower rate than my hair. Yet, much to my horror, they began to interfere with my grip on the bar.

Ten stretching toenails began to curl underfoot when they encountered the resistance of the enclosed space inside my footwear.

The wind became a screaming gale. The glider's hardware hummed and rattled. I visually inspected the vibrating parts in alarm, then rapidly calculated the rate of disintegration and analyzed how much longer my craft could take this abuse. Either the tunnel would end soon… or my time would expire.

A new sensation gradually encroached upon my existing fears. The air pressure inside the tunnel increased tremendously and I felt as though my skull was in a vise-grip. I shook my head a few times, careful to counterbalance my glider while doing so, but my discomfort increased and became debilitating. I was sure that my head was going to explode under the relentless, intensifying pressure. I gasped. I squeezed my eyes shut and a strangled cry escaped my lips.

I was sweating profusely and utterly panic stricken. My breathing came in jerky gulps as my lungs fought against the pressure that was forcing them shut. I was close to passing out. A last-ditch effort to survive caused my eyelids to flutter open weakly.

My vision was failing me. The tunnel was a riot of psychedelic colors. Miraculously, it had straightened out, and I thought I saw a black opening ahead. I drew on my last reserves of strength and forced myself to concentrate on steering.

The wind crescendoed to tornado force and roared like a freight train. The tunnel walls were a blur of terrifying movement. I fought to hang on, but my fingernails had loosened my grip on the bar.

"Noooo!" I wailed in despair as the pulsating life inside of me caused the keratin to multiply at incalculable speeds. My nails forced my fists open and my doom was assured. The unavoidable ultimately came to pass—my hands slipped off the bar.

Immediately, the glider glanced off one wall and slammed into the other while traveling at astronomical speed. The glider broke apart upon impact and I ricocheted all over the tunnel, screaming insanely until mercifully knocked unconscious.

Silent now—and limp as a rag doll—I was catapulted inexorably towards the ominous black hole.

Chapter 8

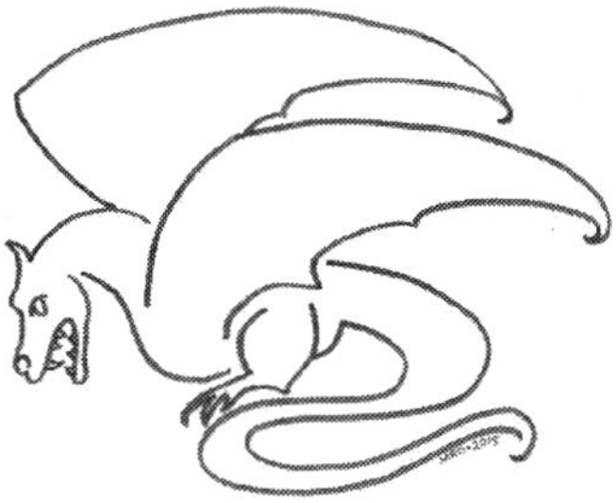

Two old women were fishing from a stone pier that jutted three score feet into Kylemore Lough. Behind them, a stone's throw from the lakeshore, a solid iron gate was set into a massive, ivy-covered stone wall. On the lintel above the gate were carved the words *An Tearmann,* which means 'The Refuge'.

In the darkness of that moonless night, the light of a smoky, whale oil lantern revealed the women's robes and head coverings to be of coarse, homemade, brown fabric. The plant fibers and animal hairs used in constructing the primitive material were visible, but the women's faces were in shadow.

The nocturnal activity of insects and small animals filled the damp air with a thrum of rustlings and whisperings. Night birds piped or cooed gently and the water chuckled playfully against the rocky shoreline and solid pier.

The old women offered occasional soft comments to one another, but were otherwise content to be.

Then a ripple—like the shadow that follows a

comet—crossed the landscape from east to west. It snuffed out all sounds of life. Animals froze in their tracks and birds took cover. The water shuddered briefly as the ripple crossed over, but then the lake surface became black and eerily still. No wind. No sounds. No movement.

The fishing lines were forgotten. The old women threw back their hoods and riveted their attention skyward. With deep foreboding, they watched as a strange tubular cloud formation unfolded out of thin air and quickly billowed into mountainous reality overhead.

"Dragon Sky," whispered Aoibh to her comrade. She was speaking an ancient tongue which bore a faint resemblance to Old Shelta.

"Dragons won't fly at night without a moon," replied Finoula.

"I don't like it. It's too quiet," opined Aoibh. She reeled in her line and started to disassemble and box her tackle.

The whistling of an invisible wind began high in the clouds above and built gradually into a tremendous roar; yet not a leaf stirred, and the surface of the lake remained glassy.

"Dragon Wind!" Aoibh's whisper was hoarse with fear. She snapped the lid of her tackle box shut and then jumped at the noise it made. She scanned the silent waters, fearful of what she may have awakened.

"Enough of your nonsense," clipped Finoula matter-of-factly. "We haven't seen a dragon around here since… since…"

"…since the last Dragon Sky," finished Aoibh hoarsely.

A high-pitched, agonized scream, epitomizing the

utmost in Human terror, suddenly emanated from the cloud. Both Aoibh and Finoula found their feet in a hurry and clutched one another.

The scream was cut off just as suddenly as it began, and a Human form rocketed out of the end of the tubular cloud and dropped like a stone to the water below.

Immediately the cloud had ejected its cargo, the roar of the wind lessened until it was no more than a whisper. The cloud formation quickly evaporated and the sky once again held only stars.

Neither Aoibh nor Finoula moved for several moments. A curlew's plaintive cry startled them out of their immobility.

"That was definitely Human," said Aoibh.

"Let's not jump to conclusions," warned Finoula.

"Well, it wasn't a dragon, that's for sure."

"We should wake the others."

But Aoibh was already untying the painter that snugged the small rowboat to the pier.

"What are you doing?" shrilled Finoula, although she knew full well. Aoibh hitched up her skirts and climbed in, then held the boat steady while Finoula tumbled in behind.

"If it's not what we think it is, we can always kill it and return it to the lake," said Aoibh. She pushed away from the pier wall and fitted the oars on their tholepins.

Finoula untied her rope belt and loosed her outer garment. A short silver sword gleamed in the starlight amongst the folds of her gown, and she clasped its hilt for reassurance.

Aoibh bent her back to the rowing.

When I was dragged ashore, unconscious, I was placed on the cold flagstone floor of a straw-strewn stable. They told me later that I was tossing and flailing at the whim of a dread fever. My clothes were drenched and my hair was hopelessly tangled around my body and limbs. I moaned and cried out, slashing at the air with wicked fingernails.

A score of wrinkled, careworn hands held me down while another pair searched through my hair to uncover my ears. Aged fingers gently traced the rounded ear tips and an elderly female voice exclaimed in excitement, "Good God! She's one of us!"

"Wait a minute. Check her eyes. She's got red hair; might have green eyes, too."

My eyelids were forced open, and a collective sigh resulted. "Brown," said Aoibh with satisfaction. "Not a hybrid."

This was followed by the murmur of many voices discussing the portent of my arrival.

"Let's trim these scythes before we bring her inside," said another.

Many hands went to work trimming my fingernails, but I was oblivious to all but the demons of my delirium. I dreamt I was being squeezed to death in the arms of a grinning giant. My ribcage was encased in iron and my brain was swollen to the point of bursting.

And—oh, God!—I hurt.

Chapter 9

When I awoke my fever was gone. I was clean and dry and very comfortable. My long hair had been braided into a thick rope to prevent me from becoming tangled in my own tresses. The weight of it prevented me from lifting my head off the pillow and seriously curtailed my efforts to look around. Every muscle in my body shrieked in protest at the slightest of movements. The ache in my ribcage forced me to take shortened breaths. Even moving my eyeballs hurt.

I couldn't remember much. My skull felt as though it had been trampled upon. The effort of thinking wasn't worth the agony. Nevertheless, a vague impression of imminent danger left me in an unsettled state of mind and I forced myself to turn my head. A groan escaped me and I regretted that, but the noise didn't bring any instant calamity down upon me, so I allowed myself to relax somewhat; yet I needed to find out where I was.

I found myself lying on a narrow cot in a small stone room with no windows and only one door; a wooden door with large cast-iron hinges, a huge keyhole, and an oversized ring pull. A candle in a niche in one wall provided little light and many dancing shadows. Everything in the room seemed to be a little on the small side, and I felt like Goldilocks in Baby Bear's bed.

Awareness gradually seeped in through my murky consciousness, and images of my headlong flight flashed upon my mind. The memory forced me up onto one elbow. *Whoa!* Was that ever a mistake. It felt like I was in command of a lump of solid iron. My rash move was punished with searing heat. It was as though molten lava had replaced my muscle tissue. I cried out loud and collapsed back onto the straw mattress, holding myself tense against the pain.

My cry brought a response from without the room. The heavy door was pushed open with barely a whisper of sound and a tiny old woman with a kindly face peered nervously in. Her blue eyes met mine and her fear morphed into concern for my wellbeing when she saw the pain written on my features. She slipped into the room and came to my bedside, speaking to me in a language which sounded familiar but was at the same time unintelligible. Her tone and manner were unmistakably kind and my fears were very much relieved. She felt my forehead with the back of her hand and smiled at the knowledge she gained from that.

She was dressed in rough, brown robes. Her head was covered with a shoulder-length nun's veil. A decorative brass strap held the mantilla in place, wrapping across her forehead and tucking behind each ear. The ears were showcased by this design, but only a glimpse of hair was revealed.

Pointing to her solar plexus, she repeated the

word 'Cáit' a few times, and from this I learned her name.

Talking gently the whole time, she removed a small leather pouch from a cavernous pocket and began applying the ointment from it onto my aching arms and neck. I was so exhausted that I fell asleep while she massaged the stiffness and pain from my battered and badly bruised body.

After two days of Cáit's tender care, I was able to sit up. The pain and stiffness were gone. I was chockfull of energy after my long bed rest and couldn't wait to get back home. Nice as she was, sweet little old Cáit was the only person I had seen during my recuperation, and I still couldn't figure out what she was saying most of the time. I needed answers—and I needed them two days ago! I wished for the millionth time that I had my Smartphone with me, but it was probably in smithereens at the bottom of Lough Corrib.

Cáit was speaking some form of Shelta; that much I had figured out. The structure was identical and many of the words were similar or shared the same roots. I was sure I could become fluent if I spent more time with her, but I had to find someone who could speak English. I needed to know where I was and I had to get word to Caroline that I was safe. She must have been out of her mind with worry when I failed to return home. The police would think I crashed into the lake. They had probably been trolling Lough Corrib since the previous day.

I couldn't believe that Cáit hadn't yet connected

the dots and linked me to the story of the missing girl that must have been all over the news. I assumed she was a hermit, living in isolation without a television or internet connection. She seemed to live very simply. There wasn't even an electrical socket in my room. So, it was up to me to make my own way back to civilization.

I sat up tentatively and my body co-operated. There was just the remnant of an ache in some of the larger muscles, and my flexibility had returned. Since my headache was gone, I decided to swing my legs over the edge of the bed. I did so very slowly, anticipating the return of the migraine, but there were no blinding flashes of pain. It appeared as though I was fully healed, despite a lingering shakiness.

I examined the coarse cloth of my simple nightgown and toyed with my bulky braid. That aspect of my whole ordeal was the only evidence that my journey through the cloud had not been a dream. Well… that and the physical agony I had endured. I pushed the plait off the bed and it tumbled to the floor.

"Wow!" I exclaimed. "It's at least five feet long!" What on Earth had caused my hair to grow like that? I could find no explanation in my limited understanding of physics and biology.

"It's going to be a pain to take care of," I muttered. Part of me was delighted by how I would look with my new hairstyle, yet the practical side of me warned how much it would curtail my activities.

Just then, Cáit arrived with a breakfast tray stacked high with oatcakes, poached eggs, rashers, sausages, fried potatoes, black and white pudding, and a mug of buttermilk. She shoved the door open with her foot and I leaped to my feet to help her. Unfortunately, help is the exact opposite of what I did.

My leg muscles acted like powerful springs and propelled me headlong across the small room. I body-slammed Cáit into the door, and the breakfast tray crashed to the floor. I ricocheted off the stunned hermit and demolished the wooden nightstand, along with the items on it. I staggered back to Cáit and tried to offer my apologies, but I wasn't finished smashing things yet. Every tiny command I gave my voluntary muscles was translated into über-action. I reached out to Cáit, but instead my arm jerked forward and I slapped her senseless! She slid to the floor, unconscious.

None but I witnessed what followed, as my stupid, masterless, alien body staggered and crashed, bounced and tripped all over that tiny room. I had absolutely no control over my limbs. I had no balance, my depth perception was messed up, and I couldn't put one foot in front of another. I was like a baby who had never walked before. What was even worse, my strength exceeded that of ten grown men. Strength without control—not a good combination.

I grabbed the thick oaken door to try to balance myself—but pulled it off its hinges! I held it easily in one hand and stared at it uncomprehendingly. I didn't want to drop it as it would have crushed Cáit, so I leaned it against the wall. But I exerted too much pressure and the door splintered into pieces. My horror mounted. I shook my head to chase away the surreal haze descending upon me.

I ultimately allowed myself to collapse onto the rush mat where I could do the least amount of damage. There I sat, next to Cáit, afraid to touch her in case I killed her. I could hear her breathing so I knew she was still alive, but I was afraid of the internal damage I may have caused. I had socked her pretty hard. I looked around at the shambles of the room and was completely bewildered by my predicament.

The pounding of feet in the corridor outside my room was followed by Aoibh and Finoula and several other elderly women of similar habit, wielding an assortment of dangerous-looking farm implements. Wide-eyed with wonder, they surveyed the damage and immediately noticed Cáit in a heap at my side. Finoula held a carving knife to my throat, but Aoibh struck it aside and admonished her something fierce.

My face told the story. Aoibh sank to the floor beside me and put her arms around me. I squeezed my eyes shut, refusing to cry even then.

They placed Cáit on my bed and a woman named Kitti examined her. After prodding gently, Kitti nodded in relief and said something to the effect that Cáit was not badly injured.

Aoibh patted and stroked my hair and murmured consolingly in a tongue I was rapidly beginning to understand. "Don't worry," she said. "You'll learn to control your new strength."

Chapter 10

Supported on either side by Aoibh and Finoula, I baby-stepped to the meeting in the refectory. Cáit led the way, encouraging me like a proud mother hen. My balance was still off kilter, and I was inclined to topple over without support.

I paused in trepidation upon the threshold and anxiously scanned the unfamiliar faces seated around the long wooden table in the low-ceilinged room. These other ladies had left me alone to recover, not wanting to overwhelm or crowd me too much. Their smiles were shy but welcoming.

Parts of my dismembered glider were displayed upon the table, and I was surprised at how much of it had survived.

One of the recluses, a regal-looking woman, stood and approached me with hands outstretched in welcome. Her smile was warm and motherly. "Welcome, Ashling," said she. I nodded, but kept my own counsel.

During my daily interactions with Cáit, Aoibh, and Finoula in the week since my arrival, I had become fluent in their language. My thoughts were like razorblades after the cell growth I had undergone, and the intricacies of language were very easily processed. It helped that I had studied Shelta as part of my university coursework.

"My name is Bróna," the matriarch continued, and held up her right hand.

Bróna was the leader of this tiny commune. I returned her greeting and showed her the palm of my right hand, as I had been taught by Cáit. I hadn't a clue why they preferred this form of greeting instead of handshakes; perhaps they were germophobic.

Cáit seated me at the table's head and all eyes were focused on my countenance. I counted twenty-one of them—all women, and all in the latter stages of life. I was head and shoulders taller than any of them.

There was a hush of breathless expectation in the room. All my hostesses were poised on the edge, awaiting the tale about to be unfurled. And I, for my part, was getting set to say goodbye. I wasn't going to wait another hour. They hadn't even known the word 'telephone' when I had asked them! Now *that's* isolation. I figured I could walk with the aid of a stout cane to balance me, and I was sure civilization couldn't be more than ten miles away in any direction.

I was now wearing the same getup as the women I thought were nuns. The coarse fabric scratched my skin unmercifully. My hair had been cleverly braided by Cáit and Aoibh, and was folded back upon itself so it fitted neatly out of sight underneath my mantilla. The ornamental brass clasp held the headpiece securely in place, and although I couldn't wait to rip it off around the first bend on the long road out of here, I had to admit that shade of brown emphasized my eyes to perfection and nicely complemented my skin tone.

"Would you like to begin?" queried Bróna.

I nodded and cleared my throat. I had already prepared my story, never imagining that any of them would understand what I had been through (*I* certainly didn't), and not wishing to be burned as a witch, or whatever their simplistic religion would dictate as punishment for someone who dallied in the type of magic that catches people up in whirlwinds, messes with their growth hormones, and tosses them out in a different part of the country.

"I was hang gliding over the lake and fell in," was my abbreviated explanation.

They stared at me in silence. Bróna frowned and shot a sharp look at Cáit. Obviously, they needed more information.

"I was out hang gliding when a storm caught me unawares," I offered. "My glider was tossed around and I lost control."

Bróna glared at me and shifted impatiently in her chair. "Child," she said, "I understand your caution, but you are amongst friends here. Your secret is safe with us."

All the women nodded and smiled, murmuring their affirmation. Now it was I who was wide-eyed.

Bróna launched into more detail. "Long decades ago, after the Fall, when menfolk on Earth were corrupted by the Fallen Ones and became dissatisfied with the power and skills that were the birthright of women, our small company came under attack. Not just from the Tuatha Dé, but from mankind as well." A few low rumbles accompanied this reminiscence. "My sisters and I fled to this remote inland valley and built this refuge with our own hands. So, you see, my dear girl, we have waged war against the very creatures you live in mortal fear of."

I just looked dumbly at her. She made no sense. I began to grasp that I may have been rescued by a group of people in an insane asylum.

Bróna could see I wasn't convinced. She became bolder and voiced the unmentionable in a conspiratorial tone: "You flew on the Dragon Wind."

Again, that sense of suspended breathing around the table. As for me, an inkling of the depth of trouble I was in started gnawing at the pit of my stomach. I was thinking about weird witch cults and savage sacrifices under a blood moon. My face must have registered a smudge of that stomach-acid taste, because Bróna smiled and patted my knee.

"No Human has ever flown on the Dragon Wind," she said with great excitement. "How did you do it? What was it like?"

I looked at the eager faces around the table and shook my head in frustration. "I don't know what you're talking about," I said. "I have no idea what happened to me, or how my hair grew so long. All I want is to go home."

So saying, I stood up and maneuvered away from the table. All the ladies got to their feet as well, with looks of concern and doubt on their faces. Bróna reached out to stop me, but I shook her hand off my arm.

"I appreciate your hospitality," I told her stiffly, "but I really need to get back home and let people know I'm all right. They must be worried sick about me, but you have made no attempt to contact them. So, I'll be off now."

I dragged the chair with me for support and balance, but had only gone a few steps before Cáit intercepted me. Her black eye was fading to yellow. I frowned at her, not wanting to have to get rough with her again, but she looked at me with deep concern and compassion.

"Ashling," she said with a long sigh. "You can't go home the same way. That was a one-way portal."

"What do you mean?" I snapped, growing defensive, expecting them to attack at any minute and carve me up for their next sun-worship ceremony. Their insanity terrified me. I had heard that crazy people could be super strong, and there were twenty-one of them…

"Your clothing and speech convinced us you were from another world," said Aoibh. "Another dimension. Possibly even another time."

I blinked my eyes and shook my head. I totally rejected her words.

"Of course, you are free to leave at any time," Bróna hastily assured me, "but it would be wiser if you stayed with us until you have learned more about our world."

Bróna was a very wise woman. She knew the guarantee of freedom would allay my immediate fears and allow me to listen to what they had to say. They had hoped I could explain to them how I—a mere mortal—had unlocked the closely guarded secret of quantum travel. They hadn't expected me to be so completely clueless about my journey. Now Bróna realized it would be a lot for me to take in. There was much explaining to be done. She indicated that the ladies should back off and give me space. They reseated themselves.

I turned the chair around and flopped onto it. I

mentally reviewed the things that had happened to me and reached the grudging conclusion that I might receive more information from these ladies than I had to offer myself. What had I to lose by listening? I straightened and looked around at their kindly expressions. What I had taken for the light of insanity in their eyes might just as easily be the spark of intelligence.

"All right," I sighed in temporary capitulation. "Enlighten me."

Chapter 11

"Our planet is Terra," began Bróna. "We live in Danaan Land, which is a northwesterly drifting section of Pangaeden. It has been three hundred years since Partholon of Greece founded this colony." She paused and looked at me for any stirring of recognition, but my eyes had glazed over, so she continued.

"It is the Year of Adam Thirty Forty-Six, twelve hundred years after the Dispersal of Nations." She halted again and scrutinized me. "Is any of this ringing a bell?" she asked.

"The phrase 'ringing a bell' rings a bell," I joked lamely. I was completely out of my depth in these uncharted waters.

"Where are you from?" she coaxed.

I burst out laughing at the incongruity of my situation. It was better than crying. They watched me solemnly, so I wrestled my laughter into submission.

"Okay, fine," I finally said. "I'll play along. Terra… okay, that's Earth. And I've heard of Pangaea. That was the huge supercontinent at the beginning of the world. It split up and the different landmasses drifted apart." The women looked excited. They were hanging onto my every word, waiting for some kind of revelation. "I am also from this planet, but I live in the year Twenty Fifteen."

The women broke into excited chatter around the table.

"Why, the crust was still heaving back then!"

"She probably knew our tribe's great forefather, Shem! He didn't die until Twenty-One Forty-Eight!"

"Perhaps she knew Noah!"

"Noah died in Nineteen Ninety-Six. She would have been a little girl."

They hushed in awe and turned back to me with a new kind of respect.

Bróna questioned me further. "What continent was your tribe drifting on?"

I looked at her with penetrating focus, my eyes mere slits, trying to read her mind. "Aahh… we weren't drifting anywhere." I answered. "We were stationary."

"Impossible," said Bróna tersely. "We haven't stopped yet."

"That whole Pangaea thing happened *millions* of years ago," I explained.

There was complete silence. Bróna's face was a study. She sputtered a bit as she tried to find words. "You're from millions of years in the *future*?" she asked in amazement.

"I doubt it," I said. "Millions of years ago, Humans were still evolving, but you look fairly well advanced."

"Evolving from what?" she asked, perplexed.

"Apes," I answered confidently.

You could have heard a mouse sneeze. After a long, awkward silence, an old biddy named Maddy snorted. That started a ripple of laughter which Bróna shushed with a stern rap on the table top and a fierce glare. Then she turned to me.

"Pay no attention to them," she advised. "When you say Twenty Fifteen, when exactly do you mean?"

"Twenty Fifteen A.D.," I clarified. *"Anno Domini.* The Year of Our Lord."

"What lord?" Bróna asked.

"Aahh… that would have been Jesus Christ. We number our years from the time of his birth." I couldn't believe they had me talking like this. I'd probably be asking them to take me to their leader next.

"What global events are happening, to give us a rough timeframe?"

"Well, Ireland is part of the European Union." I paused for effect. Not a glimmer of recognition.

"People have flown to the moon and walked on its surface." That should have shocked them if they were truly a Stone Age tribe hidden in the Connemara Mountains, but they accepted this news with a thrill, not with disbelief or surprise.

"I have so many questions for you!" Bróna exclaimed. "Obviously, Humans have been able to learn the secret of quantum travel from the Tuatha Dé. How did that come about? Did we defeat them in battle?"

Once again, I was at a loss. "Quantum travel? No, it was rocket power. Werner Von Braun."

Now it was their turn to be puzzled. I felt as though we were playing a game of table tennis, slinging surprises back and forth.

"The manner of travel is unimportant," said

Bróna. "What we would like to know is exactly when and how you learned the secret from the gods."

"You're all pulling my leg, aren't you?" I said in great annoyance. My eyes darted to places where cameras might be hidden. "I bet I've been shanghaied. This is a whacked-out Reality TV show, isn't it? Or maybe it's some extreme field lab experiment Carlyle is subjecting me to." Once again, I got blank stares and mystified looks.

"Nobody's tugging on you, Ashling," said Cáit apologetically. "We aren't experimenting on you at all."

"You flew through a portal from your world to ours," encouraged Aoibh, "and we just want to know how you did it. The gods do it all the time, but they guard their secret very closely."

"The gods?" I asked sarcastically.

"Yes. Don't you have gods in your world?" asked Bróna.

"No!" I exclaimed in disgust. When a gasp of delight tore around the room, I amended my statement by saying, "Well, some people believe in gods of various sorts. Others believe there is only one God, but I'm agnostic."

"Oh, dear," said Bróna. "We haven't made ourselves clear. There *is* only one God. The 'gods' we are referring to are only the Fallen Angels. Not only did they appear glorious to us Humans in our humble state here on Terra, but they insisted that people worship them as gods. Many people in other tribes do worship them, and live in fear of them, but here in Danaan Land the descendants of Gaodhal Glas choose to worship the one true God—the one who created us and who calls us his children."

"And we have suffered at the hands of the gods for our stubborn loyalty to God our Father," said Finoula bitterly. The other women nodded in sober agreement.

"That you don't know this is very encouraging," said Bróna with enthusiasm. "It means that at some point in time the gods have little or no influence at all. We won't trouble you with that, my dear. But please do try to explain how you came through the portal."

I shrugged and sighed. "I don't know. I was flying and I entered the tunnel and I have no idea where it came from or why it opened when it did."

"How could you travel on the Dragon Wind and not know what you were doing?" asked Aoibh. "The Hub is always guarded. Your passage would have been denied."

"I told you, it was an accident. Believe me when I say I did *not* intend to do that. I was *this close* to getting my degree in Ancient History…" I nearly choked when I realized what I was saying. It seemed that *I* was now Ancient History. "Birth certificate or not, they can't withhold my degree now!" I squawked, and then I had to cut a crazed laugh short so as not to alarm the old ladies.

"Dear, you're rambling," said Bróna impatiently. "Focus, please. Did you, or did you not have help from the Tuatha Dé?"

"Tuatha Dé?"

"Yes. The God People. You know… the Elves."

"Elves?!" I fairly screamed. "Elves are just myths. What sort of daydream are you people living in, anyhow?"

The ladies all looked at one another with a hopeful sort of disbelief. This time, the silence was elongated as they pondered a world without Elves. To their way of thinking, since I didn't know what Elves or gods were, there mustn't be any in the world or time period that I came from.

"Perhaps she's from a parallel dimension," Cáit suggested, "with different tribes, different continents, and a different history."

"Curse the Lucifer Laws for cutting us off from all that knowledge!" blurted Bróna, thumping the table and making everyone jump. She composed herself before continuing. "Okay. Assuming you chanced upon our world by accident and have no knowledge of what happened to you, we should try to explain.

"First of all, there are portals between the different worlds, or dimensions, which are closely guarded by the gods. The gods make the rules, which the God People enforce. We call them 'God People' because that's what they are, but they don't like it, so don't ever call them that to their faces if you want to keep on living…"

"Wait, wait, wait!" I interrupted. "Who are the God People?"

Bróna looked flustered, overwhelmed by the amount of knowledge she needed to disseminate, so Aoibh took over.

"Sometime during the Eden Years there was a war in the Heavenlies. One third of the Angels staged a coup, but they were overthrown and cast down to Terra, along with the Uncommitted."

"The who?" I managed.

"Angels who didn't choose a side in the battle," Kitti expounded. "They didn't commit to either side and were deemed unfaithful and untrustworthy."

"The Fallen Angels quickly subdued us Humans," continued Cáit, "and forced us to worship them, since power and glory is what they had craved in the Heavenlies."

"And you call them God People," I surmised.

"No," answered Bróna. "The Uncommitted Angels chose wives from amongst the Human women and they had offspring that were half Human and half Angel. *Those* are the God People. They are also known as Elves, or demigods, but that label elevates them higher than they deserve." She delivered this opinion with a toss of her head and something close to a snort of derision.

"Some call them Nephilim," inserted Finoula.

"They aren't immortal, like the Angels," added Aoibh, "but they live for thousands of years."

"Especially if they travel to a dimension where time is out of sync with ours, and come back hundreds of years later," said Kitti.

"Were the other Angels allowed to have children?" I asked. "You know, the ones who openly rebelled?"

This was followed by groans and grimaces from my hostesses.

"Unfortunately, yes," said Bróna. "But their offspring are horrific, unnatural beings."

"Giants, trolls, goblins…" said Cáit.

"Our mortal enemies," croaked Maddy.

My insides curled up. The word *grendel* skittered around in my fearful heart.

"Hairless, soulless, grey-skinned, Human-eaters," added Emer in a timorous voice, and hugged herself as though suddenly chilled.

"The smallest of the monsters are hairy little things with green eyes," said Bróna. "They're the worst."

"How?" I asked, not really wanting to know.

"They are evil tricksters," came Bróna's reply, "Lucifer's chief assassins, who delight in perverting Human minds and bodies."

"And they steal babies," Aoibh appended.

"Anyway," said Finoula, getting back on track, "Fallen Angels can be killed, but they cannot die of natural causes. And if they are killed in their fallen state, they become demons and are banished to Tartarus."

"Tartarus," I echoed in a daze.

"Also known as Hades. Where demons are confined until the Last Days," explained Bróna as casually as though she was giving the weather report.

"What happens when their offspring die?" I asked.

"Same fate," she answered with a shrug.

"The gods haven't interfered with us much since the Great Deluge, but they watch us carefully from their mountain top." Aoibh shuddered as though sensing unseen eyes upon her.

"The Great Deluge?" I interjected. "You mean the Flood of Noah?" Everyone nodded in affirmation. "Back in my time there is a… uh… popular book that says only eight Humans survived that. Surely all the Fallen Angels were wiped out."

"More's the pity, no," mourned Bróna. "God tried to catch them off guard and flood their Portal Hub on top of Mount Olympus, but Noah's granddaughter warned them just in time."

"Noah had a granddaughter?" I asked. "That's news to me."

"Then you are definitely not from the Year of Adam Twenty Fifteen," said Bróna with conviction.

"Noah had hundreds of grandchildren and

thousands of third- and fourth-generation descendants by the time of the Deluge," said Maddy.

"It must have been terrible for him, knowing they were all going to die so horribly," said Aoibh sadly. "He warned them to change their ways, hoping God would relent. He preached for close to one hundred years, but they all just laughed at him."

"God didn't want to kill Humans," objected Kitti. "His main target were the gods, but Human nature was perverted to such a degree that nobody wanted to hear Noah's message."

"Most people had some form of hybrid blood, too," reminded Maddy gently. "God needed to purify our species again."

A woman named Emer took up the story. "When their appointed doom was heralded by rain falling for the first time, Noah's son Bith begged his father to allow his family onboard the Ark, but Noah refused, saying that God didn't want to turn the Ark into a pirate ship."

Bróna continued, "Bith's daughter Cesair hatched a plan to warn the gods of the plot to wipe them off the face of Terra, in exchange for taking her with them when they fled through their portals."

"How did she warn them?" I asked, by now completely engrossed in the tale. How could I not be? They were telling it as though it had really happened and wasn't just a fairy story.

"Cesair and her father sailed west with a group of men and women," said Kitti, "but the floodwaters caught up with them—right here in Fintan's Highlands, in fact. They all died except Cesair's husband, Fintan. He pushed on and made it to Mount Olympus. He warned the Fallen Angels, who rewarded him by taking him with them when they evacuated."

"But how can anyone know all this?" I objected. "If it happened before the flood, and Cesair died, and Fintan went with the Fallen Angels to another dimension, where did the stories of Cesair and Fintan come from?"

"Fintan came back after the Flood," said Aoibh.

"When our tribe colonized this section nearly three hundred years ago," clarified Bróna, "they were greeted by a very old man who claimed to be Fintan."

"When he came back from his exile, he returned to the last place he had seen his wife," said Finoula. "It's a very romantic story."

"How long ago was the Flood?" I asked.

"It has been a millennium and a half since the First Rains," answered Bróna.

"How could Fintan live that long?" I quizzed.

"Apparently, the gods took him to a world where time passes slowly in relation to ours," said Bróna. "When he had been there for only ten weeks, a thousand years had passed on Terra."

"A week is as a hundred years," I whispered, as legends of Oisín and Tír na nÓg plucked at my memory.

"Precisely," said Bróna. "He lived here alone for seventy years before Partholon arrived. He claimed to be one hundred and sixty years old."

"People lived longer lives before the Flood," explained Cáit. "It was because of the air quality—"

"...and the atmospheric pressure," added Kitti.

"...and the water barrier," said Emer.

"What water barrier?"

"Water used to be suspended around the planet in a vapor barrier that deflected harmful rays from the sun," explained Bróna. "When God turned it to liquid, it fell as rain and caused the Deluge."

"And that's what eventually caused the Great Breakup," said Finoula. "All that extra water needed somewhere to go, so it seeped through cracks on the planet's surface and filled the underground caverns."

"The crust fractured and the different sections started to slide around," said Emer. "Terrashakes were constant until the planet regained equilibrium."

"The weight of all that unaccustomed water unbalanced the entire planet," said Finoula. "Terra occasionally shifted out of its orbit. It even stopped rotating for one whole day."

"That's not possible," I scoffed.

"It is recorded in the great libraries at Nineveh and Teotihuacan!" Finoula protested.

"I happen to know that the breakup of Pangaea took millions of years," I replied arrogantly.

"Ladies! Keep it civil," cautioned Bróna. "Perhaps we should go outside and get some fresh air into our lungs. We've been inside long enough." She scraped her chair away from the table and stood up.

"Oh, but I want to hear more," I protested.

"The day is young, my dear," she answered with a smile, "and the sun is shining. Let's not waste it."

Chapter 12

Midway through my third week I was walking like a pro. I had been doing a toned-down MMA workout three times a day, which I custom designed to help me regain coordination and fine motor skills, while learning how to gauge my strength in relation to my movements. I was constantly breaking things and knocking stuff down. The world seemed to have shrunk, yet in fact it was I who had grown. I was now six and a half feet tall and felt like a bear in a crystal chandelier. My hostesses at the Refuge made me fix or replace anything I broke, which turned out to be a lot of fun. They had their own forge and carpentry workshop on the premises, and insisted I learn their uses. They manufactured everything they needed on site. They even had their own flour mill!

I thoroughly explored the walled compound which contained the main house, a separate kitchen and refectory, a barn, a stable for their fleet of donkeys, a dairy, the forge, various workshops, the mill, a tannery, an orchard, and acres of vegetable gardens. There was also a chapel and a tiny graveyard. The women did all the work in providing for themselves, growing food, making clothes, and maintaining their property. They had built the entire enterprise in their youth, and had been there ever since the Tuatha Dé had destroyed their schools and forbidden them to own or dispense knowledge of any kind.

Partholon and his followers built quite a prosperous colony in this land which Moses had promised to their ancestor, Gaodhal Glas. Gaodhal was just a little boy when Moses cured him of snakebite in the Sinai Desert. He prophesied over the boy, telling him that God would prepare a verdant land for his descendants to live in, and he promised the recently traumatized Gaodhal that there wouldn't be any snakes on that faraway island. Moses called it Gaodhal's Island of Destiny, and described it as green and lush and quite the opposite of the parched Sinai. His friends added *glas* (meaning 'green') to the boy's name, and it stuck.

The leader of the Fallen Angels strove to subvert whatever God had intended for good. Lucifer ordered one of his generals—an Angel named Dana—to hunt for Partholon's disgruntled colony. Partholon and his followers were Firbolg slaves who had slipped away in secrecy aboard thirty ships stolen from their Greek masters while the gods were preoccupied with the Battle of Troy. Dana eventually discovered the thriving colony on the distant Island of Destiny. In short order, Dana and his army invaded, conquered, forced the colonists into servitude, and renamed the country Danaan Land.

Following the *modus operandi* of all Fallen Angel conquerors, Dana's army bred a race of Elven offspring to take over and rule the land in their stead, whilst they returned to their home base on a continent even farther west than Danaan Land. Ever since the Great Flood of Noah, they preferred not to stray too far from Mount Olympus.

The half-breed offspring of the Fallen Angels were cruel taskmasters. Not having the same size, skills, or beauty as their fathers, they invariably became bitter at their perceived shortcomings, and—like all bullies—took it out on those weaker than they. Because the Humans under their command were purebred and were the Children of God, the Tuatha Dé were ferociously jealous. They passed laws which dehumanized their slaves. For example, Humans honored their hair and never cut it, holding it sacred as both a spiritual link to God and the source of their strength. Bróna said that hair is an extension of our nervous system and aids in fine-tuning our other senses and abilities. So, of course, the Tuatha Dé ordered Humans to keep their hair shorn to the nub.

The ladies at the Refuge would not let me cut my hair, despite the law I was violating by keeping it long; and despite the fact that if an Elf ever saw my hair, he or she was obliged to put me to death on the spot. It was ridiculously long, however, and I secretly cut it to waist level so I could manage it. The ladies were heartbroken when they discovered my act of barber-ism, but grudgingly agreed that it was a much more sensible length and way easier to braid and hide under my mantilla.

It was springtime when I left Earth via the quantum portal, but when I arrived in Fintan's Highlands summer was in full swing. As the weather cooled and stretched to autumn, I was allowed to explore a limited portion of the forests and mountains that encircled the cloister and its lake. Daily I would set out into the forest with a small work crew of ladies and their donkeys, our purpose being to find fallen trees. We would saw the deadfalls into usable lengths and haul them home for firewood and construction purposes. Finoula was the head carpenter and always accompanied these excursions.

Because of my boundless energy, I wanted to run ahead, or in any direction that took my fancy, but I was not allowed to wander from view of the small caravan as it trudged at an agonizing pace along the worn path that led up the side of Aranafalla Mountain. I chafed at the rules and restrictions; yet dire wolves often entered our little valley in pursuit of deer and wild pigs, and I would most likely meet my death if I encountered a wolf pack while exploring alone. Dire wolves were wily and extremely vicious, and invariably hunted in packs. The pigs were dangerous too, I was told. I had seen pigs brought to market when I was a child and I knew they could grow quite large. I certainly didn't want to run into a wild boar. The ladies brought stout clubs and long staffs for protection, and always traveled in groups. Finoula told me that in their youthful days they sometimes would kill a pig, and that its meat would feed the entire commune for several months. But I thought she was exaggerating; no pig could be *that* big.

Up on Aranafalla, several thousand feet above the rooftops of the cloister, sat a sway-backed valley where pines, spruce, and mountain ash grew in abundance. I was informed that the wispy trail pushed through and past this tree-choked valley to another table at a higher elevation, where coursed a fast-moving stream with no name. The stream spilled boisterously over Aranafalla's westernmost edge and fell eight thousand feet into

Scucca Pass, which divided Aranafalla from her bigger sister, Maumseachtain. I was not permitted to venture that far, however, due to the certain danger that awaited me should I be seen by either Elf or Human; for Scucca Pass led to civilization, I was told.

My heart and mind longed for civilization. The ladies at the Refuge were all right... they were growing on me... but I was weary of women and wrinkles. I hardened my heart against them, because I knew I would be leaving soon. I buzzed with curiosity about the world beyond my mountain pale, and was constantly preoccupied with plans for my journey home. Bróna was teaching me as much about her world as she could, and was working on concocting a cover story and legitimate reason for my forthcoming travels to Mount Olympus, but she seemed to put it all on the long finger. She was in no hurry. Her philosophy that there was a season for all things clashed diametrically with my belief that time and tides don't wait for the idle.

My patience was consumed by an intense electrical energy that charged through my body. After I had recovered from my trauma and regained my balance and coordination, I gloried in my newfound super strength. I felt invincible. The obstacles Bróna threw in front of me appeared insignificant. Armies of Elves? I could run circles around them. The Atlantic Straits? I was an excellent sailor. The gods on Olympus? If God was truly for me, then who could prevail against me, right?!

I wondered whether the university had fixed the computer glitch yet. I had worked desperately hard for my degree, and yearned for the respectability it would confer upon me. I simply had to get back. I often thought about Caroline, and wondered how much time had passed while I'd been gone. What if I returned hundreds of years *after* 2015? Of course, I might just as easily have been gone only a few minutes. Uncertainty and fear of failure gnawed at my insides.

I couldn't help but marvel at the height of the mountains around our secluded valley refuge; easily ten thousand feet, if they were an inch. And their tops were jagged, not rounded. That is what eventually convinced me that I wasn't in Kansas anymore (to quote another quantum traveler from my time). I may or may not have been sent to a different dimension, but if this was Ireland, then I had definitely been sent backwards in time—close to the beginning of things, before erosion reduced the mountains to shadows of their former selves.

My strength was astounding. I could haul two fifty-foot pine logs or one thirty-foot oak at a time, although the ladies limited me to much smaller loads out of concern for my safety. I built a sled with upturned skids to prevent the logs from plowing into the earth while I pulled them. We attached chains to an old donkey harness which Kitti adapted to fit me, and I would pull the logs home without even breaking a sweat. I loved my new strength and dreamed of the day I would return to my *real* home so that I could take on all of Coach Griffin's gym rats at once. I'd beat the stuffing out of the lot of them.

As we hauled logs home one day, I questioned why the ladies did not use turf for their fires.

"What's turf?" quizzed Finoula.

"The stuff that's cut from bogs," said I.

"What are bogs?" she asked, and I looked at her to see if she was jesting, but she honestly didn't know what I was talking about. I was astonished, and hastened to explain how bogs had been formed from all the trees that used to cover Ireland—the name we would give to Danaan Land in the future.

"When the trees fell, they were compressed into watery layers, several hundred feet deep in some places. They gradually formed a dense, sponge-like substance that we cut into sections and dry in the sun. We use it as fuel."

"How can trees grow in water?"

"They didn't. The water came later, I suppose."

"What knocked all the trees down?"

"They just fell down… over time."

Finoula adjusted the forehead strap that supported the bundle of firewood on her back, and looked a little puzzled. "Trees die at different times," she said. "They decompose at different rates." She pointed at the trees all around us. "Look at these trees. The majority are standing. Each is at a different stage of life. They are not forming a bog."

I hadn't thought much about it. Who does? A bog is a bog. They were formed millions of years ago and nobody was there when it happened. *I'm beginning to sound like Professor Carlyle,* I mused.

"I don't know," I answered. "Perhaps the Flood of Noah knocked them down and piled them on top of one another."

"There has been no evidence of that," she refuted. "All the organic material and bodies were washed to the lowest points upon Terra, and were buried under hundreds of feet of mud and rocks when the floodwaters subsided."

"Surely everything was just left to rot where it died," I objected. "Why do you say it was buried?"

Kitti, who had been listening quietly while leading two laden donkeys, now chimed in. "Whole sections of Terra's crust collapsed under the unaccustomed weight when the water barrier came down. The floodwaters drained in turmoil to the lowest elevations and washed all the debris off the land with tremendous force."

I imagined how it must have been.

Kitti indicated the steep mountainsides. "That's what carved out these valleys," she continued. "Pangaeden was a fairly level land mass. There were not the extreme elevation differences that we know now."

"Where I come from," I replied haughtily, "people believe that deep canyons took millions of years to carve out."

The two women laughed as though I had just told a marvelous joke. I frowned, because I had been quite serious. Kitti noticed how embarrassed I looked and was immediately conciliatory.

"A great many years have passed in your time," she mollified. "No doubt the stories of the Beginning have been lost."

"They're just fairytales," I argued.

"But the evidence abounds!" cried Finoula. "Something must be blinding your people to the truth."

"We have our own truth, I guess."

"Lucifer has succeeded then," said Finoula sadly. "He has severed the connection between Humans and their Creator."

"All it takes is a deceiving whisper in the right ear," agreed Kitti. "And we know how he excels at that."

"There's no need to prove your strength to me," scolded Bróna one day when I arrived at the back gate with three short pine logs in tow. "Save it for when you really need it."

"And when might that be?" I retorted sarcastically. I saw the disapproval in Bróna's face and immediately felt guilty for my disrespectful tone.

"I'm sorry, Bróna," I said. "It's just that I'm frustrated." I began ticking off individual grievances on my fingers. "I've been given all this strength and energy, yet I'm not allowed to use it. I can't ask the Fallen Angels to access their portal hub or they'll kill me. I can't reveal myself to anyone or they'll report me to the Elves. I'm not allowed to explore, go into town, or travel anywhere alone, and I'm going out of my mind!"

"Hush now, child," she replied with a loving smile. "God's purpose will be revealed in due time. You are not ready to brave the gods, or the God People, or even the Humans of this world. Keep studying. Keep training. Your purpose and direction will be revealed in good time."

"I know my purpose. All I need is the know-how and a map, and I'll be gone faster than you can shake a stick at me."

Bróna smiled at me, understanding and envying my youthful impatience. "There is a reason you were sent here," she said. "You must trust, as I do, to a high-up wisdom."

I unchained the logs and rolled them to the foot of a mountainous woodpile in the yard. Brushing the dirt and woodchips off my hands and clothing, I surveyed the stack with great satisfaction. "I'll haul the knots to the furnace after supper," I said. "They should make great charcoal for Aoibh's forge."

"With your help, we've already cut enough firewood to see us through the winter," said Bróna. She sighed tiredly. "I for one am heartily glad that chore is behind us."

I stared off into the distance. Bróna watched me for a few moments before gently tugging at my sleeve, and I voiced my thoughts without waiting for her invitation. "When I was traveling through the portal I felt tremendous pressure building up. It was as though I was being squeezed tightly. I thought I was going to burst."

"It has been told that the journey is like the birth process," explained Bróna as we walked back to the main building to wash up before supper. "The pressure caused damage to your brain, which altered its electrochemical output and resulted in excessive stimulation to your muscles."

"I was brain damaged?" I asked in dismay.

Bróna chuckled. "Not unlike young children who cannot sit still. Their condition is marked by a lack of coordination and an inability to focus their attention on anything for long. However, this chemical stimulation wears off after several years as their skulls expand and their brain tissue heals."

"Do you mean someday I'll shrink back to my normal size and become weak again?"

"That's unlikely. Those changes were permanent."

"Was it the chemical stimulation that made me so sick?"

"No. That was your body detoxifying. You described the air in the tunnel as being magical?"

"The air? Yes, it seemed to flow through my flesh and bones."

Bróna nodded sagely. "You were exposed to the pure air of the Heavenlies. It cleansed your cells. Your illness was the manifestation of all the toxins being forced out of your body."

"I can't believe how much you know about medicine and science," I marveled.

"We used to have manuscripts that were passed down by our foremothers," said Bróna. "They contained all the knowledge God revealed to Adam in their daily walks through the Garden. But the knowledge was stolen from us. The gods want us to be stupid. They don't want us to remember or pass on our knowledge and skills. They burned our libraries and killed our elders."

Now it was she who stood still and stared, unseeing, at the mountains. A clatter of pans from the nearby refectory startled her out of her reverie and she shook away the memories. She noticed me waiting for her to continue, and her voice became lively again. "But that was a long time ago, my dear."

"What would happen if the Elves found your secret hiding place… all your books?" I asked.

"We would all be put to death," she said briskly. "Our Refuge would be razed and scattered to the four winds. Even our relatives and friends would be killed to ensure that not an iota of intelligence remained for our agile minds to play with."

I gulped and looked at her, the shock making ovals of my eyes and silencing my tongue.

She nodded grimly. "So, you see how our lives are mutually entwined, and why self-preservation must be our primary goal?" She peered closely at me to determine my understanding of the situation.

I drew a deep breath and blew it noisily through

my lips. I nodded at her and she was satisfied. She put her arm around my waist and drew me toward the door.

Chapter 13

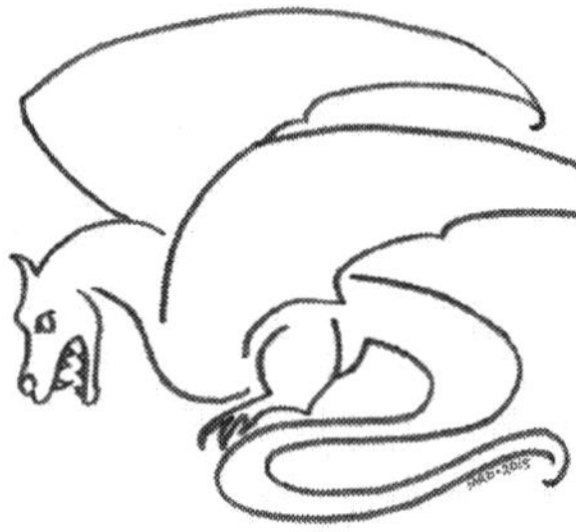

A cold, crisp day in early autumn found me helping Finoula in her carpentry workshop. Crushed shavings and wood chips underfoot released the sweet aroma of dried sap and singed wood. Our breath ghosted between shafts of sunlight where the glittering wood dust danced.

We were trying to reassemble my broken hang glider, using a sketch I had drawn from memory. Finoula and Aoibh were attempting to manufacture the several parts that were missing. I had been thrilled to learn that their knowledge of metallurgy was on par with that of the civilization I had come from. They knew the secrets of metal alloys; therefore, my glider's fiberglass rods could, in theory, be replaced with hollow steel rods of similar weight. I was worried about the potential loss of flexibility and undoubted weight gain, but Aoibh (our blacksmith) assured me that the alloy she had forged would be strong, lightweight, *and* flexible because of the addition of a rare metal called findruine.

A small trove of this valuable metal still remained from the wealth the ladies had once been in possession of, before the God People had destroyed their school and driven them into hiding. When Aoibh had petitioned the coffers, the women had unanimously given their approval to use the findruine for repairing my wings. The ladies were so convinced that I had been sent by God for a soon-to-be-revealed purpose, that they had no qualms about using their rainy-day fund of findruine. I felt guilty about taking advantage of their innocence and trust, but my desire to return home overruled any principles that stood in the way. I was willing to chance anything to get back to the twenty-first century and claim my Bachelor of Arts.

I planned to test the glider from a low hill to see how it held up. If findruine didn't work, I would try something else. Ash wood was excellent for constructing bows. That was going to be Plan B.

My headdress swung in front of me every time I leaned forward. I ripped it off so I could work more freely, but Finoula gasped out loud when she saw my braided hair exposed for all to see. She left what she was working on and picked up the mantilla I had cast onto the floor.

"You must never uncover your hair," she scolded.

"Why not? Nobody else can see me."

She just shook her head and tut-tutted as she dusted off the mantilla and placed it upon my head. Once she had secured it with the brass clasp, her old fingers traced the rounded tips of my ears. "We Humans must keep our hair short. It's the law. You cannot take the risk of anyone seeing it."

"Let me just cut it, then!"

"Oh, no. Our hair is our connection to God. The gods know this and forbid us to grow it long."

"Why are you so opposed to me cutting it short, if I risk breaking the law?" I asked in genuine confusion.

"Because you're special," she said with a smile. "Bróna thinks you have been sent here on purpose, and we are all committed to help you succeed in your mission."

I laughed good-naturedly. They had such simple but sure beliefs that I almost envied their simplicity of thinking. They believed that everything happened for a reason, even mishaps and tragedy. I could not wrap my mind around such concepts. Life, for me, was an unknowable but chronologically unfolding experience that I had the power to shape into my own destiny. The tunnel flight had been an aberration—something I could have avoided if I had been forewarned. Still, I had chosen my path at that time, and now I was planning to correct that mistake and redirect myself back home.

"Always show your ear tips off to advantage," Finoula added as she clamped a steel rod to the workbench. "The Elves like that."

"Why do they care about our ears?"

"Our ears highlight the race disparity between us, which God People see as a class distinction." She wrinkled her nose in disdain. "They think they are superior to Humans."

"Then why are they jealous of us?"

"Aye," she said, laughing. "That's the crux of the matter, and no mistaking! They are jealous of us because we are Children of God, while they are the illegitimate hybrid offspring of God's servants and messengers."

"Illegitimate? How so?"

"Interbreeding with Humans was a deliberate attempt by the Fallen Angels to corrupt our bloodlines; a cruel attempt to destroy that which God took most delight in. But there are those of us who refuse to be corrupted. We are of the same mettle as Noah and his tenth wife, Cova—our beloved Matriarch—whose bloodlines alone were found to be uncontaminated."

I lost interest in the conversation right about there. I turned my back on Finoula and rolled my eyes at the wall. I bent over my diagram, checking to make sure I had not left out any details of the glider's structure.

Finoula began filing the steel, and soon sparks were spraying twixt rasp and rod. The high-pitched whine didn't seem to bother Finoula, but I plugged my ears with my fingers. I watched, fascinated, anticipating disaster each time a spark dissolved on the brink of igniting the tinderbox floor.

After a while, Finoula straightened her back and reminisced wistfully. "We had to cut off our long, beautiful hair. We chose to wear veils rather than expose our shame."

"Why is it such a shame? I've had short hair ever since I was old enough to decide for myself."

Finoula shot me a look across the work table. "Um-hum," she said as though I had just proven her point. "And just look how scattered you are."

"Scattered?"

"You are not grounded," she said, then laughed at the humor in that. "That's probably what caused you to take flight! You had no roots, so you took to the sky."

I didn't laugh with her, but stared out the window, lost in thought.

She put down her file and scurried across the room to me. She put an apologetic hand on my arm and searched my eyes for forgiveness. "I didn't mean any harm by that," she said softly.

I broke into a grin and covered her tiny hand with mine. "No, you were right, Finoula, and I don't hold it against you. There is a lot of truth to what you said. I was cast adrift at an early age and had no traditions to guide me."

"Hopefully we can teach you what you need to know, and balance will be restored in your life."

"I don't think I can wait that long," I said. "Whatever plans you lot may have for me, *my* only mission on Terra is to get back to Earth—back to my time—as soon as possible."

Finoula looked at me with a pained expression. "You haven't yet grasped it, have you? That was a one-way portal you traveled through... an *exit* portal from your world to ours. The only other navigable portals are on Mount Olympus, and they are heavily guarded by the gods. They will kill you once your quest is known. They will kill you for having flown on the Dragon Wind, which is their realm alone. They will even kill you for setting foot on Mount Olympus." She paused and took a deep breath. "They will kill you every day of the week and twice on Thor's day. Returning home is entirely impossible, Ashling. I'm afraid you're here for good."

"And *I'm* afraid 'impossible' is not in my vocabulary," I replied with the confidence of my youth and newfound strength, and in the dangerous arrogance of my ignorance and disbelief.

Chapter 14

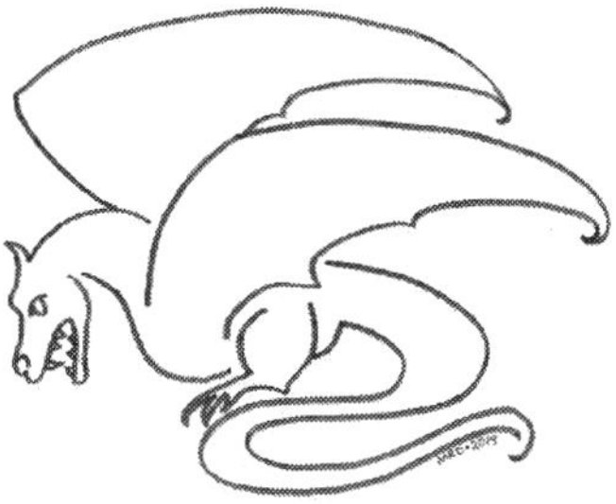

Once the hem of my robe was pulled up between my legs and tucked into my belt, it formed serviceable, baggy, Samurai trousers. I spent five or six hours each day practicing my katas, working every possible combination I had ever learned, and even making up a few new ones. I trained with staffs and knives, and wielded shortened broomsticks as swords. I longed for the bow and quiver of arrows I had left behind in Galway, but the ladies at the Refuge had eschewed all manner of weapons of war in obedience to the Lucifer Laws. They were fascinated by my martial arts, and I often had an audience while working out.

My favorite place to train was on a broad branch of the gigantic oak that overhung the stable. The branch was five feet wide and at least seventy-five feet off the ground. I could see all over the valley and to the far side of Kylemore Lough from my perch.

I exhibited uncanny balance and climbing ability, and the ladies soon outgrew their fear for my safety. I never fell. I even tried swinging and leaping from branch to branch, like Tarzan did in the Edgar Rice Burroughs books. My success at doing that gave me a special thrill. My brain sort of went ahead of me whilst I was climbing or running, and calculated each step and move before I had to make it. I was firing on all cylinders.

One particularly hot day, the lake seemed to be calling my name. I could see it glittering alluringly beneath the cloudless sky; an open invitation to cool off after my strenuous workout. I swung down to a lower level of the oak tree and leaped onto the wall of the Refuge. From there, I vaulted to the ground and ran along the pier. As I ran, I tore off my outer garments until I was down to my yoga pants and neoprene shirt. I dove off the end of the pier and struck out powerfully for the opposite shore.

The cold water was exhilarating. I challenged myself to speeds unknown to me before this time. I broke every pathetic Olympic record that had yet to be made. All that was missing were the cheering multitudes, gold medals, and breakfast cereal endorsements. I churned through the frigid lake water so fast that a sizeable wake formed behind me.

My skin was tingling and I felt unbelievably alive when I hauled myself out of the lake onto the pier after my swim. To my surprise, a welcoming committee of several scolding and very frightened women surrounded me and wrapped me in a warm blanket.

"What's the matter?" I asked as I toweled myself off with the rough blanket.

"You must *never* swim in the lake," scolded Aoibh.

"The knuckers!" screeched Cáit.

"She was probably going too fast for them," said Finoula proudly, now that her fear was wearing off.

"You shouldn't trust to chance, you foolish girl!"

That was Bróna.

"What's a knucker?" I asked midst all the clucking.

"You've never heard of knuckers?" asked Cáit in disbelief.

I shook my head.

"Wave thrashers?"

I shook my head.

"Lake monsters?"

At that reference, however, I threw my head back and laughed out loud. "Yes, I *have* heard of lake monsters, thanks to Professor Carlyle! What of them?"

In answer, an ashen-faced Cáit turned my silly self around and pointed to a huge, serpentine head on a long neck watching us about fifty yards offshore. I leaped backwards in shock and instinctively dropped into a defensive martial arts stance. For a protracted, dizzying interval, time seemed to unfold in slow motion, as though I was in a dream state. This was not the first time I had experienced that sensation since my quantum leap.

"Oh, my God, they're real!" I gasped. I looked into the beady, black eyes of the great, charcoal-colored monster out in the lake. It didn't blink, and I'm not sure I did either. It looked exactly like the Loch Ness Monster—a prehistoric plesiosaur. Then a scary thought interrupted my scientific analysis. "Oh, my *God*! I was just *in* there!"

The women started to move toward the compound gate as a group, careful not to turn their backs on the creature they called a knucker. Their actions quickly brought to mind another worrisome thought.

"Can they get to us from there?" I queried in fear.

"They rarely come ashore," said Aoibh as we

retreated toward the compound. "They prefer to catch their prey out in the water."

"So, please, dear girl, stay out of the water!" moralized the ever practical Bróna.

"All bodies of water are dangerous," said Finoula. "Grendels prefer small ponds and marshes, sea dragons haunt the oceans—"

"You should even avoid puddles, just to be on the safe side," concluded Cáit.

At the mention of grendels, I felt queasy. Professor Carlyle's readings from *Beowulf* had left a lasting impression upon me. Grendels were bad enough when presented as mythological horrors in a novel of antiquated origins, but now I was learning that Beowulf's principal antagonist in that faraway Saxon world was a living, breathing creature that I might actually bump into someday. My new world had suddenly lost its sheen.

The playful breeze that ruffled the water brought the strong and unmistakable stink of fish mixed with a dank, musty odor that I couldn't quite pin down. It was the knucker's musk that I would rapidly learn to recognize and avoid.

The lesson was over and we had all lived to see another day. Before closing the gate behind us, I locked eyes once more with the serpent in the lake, and shuddered.

The monster submerged with barely a ripple.

Chapter 15

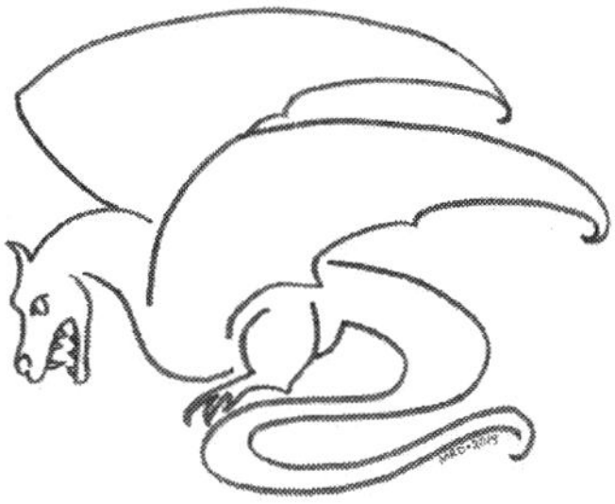

I woke with a start and leaped out of bed all at the same instance, grabbing my wooden staff in midair and spinning it into a defensive position before landing on both feet, facing the door. I had no idea what woke me, yet subconsciously knew that something was wrong.

I waited… listening… barely breathing… but nothing happened. All was silence. I opened the door carefully and peered cautiously into the corridor. Cáit was waiting outside and immediately pushed me back into the room. She followed me in and shut the door, shushing my protests with a finger over her lips.

"What's wrong?" I asked in a whisper, all my senses on high alert.

"Visitors," she whispered in return. "They mustn't see you. You have to stay in your room until they leave."

Somebody new! And I couldn't meet them? Couldn't get news from outside the valley? I desperately needed a pulse reading of the political goings-on to assist me in my return to the future. If nothing else, just a chance to see a different face, for crying out loud!

"Why can't I see them?" I pressed. "I'll keep my headdress on and I won't speak a word. I just want to look at them!"

"No, Ashling," she said firmly, and I detected fear in her voice. "If they see you, they'll notice you're a lot younger than the rest of us, and they'll start asking questions… No, absolutely not."

"But I want to know what's happening in the outside world—"

Cáit anticipated my desire and answered me swiftly. "We all do, loveen. As soon as ever possible we will pry every last speck of information out of them, don't you worry." I could sense the underlying fear that stilted her voice and caused her movements to be agitated and jerky.

"How long will that be?"

Cáit shrugged and pulled a chessboard from under her habit. "I don't know, but I brought something to keep us busy."

I groaned loudly. "I'll go out of my mind if I can't go outside."

"It's the middle of the night. Why would you want to go outside?"

"Good point," I retorted. "Why are strangers dropping by for a midnight visit? They can't be up to any good. Let me go out and mingle with the other ladies, just in case there's trouble."

"Bróna knew you'd want to do that. She sent me to tell you that it would be safer for everyone if you stayed out of sight. Please, Ashling. Trust our wisdom on this one."

"Okay," I agreed reluctantly. My every instinct told me there was danger in the wind. I knew I should be outside, patrolling the perimeter. Staying inside, with ears and eyes shut off from my surroundings, was a lousy tactical position. "Who are they?" I persisted. "Why can't they see me?"

"Because they're Elves," was Cáit's tremulous response.

So, that's why she was so afraid! The mortal foe of everyone in the Refuge had come knocking on the door in the middle of the night. My eyes widened in excitement and alarm. "What do they want? Is it an inspection?"

"They have come here seeking refuge."

"But they're your sworn enemies! You built this place as a refuge from *them*."

"Yes, but what can we do?" she asked, sounding torn about the decision.

"Send them packing!"

"That might bring us unwanted attention."

"What are they seeking refuge from?" I had only just realized how strange it was that the lords of the land had come to a wild and isolated valley high in the most inhospitable mountains in Danaan Land, seeking aid from a group of lowly Humans at the eleventh hour of a most disagreeable night.

"They were attacked by Fomorians on the Dún Aengus road, and many are wounded. We can't turn them away. There are rules about hospitality that are inviolate."

My excitement was stilled by her use of a word I recognized from my history lessons and that my memory had tainted with negativity. "Fomorians?"

Cáit nodded distractedly while setting up the chess pieces. "Yes… Giants."

Less than an hour later, Cáit was fast asleep on the bed beside the chessboard. I plaited my hair and donned the brown robe over my skintight neoprene sports attire; then slipped silently into the corridor, pulling the door softly shut behind me.

I left my homemade weapons behind. If the Elves spotted anything more sinister than sawblades in our possession, we would be put to death. Besides, there was no point in bringing a stick to a swordfight—if fight there be.

I sneaked outside through a little-used side entrance. Torrential rain covered the sound of the squeaky hinges and no one noticed my exit. I stood for a moment under the eave until my eyes adjusted to the darkness.

Around the corner, a yellow glow beckoned. That's where the stable yard was, and no doubt the Elves would be taking care of their horses. I ran behind the smithy and shinned up the far side of my huge oak tree. When I reached an ample branch about twenty feet off the ground, I stretched myself along its length and peered apprehensively over its girth for an unobstructed view into the open-fronted stables below.

Words cannot describe my awe when at last I set eyes upon those marvelous creatures of myth and legend—unequaled in science, the arts, and war—the Elves of Tolkien, the demigods of Roman and Greek history and Viking legend, and the bane of the Human race.

The scene was lit by a lantern suspended from the

roof. Three male Elves were deep in exhausted sleep beside several horses similarly occupied. A sword was stuck into the ground by each Elf's side for immediate access, and I knew intuitively it was the way they slept during wartime, for that's what I would do myself.

They were taller than I, averaging about seven feet; with smooth white skin, long hair, and—wonder of wonders—long, pointy ears. Beautiful was the only word to describe them, despite the fact that they were males. Their features were finely chiseled and quite symmetrical. Their clothing looked to be very expensive: soft material of varied hues, very pleasing to the eye, richly embroidered with silver and gold thread… and heavily blood splattered.

A suggestion of sound caused me to look toward the lake. Seeing nothing, I turned my gaze back to the sleeping Elves.

Another noise from the lake. I swiveled quickly to look. Knuckers rest at the bottom of the lake at night and surface for neither love nor money. Whatever had made that noise was large and unfamiliar to me, and had definitely originated out on the water. I squinted futilely through the gloom and cupped my ears to focus the sound through the pouring rain. After an interminable interval, a faint, rhythmic splashing reached me, growing louder as it neared.

Thoroughly alarmed, I somersaulted from the tree onto the boundary wall and crouched in the shadows, waiting.

The unmistakable sound of heavy boats scraping on the gravel shore reached through the darkness. Almost simultaneously, the beach filled with hulking shadows, crunching footsteps, and muffled clangs. The odor of mutton grease reached my nostrils. I hesitated but a second before casting off my bulky robe and raising the alarm.

"To arms! To arms! The Fomorians are upon us!" My stentorian cry cracked the night wide open, echoed across the lake, and ricocheted off the mountains.

Trusting to my warning to awaken the slumbering Elves and give my friends enough time to flee to safety, I sprang to the ground and positioned myself outside the gate of the Refuge, determined to defend my home against these invaders… or die trying.

As soon as their surprise was foiled, the Giants rushed the compound with a battle cry that almost melted my bones.

I met the assault with every ounce of martial arts skill I possessed. This was what I had trained for. Twenty-one elderly women were counting on me to protect them. I was more alive than I had ever been. My determination was unconquerable. Sheer energy alone should have disintegrated every living thing within a fifty-foot radius.

I struck the first Giant in his solar plexus with my right fist, and a bolt of electricity jumped from my hand when I yelled my *kiai*. Karate students learn to envision their punches striking through their victims, rather than just landing the blows. Because of the sheer volume of pent-up power that I unleashed on that creature, the energy of my blow severed his spinal cord and turned his internal organs to jelly. I snatched the sword that had been about to cut me in two, even as its former owner crumpled lifelessly at my feet. Without pause, I reversed the sword and rapidly disemboweled the Giants on either side of the first.

The battle was engaged, and it was fierce, and it was bloody.

My mind disconnected and allowed my body to perform the moves it had mastered through many years of practice. With a sword in each hand, I disabled the front line of attackers and used their weapons to butcher the next group. Time slowed to a hearse pace. The world was cast in indigo. Sounds were silenced save only the slow, steady rhythm of a heartbeat in my ears and the shattering of individual drops of crystal rain. My soul detached from its physical confines to watch the scene from afar. I dodged and weaved lithely, easily avoiding their slow, awkward strikes and thrusts. The wind lashed me with religious fervor and I swung my weapons in a brutally choreographed death dance that resembled someone else's gothic nightmare.

The gargantuan bodies piled up around me and I had to vault over the carcasses in order to stay in the fight. In the dark, sleeting rain I noticed seven or eight Elves fighting alongside me, their swords flashing and hacking. I don't remember at what point they joined me; my brain simply registered their presence.

We fought a good fight, my allies and I, yet one by one my comrades-in-arms were overcome and defeated. I registered their deaths somewhat like lights being extinguished, and incorporated the losses into my overall battle view as irreversible, negative statistics.

But I was a raging inferno and stayed the field.

After an unknowable passage of time, the Giants retreated without warning. They faded into the stygian reaches of the storm and left me alone on the field of slaughter, wielding a captured sword in each hand and shouting my challenge to the empty night.

Chapter 16

Dawn illuminated the horrific scene. The bodies of approximately twenty Fomorians were strewn across the beach, marking the advance I had made as I drove them back to the lakeshore. Dead, as well, were seven noble-looking Elves. A scan of the horizon reassured me that the coast was clear. With no more enemies in sight, my battle lust ebbed.

I was standing guard in front of the Refuge gate, sword in hand, resting against a spear that was twice my height. At some point during the cold hours preceding daylight, my soul had cautiously reentered my body, and I was busy trying to connect the scattered pieces of fragmented battle memories.

It had stopped raining. Sparrows and thrushes were chirping and going about their normal business, completely oblivious to the carnage on the beach.

The stench of spilled stomachs and intestinal corruption mingled with the sickly odor of gore. The bodies were crawling with crabs. Scores of shrieking seagulls blew in with the early morning breeze and landed on the rocky beach to sample the smorgasbord.

Two or three dead Fomorians were floating in the blood-red lake water lapping the shore.

To my utter amazement, a pair of leather-winged pterodactyls landed on the bobbing corpses and began feasting, and I experienced that out-of-body dizziness again. Science books of the future had nearly everything wrong. It was apparent that pterodactyls had *not* become extinct before homo sapiens appeared on the scene. I cringed, remembering the contempt I used to exhibit whenever I came across reports of weird creatures in ancient Irish manuscripts. I had studied history with great disdain for what I considered to be fanciful accounts written by simple-minded lackeys. How narrowminded of me; how unforgivably arrogant.

Clear mountain light reveals details with a harsh, unbiased reality and I had an unforgettable first look at my enemies. The Giants averaged ten or twelve feet tall. Their skin was ash-grey. Pale, colorless eyes highlighted the network of blood vessels in their eyeballs. Although resembling Humans in general conformation, they were bulky creatures and awkwardly put together. Ropey, blue-colored veins disfigured their bald scalps and hairless bodies much the way beetle infestations mutilate tree bark. Closer inspection of their deformed hands revealed six fingers on each. Slack-lipped, shapeless mouths housed over-sized, brown-stained, gappy teeth which were filed to a point. Their clothing was primarily dyed wool accessorized with leather, bronze, and fur. Their jewelry comprised copper, leather, shell, and bone. No rich fabric or precious metals or gems adorned their persons.

I admired the exquisite craftsmanship of the Elven swords and compared them to the blocky, iron, Fomorian imitation in my hand. Suddenly repulsed, I flung the bloody weapon far out into the lake.

My face was caked with something that felt like heavy makeup drying in the morning sun, so I reached up to wipe it away from my eyes. For the first time, I noticed that my hands and arms were coated with congealing gore. A quick examination of my torso, legs, and feet revealed an identical lamina, and I knew without a doubt that the mud-like substance that clogged my eyes and restricted my facial movements was blood. That knowledge produced an instantaneous response: I bent over and heaved up the contents of my stomach. When my misery had passed, I straightened and turned toward the Refuge, and studiously avoided looking at the cadavers.

The heavy gate remained ominously shut and no sound of life stirred beyond the walls. Had I failed, then, to protect my dear companions? Had the Fomorians bypassed me in the heat of battle and darkness of night, and were all the ladies of the Refuge lying dead behind the walls?

Dreading to know the answer, I couldn't bring myself to climb the wall and peer over. Instead, I rapped on the iron door with the head of the spear I clutched, and called out with vain expectation to those within.

"Hello, ladies! The coast is clear. You can open the gate."

The answering silence was unbearable. I tried again, striving to prevent my voice from shaking in its terror. The resulting sound revealed a lonely and frightened little girl who was lost and far away from home.

"Please?"

I heard the screech of a weighty bolt sliding back, and the gate opened wide. Just beyond the threshold, the stern-faced women of the Refuge were arrayed in battle formation, wielding swords, shields, and spears. Tunics and leggings had replaced the familiar brown habits and veils, and they looked like they intended to inflict damage. And although stupefied by the unanticipated unveiling, my brain registered the fact that they all had long hair.

I was completely floored. Then I smiled hugely with relief. "Who are you?" I joked weakly. "And what have you done with those sweet little old ladies?"

With a surprising display of discipline and training, five of the women—led by Bróna—executed a sortie to survey the killing ground beyond the gate, and the phalanx reformed behind them.

"Is that all of them?" asked Bróna tersely.

"For now. But I think they went back for reinforcements."

Bróna lowered her sword and surveyed the apparition that once was Ashling MacGillycuddy. She pursed her lips—appalled by my appearance—but nodded her approval. "You were sent here for a day such as this. How are you holding up?"

I could only bob my head and shrug. I had no words for how I felt after my first real battle that involved blood and guts and the ending of lives. How could I relate the finality of death, and my self-loathing? I had played at war before this, during martial arts competitions, but my soul had not been prepared for the experience.

I could not create anything as intricate and alive as a Fomorian Giant, no matter how repulsive, and yet I had the unmitigated gall to destroy them. I didn't know anything about the beings I had slaughtered. It was not my fight, yet I had embraced it, choosing sides without knowing either the facts or the stakes. The Giants were after the Elves; we could have just handed them over and stayed out of their quarrel. Surely we could have convinced the Fomorians that we—as the subservient species—had been obliged to house the Elves. And yet, the Giants had attacked without warning. They had sent no emissary to discuss terms of surrender. Would they have spared the innocent?

No doubt I had made lifelong enemies of the monstrous creatures who had retreated to regroup. I had brought undying trouble upon my friends at the Refuge whose valley was no longer a secret and, thanks to me, would never be safe again.

The other women stared at me grimly without speaking. I felt the weight and confusion of their thoughts.

"You'll forgive me if I don't embrace you," Bróna said brusquely. "Why don't you wash yourself off in the lake? Emer will stand guard. Now, ladies, let's bury the Elves and get ready to evacuate."

"What shall we do with the Giants?" I asked.

"Leave them for the knuckers," she snapped contemptuously.

"No love lost there, I see," I observed.

"Not a drop," she said. "That's one thing we Humans have in common with the God People of Dana."

Chapter 17

Cáit shook me awake that night and placed a large bowl of stew on my nightstand. The hearty aroma elicited growls from my stomach.

"We're almost ready to leave. Get up and eat something," she said.

I had slept all through the day while the ladies prepared supplies to take with us into the mountains. It had been decades since circumstances had dictated an evacuation, and they went about their work with a mixed sense of excitement and dread. Old age and arthritis dampened any enthusiasm they might have felt.

Kitti was standing behind Cáit, holding up a dark-green, felt tunic with a beige wyvern appliqué. She beamed at me. "I made this for you."

"You made this?" I asked in astonishment. I traced the dragon pattern on the tunic with mingled disbelief and delight. Nobody had ever made clothes for me except my mother. Since her death, I had only worn hand-me-downs, cast-offs, and charity-shop bargains. I struggled for words. How does one express adequate thanks to a person who has devoted such time, creativity, and energy into a gift for another? This was the first time I had ever been at the receiving end of a gift. Feelings of inadequacy shriveled me. Doubts about my worthiness unbalanced me. My head spun while my heart knocked upon the door of emotions that had been locked away and forgotten.

"She has been working on that for weeks," said Cáit, smiling at my confusion.

Kitti thrust the tunic at me and held up a pair of black leggings, a heavy cloak, and lace-up boots made of soft-tanned leather. "And these," she said shyly.

I clutched the gifts tightly to my chest. My eyes glimmered with tears but my tongue had lost its skill.

Kitti laughed softly, taking pleasure in my reaction. "I didn't have any gold cloth for the wyvern, but beige is closer to their real color anyway." She sounded apologetic.

"You made this for *me*?" I managed to finagle past my uncooperative, strangulated voice box.

"These will be warmer than those strange skins you wear," she said.

"Not as revealing," added Cáit, and we all laughed.

The shell around my heart began to crackle.

"Maybe now we can let people see you," giggled Kitti.

"My own custom-made MMA outfit. Definitely better than neoprene."

Cáit and Kitti conversed silently with one another, using facial expressions and body language that read: "What did she say?" and "I haven't a clue."

I smiled and awkwardly ejected the words, "Thank you, Kitti." I was rewarded with a hug from that dear soul, and my spirit experienced peace for the first time in forever.

Outside, the rain had stopped. Lantern light reflected off puddles in the stable yard where a caravan of fifteen donkeys waited patiently. Each canvas-covered pannier bulged with supplies. The feeblest of the women were sitting astride donkeys, heavily bundled against the cold. The other women were outfitted for a long hike. I was wearing my new clothes and boots, as well a sword on each hip.

Aoibh was putting the finishing touches to a clever, two-wheeled, travois-type barrow that was hitched behind a magnificent Elven horse. On it, bundled in blankets and a waterproof oilcloth, was a long figure whose face was hidden in shadows under a rain canopy. I was instantly curious. One of the Elves must have survived!

Bróna was conducting a last-minute check of the supplies and called me over before I could visit the injured Elf. Most of the women were now openly wearing their battle attire, which included swords and daggers forged at the Refuge. Several sported a quiver of arrows and a bow slung on their backs. You may be able to imagine my delight when Aoibh presented me with my very own bow and quiver. The ladies had kept the weapons a secret until I had proven myself. They hadn't wanted to reveal everything to a complete stranger because of the possibility that an unintentional slip in casual conversation with the wrong ears might bring calamity upon them. But now their secret was out, their lives were in mortal peril, and they were better served with the swords at their waists than mouldering in a vault.

"You ride rearguard," said Bróna, "and I will take the van."

"You found a survivor?" I indicated the travois.

"It has a broken leg from its first run-in with Fomorians down by the coast."

"It?" I asked pointedly.

"It's an Elf, isn't it?" she replied huffily.

I didn't have time to debate the issue in the face of our imminent demise.

Underneath the rain canopy, the shadowy Elf appeared to be listening.

"Aoibh says you're leaving the other horses behind," I challenged Bróna.

"We can't take them. The Lucifer Laws forbid Humans to own or ride horses."

"You forged swords and daggers despite the law," I argued. "And you let your hair grow long again."

"Those are things we can hide," she said.

"Well, I'm not leaving them for the Giants to eat!" I told her firmly. "We're taking the horses, and I will bear the blame for it."

Half in shadow, the long-eared, white-haired Elf smiled.

While I was saddling one of the seven other horses, Finoula approached with a long bundle wrapped in oilcloth. She looked inordinately pleased with herself.

"Here, don't leave this behind." She thrust the parcel into my arms and the horse shied away a few steps.

"What is it?" I asked as I calmed the horse.

"Aoibh was able to make the missing parts in her forge, and I rebuilt your wings." Notwithstanding our dire situation, Finoula was so delighted to be able to grant me this wish that she glowed with happiness and pride.

I grinned and gave her a quick squeeze. "You're the best," I said, and tied the long parcel onto the saddle. "What about the rest of the weapons?"

"We emptied all our hiding places and packed them on the horses, just as you ordered." Finoula seemed deflated by a sudden thought. "I hope the Giants don't destroy our home."

"You can stay behind and talk them out of it, if you like," I suggested.

We grinned at each other. Then I lifted Finoula onto the horse's saddle and she squealed in surprise. I slapped her lightly on the leg and laughed up at her.

"Don't worry, Finoula. I'll take the blame for this, too." I handed her the reins. "You take the rearguard for me. Push them as hard as you can, okay? We need to reach Scucca Pass before dawn."

Up ahead, Bróna gave the order to move out.

"What are you going to do?" asked Finoula.

"I'm going to be all over the place, making sure we're safe. I can't be tied to the caravan."

Finoula nodded gravely in agreement and kicked the horse as the caravan jolted to a start.

Chapter 18

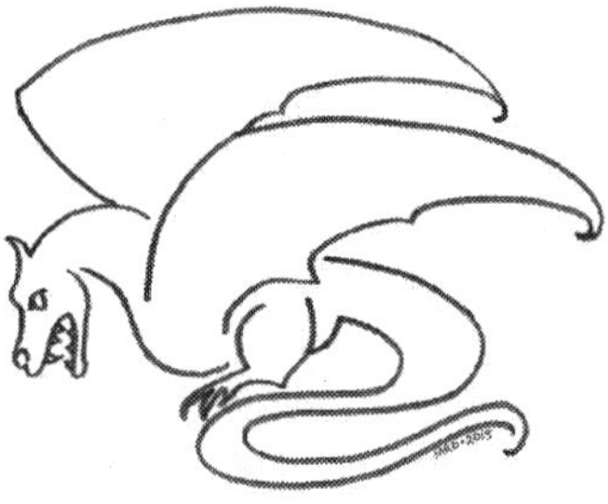

The ladies walked all night.

I ran ahead on foot and verified that Scucca Pass was safe. There was neither sight of a Fomorian nor whiff of mutton grease. After moving a downed tree that would have posed a problem, and rolling some boulders aside to widen the path, I sprinted back and took up position on a forested ridge high above the Refuge. Leading the horses and donkeys, the ladies labored up and across the flank of Aranafalla on hair-raising switchbacks, and I carefully watched our back trail while a crescent moon struggled to scatter the rainclouds.

When morning arrived, a heavy mist veiled the lake. Overhead, an ominous cumulonimbus layer blocked the sun. A family of plesiosaurs lumbered ashore to feast on the bodies in front of the Refuge. I watched in fascination from my perch on the ridge. My vision was so good that if I focused and strained and willed the images to me, even distant objects became detailed. The largest of the knuckers was busy dragging a Fomorian into the water when a bestial warning cry sounded from out on the lake. The knuckers immediately abandoned their meal and crawled clumsily to the water's edge. Once in the water, however, they transformed into graceful swimmers and glided swiftly away.

Within moments, scores of boats emerged from the mist and ran aground on either side of the stone pier. Soon the beach was swarming with Giants. There were hundreds of them. Bróna had surmised that they would have to go far to get reinforcements in any great number, since their island stronghold was two days' sailing to the northwest. But Bróna had been wrong; there must have been a large contingent of Giants within a few hours' march of our secluded valley. What were they doing in Fintan's Highlands, I wondered?

The Giants oozed like spilt treacle over the walls of the Refuge and throughout the compound. Within minutes the house and barn were ablaze. They even set fire to my log pile. I gritted my teeth in anger. We had not asked for this. We had done nothing to deserve the Giants' wrath. It was the Elves they wanted, not a group of harmless old women. Yet Bróna had made it clear that when Giants went on the rampage they usually destroyed everything in their path.

Then the Giants discovered the little graveyard. A row of upright swords marked seven fresh mounds of dirt. The Fomorians began unearthing the Elves' graves with their swords and bare hands. Their leader checked each body as it was uncovered, and then tossed it aside. This Fomorian, an ugly hulk named Py-Rhatt, could be distinguished from the others by a red bandana wrapped around his skull and a red satin blouse that he wore under his leather jerkin. I focused on his face, and his bulbous features came into view. He seemed pleased by what they had unearthed, yet puzzled at the same time. They appeared to be verifying the identities of the slain, but something wasn't adding up for them. I prayed fervently that they would find whoever they were looking for and leave us alone.

While they were exhuming the bodies, another Giant trotted back and forth in the meadow behind the compound with his head down, studying the ground. He eventually found what he was looking for, and followed the footprints for thirty yards before stopping to scan the mountain. I ducked behind some boulders in a knee-jerk reaction, even though he probably couldn't see me from that distance.

I allowed myself a quick peek and saw the tracker talking to the Fomorian leader and pointing to the mountain trail. My heart sank. What a blow! These creatures were young and powerful and could cover ground in a fraction of the time that Humans could. I would have to push the old ladies hard and start caching weapons at various fallback points along our retreat. It looked as though I was going to have to mount a one-woman, running battle of hit-and-run attacks and boobytraps.

Within minutes of discovering our escape route, the Giants were on our trail—and covering ground at a mile-eating lope. I dodged over the ridge and made sure to break some track records of my own.

The rain that had threatened all night was finally unfettered—too late to wipe out the evidence of our passage and just in time to curtail our progress.

I caught up with the caravan in Scucca Pass, a densely forested gulch that snaked between Aranafalla and Maumseachtain.

Bróna had halted the caravan at the base of the Notch, a nasty cut in Maumseachtain's treacherous cliff face. The wall of rock revealed tumbled stratification, evidence of a violent upheaval in the not-too-distant past. The conglomerate rock seemed loosely connected and unsettled. Here and there, a scraggly spruce clung to cracks in the cliffside and reached its distorted limbs toward the meager sky.

The ladies of the Refuge had started to build fires and unpack food.

I skidded to a halt beside Bróna. "We can't stop here. The Giants are on our trail and gaining fast."

"But we are exhausted!" exclaimed Bróna. "We *must* rest for a while."

"There's no time, Bróna. You have to keep going. Get into the Notch and climb as high as you can. There's no other defensible ground."

Bróna knew I was right. In her youth, she had led warriors through many battles. She drew upon a rapidly diminishing store of military discipline to shove aside the weariness of old age and exhort her companions. "All right, ladies! Get up! We must press on or die where we sit."

"I'll cover our tracks," I said. "Hopefully, they won't see where we turned off."

"Is our home still standing?" asked Finoula as she repacked a kettle into a pannier.

I shook my head sadly. "They set it on fire," I said softly.

"Well," said Aoibh, ever hopeful. "This rain will probably put it out."

It certainly was coming down hard. Visibility was reduced to fifty feet.

In the snug travois, the Elf watched and listened.

Sorrow and exhaustion was evident on the faces of the elderly women as they broke camp and prepared to carry on.

The most difficult part of the journey lay directly ahead, and up. The Notch was a gash in the cliffside which hid a steep, narrow, and convoluted trail that was known to only the ladies. They had used this escape route in the past, but it had not presented a problem to them in those bygone years. They were all in their sixties or seventies now, and a few were even older. This climb was going to be tortuous for them, if indeed they could make it at all.

Aoibh and Finoula unloaded half the weapons and left them on the ground for me to distribute as I saw fit. There were woefully few. We would definitely run out of arrows before we ran out of Giants.

The women, donkeys, and horses struggled into the Notch and began their trudge up the muddy path in the pouring rain. I busied myself with eliminating our tracks. I scattered the campfire stones, dragged a tree branch through our prints, and strewed leaves and pine needles over the drag marks. Fortunately, the animals had been too tired to move around, yet the mud was deeply churned where they had stood. I was nearly paralyzed with anticipation and fear, and worried that I would do a shoddy job. I hefted a large deadfall across the place where the caravan had turned off the trail, and was at last satisfied with my hasty work. There was no time for anything else, so I left the rest up to the pounding, blurring rain.

I chose to make my first stand at the entrance to the Notch, and accordingly cached several weapons behind a boulder at the first bend in the narrow split. After that, I dashed and sprang from one vantage point to another, higher and higher, stashing weapons at various points.

When I leapt from one particular shelf, my weight loosened the rock where it jutted from the wall. I made a mental note of it.

With my preparations finished, I returned to the boulder that overlooked the trail in the pass. I checked my weapons, nocked an arrow into a bow, and crouched down, waiting. The rain lashed me unmercifully. I was soaked to the skin and as soon as I stopped moving around, the cold crept in.

What had taken my companions all night to traverse took the Giants less than two hours. Within minutes of my settling behind the boulder, several hundred Fomorians poured into the pass at an untiring trot. I held my breath.

With their tracker out in front, the long line of Giants passed the entrance to the Notch. They had overlooked our turnoff! I welled up with exhilaration. The last of the Fomorians was almost out of sight when a piercing scream rent the air. I swiveled my head upwards. The anguished scream had come from inside the Notch and it boded ill for one of my friends—and most assuredly for all of us.

Py-Rhatt halted his troops and listened. One of the Fomorians pointed to the Notch and the whole line about-faced and charged toward my hiding place.

To my greatest horror and lifelong grief, the brown-robed body of one of the old ladies came bouncing and tumbling down the ravine. I leaped out of hiding to grab her, but slipped on the mud and missed my objective. The hapless woman slid past me, tumbled out of the Notch, and rolled lifelessly to a stop at the feet of the Fomorian horde. Because it was their wont to act impulsively and brainlessly, one of the Giants ran her through with his sword before turning her over with his foot. It was my dear friend, Finoula.

My soul was fit to burst. The pain surged upwards from my depths and I wailed aloud.

Py-Rhatt's eyes opened wide in astonishment at the sight of me, standing tall on the slope and plastered by the rain. There was a momentary pause. Then the Fomorian chief brayed something in a gravelly voice.

His shout jerked me out of my inertia. I jumped back behind the boulder and snatched up the bow I had dropped. I quickly nocked an arrow and drew a bead on Py-Rhatt, but to my horror the wooden bow snapped in two and the arrow clattered uselessly amongst the rocks.

Py-Rhatt glared at me and gave voice to his battle cry. His bellow was taken up by the Fomorian legion and the tremendous roar reverberated throughout the mountains. They clashed swords against shields. The clamor chilled me to my core. While their vociferation echoed around me, I pivoted and fled, and they came after me with all the ferocity they could muster.

Big as they were, those Giants were amazingly limber, and the gap between us closed more rapidly than I was prepared for. Rather than fumble with a spear at close quarters, I decided instead to beat a hasty retreat up the canyon with the Giants nipping at my heels. I parkoured from rock to boulder, while the mud and the steep grade and their own jostling numbers contrived to slow the Fomorians down.

When I arrived at my second weapons cache, I

grabbed a spear and turned just in time to auger the nearest Giant. He was less than fifteen feet behind me. The Notch was jammed with Giants. The muddy trail was treacherous, but this worked in my favor. The Fomorian I speared acted like a bowling ball on his downhill tumble, resulting in quite a few cracked skulls and broken limbs in the ensuing pileup.

While they were disentangling themselves, I picked up a new bow and began shooting at high speed. My victims were sitting ducks. My first shots were off the mark, but my hands and eyes quickly remembered their old skills, and vital targets soon began luring my arrows.

Below the pileup, Py-Rhatt ordered his warriors to unplug the gorge by hauling the dead and injured out of the way.

Meanwhile, I ran out of arrows and had to abandon my position. I bounded up the slope and around a sharp bend in the Notch.

Py-Rhatt himself led the second charge. He barreled around the bend, practically on his hands and knees in the steep scrabble of the incline. I was waiting, and launched a spear at his chest with full force, but he slipped in the mud and the spear transfixed the Giant behind him.

The rock ledge I was standing on shifted slightly with my spear thrust and I spread my feet to restore my balance. I immediately hurled another spear, but Py-Rhatt rolled behind a boulder and the missile zoomed harmlessly past him.

The force of my second throw caused the rock to slant sharply. It tilted me forward and I slipped down the slick granite surface and onto the muddy trail. I landed on my feet, but momentum carried me down the slope like an out-of-control skier—standing upright, with arms windmilling like crazy—directly toward the oncoming Giants.

I arrested my downhill slide by grabbing onto a rowan sapling. My feet slid out from under me and I twisted around onto my stomach. Py-Rhatt chose that opportunity to leap from his position. He sprawled on top of me and wrapped his arms around me in an iron grip. I clung to that rowan sapling for dear life. Whatever chance I had at the top of the trail, I would have no hope whatsoever if I slid down amongst the rest of the Fomorians.

My run-in with O'Grady back in Galway had traumatized me so much that Py-Rhatt's vise-like hold triggered serious psychological distress. Memories of dried urine and sour cream, aftershave and garlic clouded my brain, but were gradually overwhelmed by the revolting stench of rancid mutton grease. I was thrown into a blind panic and fought like a wildcat. I am proud to say I made that hulk pay dearly for his decision to capture me. I gouged his eyes, raked his face, and bit his leathery ear in half. We struggled in an epic embrace and our combined weight caused the rowan tree to snap in two. Without that anchor, we hurtled down the slope, locked together and fighting all the way. I was pummeled and nearly suffocated under Py-Rhatt's incredible bulk.

It was Py-Rhatt who unintentionally saved my life and brought about his own demise. He flipped onto his back and braced his feet against the sides of the narrow gorge to halt our descent. Now I was on top. My heels were level with his groin and I didn't hesitate to make use of that advantage. Oh, but I kicked him hard! He grunted in pain and released one hand to protect his crotch, and I twisted out of his grasp. I regained my footing and spun to face him, drawing my sword at the same time.

The unfortunate Giant sat up and lunged for me, but his roar of anger turned into a gurgle when an Elven arrowhead pierced his throat.

Other Elven arrows hissed overhead in quick succession from further up the ravine, rapidly picking off the Giants that were charging my tenuous position.

I paused to see where the arrows were coming from and Py-Rhatt grabbed the hem of my tunic, his eyes bulging. He wasn't dead yet, and I had a lot to learn about turning my back on an injured Giant. Time did another one of its slow-motion lapses, and I gazed into his angry eyes for an interminable moment, all the while raising my sword above my head in a slow, graceful arc.

"Primrose Prendergast sends her regards," I heard myself saying, then time caught up with me in a *whoosh* as I swung my sword and lopped off his head. Without a backward glance, I turned around and raced up the slope. Behind me, Py-Rhatt's body succumbed to gravity and slid downhill in pursuit of its rolling head.

Up ahead, hunkered down behind one of my fallback points, a young Elf with long white hair and blue eyes was sighting a nocked arrow in my direction. I stopped short in consternation. The Elf who had just shot Py-Rhatt, the Elf who had been injured by Giants on the Dún Aengus Road, was a female! She motioned me to move and I ducked as she released the arrow. The deadly missile zipped past my head and struck the chest of a Giant whose spear tip was mere feet away from skewering me.

I resumed my upward dash with impetus. The Elf's motions were continuous and smooth as she nocked, drew, and released arrow after arrow. I have no doubt in my mind that her intervention saved my life.

I leaped over the rock barrier and crouched beside the Elf. Foregoing a formal introduction, I immediately grabbed a bow and arrow and brought them into play. After I had nailed a few Giants on the slope below, I paused to smile at my new ally.

"Thanks," I said.

The young she-Elf returned my smile. As the Fomorians were still bent on our destruction, we continued shooting.

"You were doing quite well by yourself," she said. From the sound of her accent, I could tell that Shelta was a second language for her.

"There are too many of them. I would have been overpowered if you hadn't helped out."

The Giants were cautious now. Once they registered the death of their leader, they halted their charge. They took cover and showed themselves infrequently, which gave us a breather.

"I have never seen a Human kill a Giant before," said my new friend. Her annunciation was perfect, which meant she had learned Shelta in school but hadn't had much opportunity to practice it. She didn't use contractions or other shortcuts, and pronounced each word completely, clipping the ends neatly.

"You need to get out more," I jested.

She grinned, then sobered up again. "I sent the other women on ahead. Where is Finoula?"

My heart lurched. The heat of battle had driven all thought of Finoula from my mind, and the returning grief seared me painfully. I swallowed a large lump that threatened to choke me before I could answer.

"Dead."

The Elf woman looked at me with compassion. "She was leading the horse over a difficult spot," she ventured to explain. "The horse in front of them slipped and knocked Finoula off her feet. She slid down the path and out of sight."

I shot my last arrow into a Giant who had peeked around the bend, and then I leaned back against the rock in weariness. The Elf kept firing sporadically.

"I am almost out," she said after a short while.

I examined our surroundings. "We need to block the gorge," I decided. "The mountainside around that shelf is unstable, and the rock itself is loose. Let's try to dislodge it."

The slab was barely attached to its base, and the weight of the mountainside was resting upon it.

"A rockslide would surely hold them off while we escape," agreed the Elf.

"Yeah, if it's big enough," I said.

We got to our feet. The Elf's leg was in a gypsum cast but she was able to hobble. I wrestled a boulder over my head and heaved it at the rock shelf below. A direct hit! The ledge moved. The Elf used a spear to pry another boulder loose, and it tumbled down and smacked the gully wall. Our efforts produced an average-sized rockfall which drove the Giants downhill in a scurried retreat; yet it was not sufficient to close off the Notch.

While my newest acquaintance toppled more rocks down the slope, I took a spear and aimed for the widening gap behind the tilted slab. I cast the spear with all my might and it rammed home, burying itself deep and severing the last link between the slab and its base.

The rockslide that followed was a thunderous cataclysm. The entire mountain shook and roared as tons of rock filled the Notch. A volcanic cloud of debris was blasted skyward and a column of dust engulfed us. The Elf and I were terrified by our proximity to the disaster. Without asking by your leave, I grabbed the Elf and heaved her over my shoulders in a fireman's hold, then hot-footed it up the trail.

Chapter 19

The sun was coaxing steam from a small lake in the tiny hanging valley at the top of the Notch, where last winter's snow still slept in pockets. There was no way in or out of the cirque except via the slim fissure we had just climbed. Towering cliffs of unscalable granite encircled the glacial amphitheater. The northern end of the cirque dropped off sheer to a scree flank several thousand feet below. Far away and looking like puddles, Lough Fee and the Killary Inlet sparkled like jewels between the cloud shadows.

The rain was temporarily spent, but the cumulus clouds were lowering. Bróna posted two women at the neck of the Notch to warn of any danger, and the rest of us set about building a shelter. We worked in gloomy silence.

The cirque had a nice little stand of quaking aspen and mountain ash trees. I chopped down several saplings and hacked the branches off to form tent poles. The others busied themselves unloading the donkeys, building a cook fire, and gathering leaves and heather to make beds.

The she-Elf sat apart from the others, sorting and cleaning the remaining weapons. There was a cold aloofness between her and the ladies from the Refuge. They could not bring themselves to trust an Elf, and she was all alone amongst ancient enemies and was unsure how to proceed.

I hammered A-frames into holes in the ground and lashed ridgepoles across the tops to form two tents, each approximately twenty feet long. The other women covered the tents with oilcloths which they secured with rawhide thongs. They piled dead leaves, grass, and heather inside the shelters and spread waterproof groundsheets on top.

Next, I built a lean-to for the animals out of poles and branches. It wasn't completely weatherproof, but at least it was a shelter. There was no need to picket them since there was nowhere for them to wander, so our little herd grazed happily on the long grass.

Cáit tended the fire and stewpot under an awning slung between the two tents. The others gathered firewood. All the food and blankets and spare clothing were brought inside. Everyone changed into dry clothes and hung their wet garments up on makeshift clotheslines.

Bróna divided the coming night into four-hour shifts and assigned the women to stand sentry duty in pairs.

Nightfall found us inside the tents, eating our stew in silence. Rain thrummed on the oilcloth overhead and dripped incessantly from various junctures in the canvas. Despite our woolen cloaks and blankets, we remained cold and damp.

I sat next to the Elf. "Ashling," I announced,

tapping my sternum.

She raised her right hand, fingers splayed in greeting. "Séú of Elasippus," she said.

I hastily mirrored her gesture. "Why were the Fomorians chasing you?"

"My brothers and kinsmen were taking me to the King of Danaan Land. I am to marry him in order to cement the alliance between this land and mine. Py-Rhatt ambushed us outside Dún Aengus, intending to steal the King's betrothed and provoke a war."

"Who is Py-Rhatt?"

"The Giant whose head you removed today."

"So, your brothers and kinsmen…"

Séú's eyes reflected terrible grief. Her voice was a whisper. "The last of them fought and died beside you at the Refuge."

"I'm so sorry, Séú." My own voice was hoarse with sorrow. I had seen a lot of death in the past two days. The loss of Finoula weighed heavily on my mind, but Séú had lost so much more than I.

"They were great warriors," she said. Anguish and perplexity were comingled in her voice. "It is inconceivable that a Daughter of Cain should survive when the finest of Elasippus succumbed."

Where had I heard that phrase before? My brow furrowed. "Are you calling *me* a Daughter of Cain?"

Séú stiffened. "Forgive me. I meant no disrespect."

"Oh, I don't mind. I just wonder what you mean by it."

"You are white-skinned," she explained carefully as though I was slow-witted.

"Right. But who is Cain?"

Now it was she who wrinkled her brow. "He who

was marked by God after killing his brother."

"I'm not descended from that murderer!" I exclaimed, indignant at her audacity. She was referring to the sons of Adam and Eve from the book of Genesis. It was a story that all Irish Catholics knew well.

"All white-skinned Humans are."

"Why?" I couldn't help but be interested.

"When Cain killed Abel, God put his mark upon Cain so that nobody would exact revenge for the crime."

"What kind of mark? A scar?"

"No," she replied, astonished that I had not heard the story. "God promised to protect Cain from vengeful Humans, so he changed Cain's skin color to white, to make him look like one of the gods. Humans revere the gods and would never strike one for fear of retribution."

"But wasn't Cain already white? I mean, Adam and Eve were white, right?" I hadn't given it much thought. All the religious paintings hanging in the Louvre depicted white-skinned participants in the biblical stories.

Séú shook her head several times and gazed at me through eyes that doubted my sincerity. "Are you joking with me?" she asked, flashing a nervous smile.

"No. Please tell me."

"Adam and Eve were created without color."

"What do you mean, 'without color'?" I scoffed. "Were they see-through, or something?"

She laughed a little at that. "They were black, which absorbs light but transmits no hue."

"Black is a color," I said with a superior air.

"Black is the absence of reflected color," she corrected.

I had bitten off way more than I could chew. I dug

into my bowl and scarfed its cargo until my spoon scraped the bottom. Then I tore into my bread roll. I guess you could say I was pouting. It seemed that my worldview had been painted by frauds and charlatans. Why couldn't scientists and historians in my time have gotten things right? Every time I opened my mouth here, I made a colossal fool of myself.

While I was catching up on my history, Séú was calculating how to resolve our current dilemma. She visibly shook off her depression, becoming brisk and purposeful. "I must get word to the king," she said. "We were not due in Tara for another few days, so we cannot expect help to arrive for at least a week."

"That is, if they even know where to search," I amended.

"That is true. We were chased far from our designated path."

We fell silent. The sounds of subdued weeping trickled around the tent. Aoibh's head was resting on Bróna's shoulder. Bróna's lips were set in a grim line and her brittle eyes pierced the fabric of time as she gazed off into distant memories.

"They grieve for Finoula," said Séú quietly.

I could only nod. The struggle to maintain composure had constricted my throat.

"I am moved by the incredible spirit of the Human being."

"You sound surprised."

"I was not raised around Humans. My kinsmen do not have a high opinion of your race."

"Not all of us deserve a high opinion."

"It is the same with Elves," admitted Séú.

"Then we have more in common than most people

think."

"After only a short time amongst you, I have to agree."

"So, where is Ee-la-sippicus?" I mispronounced.

"Elasippus. My homeland is over the sea, three days' sail to the west. Danaan Landers call it Hy-Breasil."

"Huh. I thought that was just a mythical place."

"How could you think that, with all the ships that ply between our coasts daily?"

"I just can't picture where it would be. Is it shaped like this? Look, here's Danaan Land..." I proceeded to scratch rough outlines of modern-day Ireland and North America on the canvas groundsheet with my fingernail.

Séú frowned and shook her head. "Your education has been neglected, I fear," she began, then caught herself and apologized. "Forgive me, Ashling. It is not your fault that Humans are forbidden to attend school. Here, let me show you..."

She proceeded to enlarge my rendering of what I knew to be Ireland, until it encompassed the shape of England and Scotland as well. Then she drew a wide, serpentine continent in the center of the Atlantic Ocean, precisely tracing the path of the Mid-Atlantic Ridge. When finished, she looked at me expectantly.

I stared at the map with dawning realization and at Séú with renewed fascination. When I dared to speak again, it was in a whisper to lessen the enormity of my embarrassment should I prove, once again, to be wrong.

"Tír na nÓg?" I asked hesitantly, while pointing to the mid-Atlantic continent.

To my great astonishment, Séú beamed and nodded with satisfaction. "Ah, so you *have* heard of us!" she exclaimed.

I was flabbergasted. I was going to have to start writing all this information down so I could explain Earth's early history to people in my time period when I returned home. "But you've drawn an actual, physical continent," I said.

"Of course! What else?"

"I dunno. I heard it was under the sea."

"Ships look like they are disappearing under the sea when they sail over the horizon, but that is because the Terra is a sphere."

"I know *that*," I responded scornfully.

She shrugged. I fell silent, ruminating upon the truths I had learned about Earth's past. Eventually, I voiced my shaky conclusion.

"But if Tír na nÓg, and Fallen Angels, and Giants really do exist—what about all the other things I've scoffed at?"

"There is no draconsfeura without a dragon," said Séú.

I looked sharply at her. Did she just say 'dragon'? Was she *kidding*? Before I could collect my thoughts and formulate questions, Bróna interrupted angrily. She had been consumed by worry about the dangers that faced our doomed group, and when our whispered conversation seeped into her consciousness, her legendary patience reached its breaking point. She proceeded to unload her emotional burdens and grief upon us youngsters.

"You don't have an ounce of brain cells between the two of you!" she snapped. "Whose great idea was it, sealing up the only escape route out of this valley, with winter coming on and Giants laying siege in the pass?" She directed her next comment at me. "You, of all people, should be worried about our food situation."

I blushed furiously and turned my back to them all. I pretended to settle down and go to sleep. My greatest weakness was how much I worried about food, and Bróna had cut me to the quick. I did have a voracious appetite and ate more than my fair share of food at the Refuge, but I also was bigger and more active than the others. I wasn't a glutton, or anything of the sort; I just felt better when I knew that my next meal was secure. Yet strangely enough, I hadn't thought about food until she had mentioned its scarcity just then.

Chapter 20

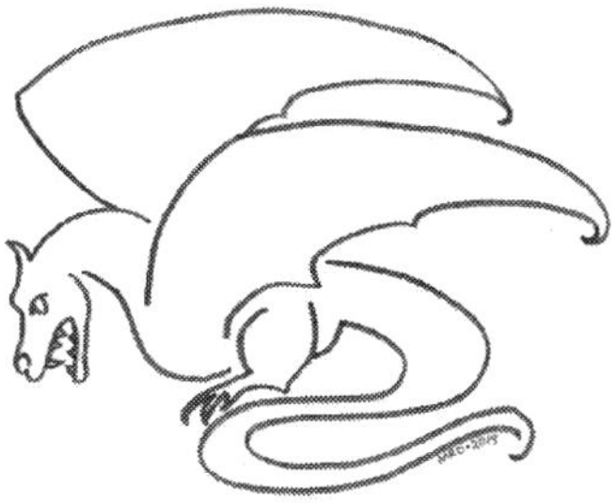

I lay awake for a long time, debating how to extricate us all from the mess I had helped get us into. Despite the ground sheet and tent, the rain was omnipotent, and I was damp and miserably cold throughout the stormy night. In the morning, after a fitful sleep, I woke up to the only logical—although terrifying—solution.

We had enough food for one week, tops. If we rationed those already meager supplies, we could stretch it out for two, maybe three, weeks. After that, we would have to start butchering the horses, and then the donkeys, although the old ladies loved their donkeys so much they would rather starve than take that road.

I idly contemplated what the punishment would be for a Human to eat an Elven horse. Death would be too good for such a sacrilegious crime, I suspected. I imagined a group of emaciated survivors being fattened up by the Elves so they could torture us cruelly before putting us to death again.

I accepted responsibility for the group's survival. If even one more of them perished, I would rather die than live with the guilt. Blast it all! I didn't need that kind of baggage! I didn't want to be tied to this horrendous world by feelings of guilt and responsibility! I had a plan for my life; I was going to earn a degree and show the settled community all the qualities that prejudice had blinded them to! They would *have* to accept me. I was going to get their respect, one way or another. And then this had to happen. Well, I wasn't about to let a time/dimension anomaly come in the way of my dreams. No wormhole was going to determine *my* fate. Therefore, my priorities must be carved in stone and my goals pursued with a heart to match. First on my list had to be escape from this mountain peak. For the next few hours, no matter how I twisted and kneaded the options, only one viable solution presented itself.

The morning meal was a depressing affair. Each of us was wrestling with her mortality. I ate a light breakfast. We all did. Bróna had already rationed the food.

During a welcome lull in the rain, I ventured to the northern lip of the cirque and studied the landscape far below through intermittent, low-level, cumulus clouds. The ladies thought of me as a dauntless flier, yet the height that presented itself on Maumseachtain that day terrified the living daylights out of me. At a very rough estimate, our altitude was ten thousand feet above sea level. Back in the future, I had prided myself on my daring. I loved to leap from the highest prominences wherever hang-glider pilots gathered to compete. I had launched from Carrauntoohil, Ireland's highest mountain, and used to dream of better challenges. Well, Carrauntoohil was only three thousand feet high—a mere hillock. This was what I had always dreamed of, and now that I was here it seemed more like a nightmare. I scooted back from the ledge in fear.

What's wrong with you, Ashling? Losing your nerve? I taunted myself.

No. Just finally coming face-to-face with my limitations, the new Ashling argued.

You have no choice. It's do or die.

It may well be do and *die.*

True. But you'll die for sure if you don't try, and so will all the others.

I took a deep breath and my lungs filled with that intoxicating 'something' that laces every sea breeze; that spiritual narcotic that captivates sailors and lures them beyond every horizon. My heedless heart answered the call and a tingle shivered its way from head to toe, but my fearful brain squelched the spark. I heaved a sigh and turned away from the edge. I strode back to the campsite and with each purposeful step willed myself through the forthcoming ordeal.

At the campfire, Aoibh had returned from the dawn watch and was reporting to Bróna. They both seemed to have aged overnight. They appeared frail, and I knew their night of tossing and turning had fed them only hopelessness and despair. They had started to await their deaths.

"Well? Have they gone?" asked Bróna.

"No, they have encamped in the pass," replied Aoibh.

"Have you any good news for me?"

"A large number of them left at first light."

"To scout another way in here, no doubt. Well, they won't find one. If there was a way in, there'd be a way out."

I walked past them and ducked into the tent. Bróna's eyes were upon me; I could feel the two holes burning in my back.

"She's up to something," Bróna confided to Aoibh.

"You've been very hard on her."

"I know," Bróna said with a sigh. "What with Finoula's death and getting trapped in here with only a few days' worth of food… She's got to understand how desperate our plight is."

"She knows," interjected Cáit without looking up from the pot she was stirring.

I reemerged with the folded hang glider under my oxter. It made a brilliant splash of red and gold amongst the earth tones surrounding me. All the ladies in sight halted their work and conversations. Cáit straightened up from the cooking pot. Bróna got to her feet and looked at me suspiciously. Aoibh's hand flew to cover her mouth, and her eyes widened in dismay.

"What are you up to, dear?" asked Bróna in a deceptively mild tone.

"Finoula fixed my wings before she died," I announced. "I plan on flying off that cliff and going for help." My voice brooked no argument. The time for discussing the rights or wrongs of my plan would have to come later. If I stopped now, I would never have the courage to follow through with it. I could only hope my actions would allow us to discuss my foolhardy plan at a later date.

Aoibh stepped in front of me and I halted. I gazed at her through the steely film of death that already separated me from those who would continue living. It was a distancing mechanism that enabled me to switch off my survival instincts and take the plunge toward certain death.

"Well, you can't," said Aoibh firmly. I just looked at her, without really seeing her.

"We won't let you," added Cáit. She had joined Aoibh's blockade.

"Finoula didn't know anything about wings," said Bróna, querulous in her fear. "What if they don't work?"

"If she followed my diagram they should work fine," I heard myself say from the other side of life.

"Finoula gave her life in this adventure of ours," argued Bróna. "She wouldn't want you to give yours as well."

"*All* our lives will be forfeit if I don't try," I answered. I could not afford to let them dissuade me. "Now, who should I go to for help?"

All the ladies had gathered by this time, and surrounded me in silence. Many were weeping quietly. They knew it was our only chance. They also knew, as I did, that we would probably never see one another again; that I would be killed in my fall and they would starve to death, unwept and unsung. They pressed in around me, hugging and touching and saying goodbye without words.

Finally, Aoibh spoke up. "My grandson Cathal has a smithy in Tubber, on the north shore of Lough Fee. He's one of us."

"A Human?" I asked.

"No, a rebel," said Aoibh.

"Excuse me?" This was news. There were rebels?

"Well, he's Human, too," amended Aoibh.

"That is debatable," said Bróna dourly.

At Aoibh's outraged expression the entire assemblage burst out laughing. It was a great relief from the grief. It warmed me and pulled me back from the spiritual brink I was teetering on.

"Aoibh has been training him in the art of metallurgy—and swordplay," explained Cáit.

"He has been training other young men from the surrounding villages," said Aoibh proudly.

"Training for what?" I asked.

"For the time that is coming when things start to change," said Bróna.

"And we could surely do with change right about now," said Emer.

"How many men can he muster to our aid?" I questioned.

"About thirty-five," responded Aoibh proudly.

"*Only thirty-five*?!" I yelped.

"There are men in other villages who would come to our aid," said Bróna.

"We can't charge a thousand Fomorians with only thirty-five farmers!" I exclaimed.

"They're not *all* farmers," said Aoibh defensively.

There was a pause. I waited hopefully for good news in the details.

"Some of them are fishermen," finished Aoibh lamely.

I let out my breath as though I had been deflated. I bit my lip. But still, thirty-five able-bodied rescuers was a better number than zero. Then a voice spoke up from inside one of the tents; it was Séú. We had forgotten all about her, lying injured, nursing a broken leg.

"The King of Danaan Land has ten thousand Elves at his disposal," she said regally. We all spun around as Séú lifted the tent flap and hobbled out with the aid of a crutch. "He may be willing to commit his troops if the prize is the return of his promised bride."

"How can *we* find a bride for the king?" Bróna asked in consternation.

"I am standing in front of you," replied Séú.

"*You* are the king's *bride*?" Bróna sounded incredulous.

"I am promised to him," allowed the Elf.

"Would he be willing to go to war with the Fomorians over you?" I asked, treating the information as a general would, and analyzing it for potential value in our war; but Séú was insulted. Anger suffused her demeanor and I hastened to placate her.

"No offense," I explained. "I'm just trying to gauge the strength of his love for you and how it could best be put to use in extricating us from this dire circumstance."

"It is not a love match," Séú admitted grudgingly, "but King Ampherat is very proud and will not allow Py-Rhatt's insult to go unpunished."

"In that case," said Bróna, "the war has already begun. The Fomorians struck the first blow."

"But where will Humans stand in a war between Elves and Giants?" I asked.

"I think the Fomorians have decided that for us, too," said Séú.

"I never thought I'd see the day," mused Bróna.

"*I* never thought Humans could fly," said Séú pointedly.

How much had she overheard inside the tent? What exactly had we said to one another about who I was? And how far was this Elf willing to go to uphold the Lucifer Laws? Séú and I regarded one another with doubt and distrust. The women from the Refuge were worried.

"I understand that you God People don't like to share the skies," I said finally, throwing caution to the wind. After all, what could she do? If one of us *didn't* fly, we would all sit around glaring at each other until death did us part.

"We don't like derogatory terms like 'God People'," said Séú in anger.

"How is that derogatory?" I threw back.

"It reminds them that their ancestors were cast out of Heaven after a failed coup," said Bróna, but that merely lobbed fat onto Séú's fire.

"You know, I would rather give myself up to the Giants than be insulted like this," she fumed.

All of a sudden I felt remorseful. We were all in this together and it was difficult enough without being at each other's throats. I tried to smooth things out.

"I'm sorry, Séú. I didn't know that was an insult to an Elf. I've still got a lot to learn about this world."

"This world?" repeated Séú, and I instantly realized my blunder. "What do you know of the other worlds?"

The old ladies looked extremely perturbed.

"Oh dear," muttered Cáit.

There was a long and painful pause, during which I decided to trust Séú. After all, she had saved my life the day before, not hesitating to jump into the battle even though encumbered by a broken leg. We could die together with our secrets, or share them and live.

"I flew into this world by accident on a Dragon Wind," I told her. Séú's eyes widened in amazement. "And now you hold my life in your hands," I concluded humbly.

Séú shook her head in disagreement. She placed her hands on my shoulders and looked me steadily in the eye, willing me to believe her. "I owe you my life… and continue to do so," she said. "We are blood-bonded under the Warrior's Code. I could never betray you."

"You say that now," I said in disgruntlement, "but you've seen our hair and our weapons. You've heard our treasonous talk…"

"I do not know what you have heard about Elves," Séú interrupted quickly, "but it sounds like you have been misinformed. When we give our word, it is a bargain sealed for life." Her glance embraced the entire group. "You gave my people succor in our time of greatest need." She looked at me. "You fought alongside my kinfolk and risked your life for strangers." She swept the assembly once more. "You were uprooted from your home and thrust into this atrocious predicament rather than hand me over to my enemies." She paused for a moment to gather her composure. "It is not in my creed to betray such loyalty. You have my undying word—and everlasting gratitude."

A wave of relief passed through the gathering. Séú removed a gold pendant from her neck and tied it around mine. It bore an intricately crafted horse icon.

"Wear this as my token," she said. "No Elf will raise a hand against you whilst you represent the House of Elasippus."

By the time my preparations were completed to the satisfaction of the old ladies, a thick mist had enveloped the hanging valley. I was glad of this, the truth be told, since the fog obscured my view of the terrible plunge I had to make.

My glider had been assembled and I donned my parachute satchel. I folded my woolen cloak and secured it in front of me under the parachute straps. I dared not take any weapons beyond the dagger which I shoved into my belt sheath, for I feared that any extra weight might unbalance my flight and stress the glider's findruine components. The new hardware was untested—that was my primary fear. The aerie I was about to leap from was a far cry from the low hill I had originally selected for the test flight. Aoibh and Kitti argued strenuously against my decision to leave the weapons behind, but ultimately agreed that I could get weapons from the rebel fighters at Tubber once I made it to the ground. A safe flight should be my first concern. It was for the same reason that I left my food pouch behind. If my flight was successful, I could always get food at Tubber; and if I crashed and died… well, I wouldn't need food at all then, would I?

I strapped myself into the harness beneath the golden wyvern. All the women were watching, except Séú, whose leg hurt her too badly to leave the tent. Bróna had given her something to combat the pain and it had put her to sleep.

Bróna and Aoibh held the wingtips steady. A strong wind buffeted the hang glider and I eyed the patched sailcloth and replacement cables with misgivings.

"Do you think it will hold?" asked Cáit, reading my mind.

I indicated the parachute on my back and forced myself to sound reassuring. "I have my backup wings, just in case," I said cheerfully.

"Won't this mist saturate your wings and cause you to sink?" asked the science-minded Bróna.

"The fabric is synthetic," I said. "The moisture will just run off."

"How will you stay aloft?" asked Emer. "Your wings are stationery; you won't be able to flap like a bird."

"Warm air rises, as you know," I said, "and is especially active inside clouds like this, due to the latent heat that's released when water vapor condenses. Plus, the ridge lift and sea breeze are strong. I might actually go up higher at first, before I can start my descent." My insides somersaulted at the thought.

Before I could come to my senses, I gave the prearranged nod to those steadying the glider and we all ran together toward the cliff edge. The wind wrenched the glider off the ground after just ten steps. Bróna and Aoibh let go the wings and I disappeared into the mist.

Back in the cirque, the group of ladies held their breath and clung to each other. They strained their every sense to learn of my fate. An overpowering mood of impending disaster was mixed in a confused combination with hope, and tore their normally stolid composure to shreds.

When my exultant yodel echoed back from the obscuring cloud, the women leaped and cheered aloud to hear it. Then they lapsed back into silence, still waiting at the cliffside.

"Do you think she'll come back?" asked Maddy,

her voice quavering.

Nobody answered for a few moments. Obviously, the fear was universal.

"What if she finds another portal in the mist?" asked another.

Then Bróna spoke. "She has not accepted the twist of fate that brought her to our time, and likewise she does not recognize us as family," she said sadly. "Ashling does not feel allegiance to anyone here. Her old world keeps drawing her back."

"But she fought so hard to protect us from the Giants," argued Aoibh.

"She's been building for a fight ever since she arrived at our door," said Kitti.

"She was defending herself as much as us," said Bróna.

"But she was trying so hard to fit in…" Cáit's voice trailed off.

"She might leave and never look back," worried Emer.

"Not Ashling!" declared Aoibh stoutly. "She is not that kind of person."

"Not even Ashling knows what kind of person she is," said Cáit.

The old ladies looked at one another with dread.

"Her task is impossible," admitted Kitti.

"She doesn't even have a plan of action," added Maddy.

"If she survives her leap of faith," concluded Bróna, "she may well decide to leave us to our fate."

"There's more to that girl than meets the eye," said Aoibh staunchly. "She will surprise us all—even herself. You'll see."

Chapter 21

I was petrified. The last time I had flown, my life on Earth had ended. In the past few days I had become intimate with death, had made my acquaintance with frailty, and finally understood how insecure was my tenure in any world.

I was afraid to die.

When I leaped blindly off that precipice, I was tense and inflexible. My eyes were squeezed shut. When I didn't crash and my glider didn't disintegrate, I lifted one eyelid and peered cautiously out. I was flying! I wasn't dead! That old, familiar joy surged through me and I released a cry that bubbled up within. Behind me, quite some distance away, I heard the ladies cheering. I smiled to hear it. I couldn't see anything through the fog, but was able to judge from the cheering approximately how far from the mountain I had flown. I surmised that my craft was substantially clear of the cliff face for me to avoid crashing into it. It was my first time flying without instruments and I felt naked and blind—completely at the mercy of fate. For such an independent and self-reliant girl as I was, that kind of vulnerability was unfamiliar and unwelcome.

I was sailing through a murky cloud on a slow descent to the rolling hills around Lough Fee. As soon as I cleared the pea soup, I would take my bearings and head generally northwest until the village of Tubber came into sight. It was the only place of Human habitation for miles around, situated at the western tip of the lake. I planned on landing several miles from the village and hiding my glider before walking into town.

Suddenly, something brushed against my wingtip. Fear shot through me and I angled my craft away from the potential impact zone. Had I circled around, unbeknownst to myself, and come into contact with a spur of Maumseachtain? What should I do? If I altered course too much I might just as easily propel myself into the mountain as away from it. My heart thumped painfully. I braced for a crash; every sense on high alert.

I heard a *whoosh* and felt a strong breeze stirring underneath. *What was that?* I twisted this way and that, searching the fog beneath me, but all I heard was the wind. My head was on a swivel, watching for danger and listening for the minute changes in reflected sounds that would indicate the proximity of a large object.

A horrendous screech split the air above me. I immediately swerved and initiated a sliding dive, instinctively knowing that the devil overhead was a lot less threatening than a possible devil beneath… but I wasn't quick enough. Something colossal grabbed my glider from above. The sailcloth shredded loudly as two sets of gigantic talons tore at the gold-painted wyvern on my red glider.

I warped into survival mode. The reasoning part of my brain shut off and the reactionary portion kicked into high gear. I knew I had to put distance between me and my glider as soon as possible. I suspected that I was not the target of the attack, but I would indubitably become collateral damage unless I unhooked my harness. The enormous creature clutched onto the glider's frame and heaved it around, ripping it asunder. I was whipped from pillar to post—a puppet on a string—and the harness became irreversibly tangled.

All the while, we were plummeting to the ground in a spiraling death dive, to the tune of the great beast's growls, shrieks, and snarls. A ferocious muzzle with a full complement of six-inch-long teeth started ripping chunks from the glider, and I could smell burnt venison on the dragon's breath. For it was, without a doubt, a dragon. The extensive, leathery wings flapped all about me, filling the air with the pungent odor that was pure draconsfeura.

One of the harness straps was severed by the razor-sharp fangs, and that gave me an idea. I pulled out my dagger and sliced through the other strap. As I fell away from both the wreckage of my hang glider and the scaly monster destroying it, I glimpsed a thirty-foot-long, buff-colored wyvern with a sixty-foot wingspan, just before its forty-foot tail whipped around and knocked me keel-over-teakettle into the enveloping mist.

I spread my arms and legs to steady my tumbling and slow my descent. When I leveled out, I gripped the parachute's ripcord with one hand and my dagger in the other. I wanted to wait until I cleared the cloud cover before opening my 'chute, to put more distance between me and the monstrous reptile. If I opened my 'chute too soon, the wyvern might see it and come after me again. My blood was pounding and I craved speed more than anything at that moment, yet I also had another concern—what if the cloud extended all the way to the ground? I might have to pull the ripcord *before* clearing the mist. What should I do? When should I open the parachute?

Suddenly, the issue was decided for me. My fate was taken out of my own hands, once again. With a jarring thump, I struck something in midair. The dagger bounced out of my hand and I instinctively clung to the scaly surface that had arrested my fall.

Clinging desperately to spiny projections on the back of this bigger, stronger wyvern, between its immense, beating wings, I prayed to God for deliverance. The dragon twisted and rolled, trying to dislodge me, but my clothing was hooked onto a cluster of curved spikes between his shoulder blades, and I couldn't have fallen off if I tried. He performed some impressive and terrifying loop-de-loops before changing tactics and diving straight for the ground. We broke through the cloud cover and skimmed over the undulating hills by the shores of Lough Fee at breakneck speed.

This was a two-legged dragon, like the one on my family crest; yet this dragon's body was fifty feet long and its wingspan was easily one hundred feet. It was almost twice the size of the one that attacked the glider. There was a stupendous difference between the stylized drawing of the wyvern on my coat of arms and the actual creature in real life. I could feel prodigious power in the wing muscles which bulked up his shoulders and chest. Scales in various shades of sand and cream covered his entire body and gleamed like quartzite where the sun struck them. His head was huge and blocky; rectangular in shape, with nostrils on the point of the muzzle and a maw like that of a Tyrannosaurus Rex. There was a bony ridge above each eye. The ears were long and very expressive, with a tuft of golden-brown hair growing out of each pointy tip. They stood up on either side of his head and pivoted this way and that to pick up sounds, the way a horse's do. His heavy tail tapered to a wicked-looking spearhead that curved like a scorpion's stinger, and he used it as a rudder while flying.

The dragon fled in fright over the lake. He twisted and zigzagged in an effort to dislodge his unexpected passenger. However, I had a tight grip and couldn't be budged. The wyvern banked toward the shore and skimmed close to the ground, following the contours of the hilly terrain and closely avoiding obstacles. His initial terror was dissipating since I had not harmed him in any way.

When I discovered that I wasn't going to fall off, and when the dragon didn't fricassee me, or eat me, or impale me on his deadly tail, I actually began to enjoy the ride. We had bypassed the weirdness point. My out-of-body sensation was fading as it adjusted to and accepted this new normal. The longer we flew together, the less strange it seemed to both of us. I sat up a little and started looking around.

We blasted around a wooded copse and zoomed across a meadow—and mowed down a cadre of men practicing swordsmanship. As the fighters scattered left and right, shouting their fear, I was overtaken by exhilaration and gave vent to my full-throated, ululating yell. It felt excellent to discharge some of the pent-up tension that had almost paralyzed me ever since jumping off the mountain.

At the sound of my voice, the wyvern shivered

from stem to stern. I began laughing with unbounded delight. My father and I used to ride horses together, with me sitting in front of the saddle and his strong arm around me. He used to tell me, "Pat the horse, Ashling. Let him know you appreciate him." I reached forward and patted and caressed the dragon's neck. In response, he slowed his pace and controlled his labored breathing. His pinned ears perked up and swiveled toward his rider.

"Maith an buachaill," I said to my scaly steed. *"Is mise* Ashling. There's no need to fear me."

Chapter 22

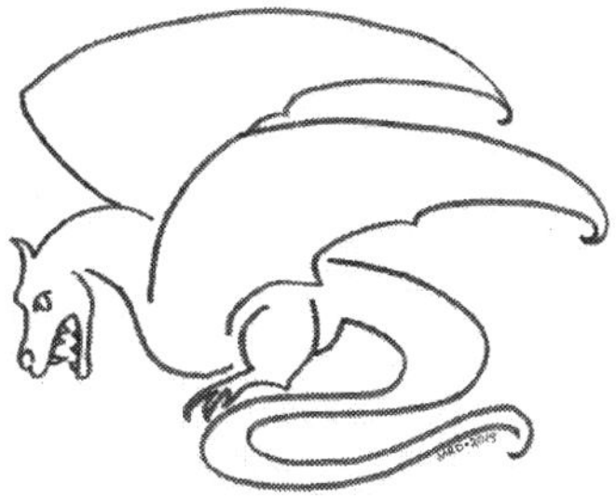

THe swordfighters in the meadow picked themselves up and ran to the safety of the trees. They were dressed in leathern tunics and woolen leggings. All except their leader had close-cropped hair.

Cathal the Smith, mid-twenties, was handsome, tall, and muscular, with piercing blue eyes and long blond hair. He got to his feet and gaped after the dragon in astonishment. Cathal's second-in-command, Niall of the Boats—a black-haired man of similar age—thumped Cathal on the back, alive with excitement.

"That's the one I was telling you about—the young male—the one who watches us all the time. He's never come this close before."

"Did you see the girl?" asked Cathal in extreme agitation.

"All I saw was Farra's scaly belly!" exclaimed Niall. This close encounter with a dragon was unheard of and he thought it boded well for their efforts; a sign, of sorts.

"The girl… the redhead… the girl who was riding

him. Did you see her?" Cathal appeared not to have noticed the dragon that had flattened his field of fighters.

Niall looked at his friend in concern. "A girl? On the dragon?" he asked, scratching his head.

"Yes!" said Cathal. "The beauty on the beast! Surely you saw her? She's the one who made that chilling war cry."

"That wasn't the dragon?"

Cathal pushed Niall in frustration. "No, it was a gorgeous woman."

The other men looked at each other in puzzlement. Niall twirled his finger close to his temple and nodded in Cathal's direction. Some of the men laughed, but most of them were too scared to see humor in anything. They searched the skies fearfully, expecting dragons to pop out of the low clouds at any moment.

"You mean none of you saw her?" asked Cathal in disbelief.

Shaking heads and shrugging shoulders were his only answer. Then Fergus, a boy of fourteen, pushed through his elders to stand in front.

"I saw her, Cathal. A redhead, just like you said."

"Aw, shut up, you little arse-kisser," snarled Niall. "You didn't see anything."

"I did!" the boy protested. "She had on a green tunic."

"How did *you* see her and I not?" asked Niall scathingly.

"I was the only one who wasn't flat on my back, is why," retorted Fergus impudently.

Niall pushed the lad and knocked him to the ground. "Well, you're flat on your back now, aren't you, pup?"

Cathal pulled the boy to his feet. "Did you get a look at her ears, Fergus?" he asked, still consumed by the vision he saw.

"Naw. She went by too fast."

"Do you think the Elves are on to us?" Niall asked, suddenly worried. This use of dragons could be a new method of spying on their subjects. He wouldn't put anything dirty past the Elves.

"It could be," agreed Cathal, finally coming back down to Terra. He gazed in the direction the dragon had flown and quickly made his decision. "Send word to all the villages to prepare for another surprise Elven inspection," he ordered. "And we need to send a runner to Tully Cross to find out what's stirring."

He paused, still searching the sky, and his men began packing up to leave. "Things have been way too quiet lately," he mused.

Chapter 23

I sat up confidently between the wyvern's wings and raised my face to the sun. I was either dead and in Heaven, whereby no harm could touch me, or else I was asleep and dreaming. There was no way I was actually flying across the sky on a gigantic dragon. So, I felt at peace, confident that my situation was good.

I started humming. The tune gained in shape and strength, and the lyrics came to me as naturally as balancing on a dragon. The melody fit my mood to perfection, feeling ancient and futuristic, and wailingly lost while yet solidly belonging.

Through the tunnels of time I have traveled
Back to The Beginning, I'm told
Great things once awaited, now I'm trapped in the past
Watching as history unfolds

With hindsight I look to the future
And dread what we've yet to go through
Lies and deception will make us forget
As we're blinded and deafened to truth

Time stretches like truth through the ages
The story rewritten and spun
A week is converted to one hundred years
A thousand years pass like just one

Quantum physics is spiritual science
Space and time are both infinite
Our dimension is one of so many
Separated by darkness and light

My future was granted to me by degrees
I was climbing and on the right track
I took a wrong turn, with so much at stake
And now I can't find my way back

My tumble from grace wasn't really that far
My truths were all built on a lie
Now I soar to the heights on this dragon I fly
By degrees have I reached for the sky

The wyvern responded well to my singing. He flew steadily and banked smoothly, careful not to lose me. And I could have sworn he was humming along! I felt rather than heard a deep-seated vibration coming from within him, like a cat's purr. There was a surprising amount of heat radiating from his body, and I was kept warm despite the cold air in the higher altitudes.

The rough map that Séú had scratched onto the canvas groundsheet the night before sprang to life beneath us as Farra soared into the atmosphere. The land of the Tuatha Dé Danaan bore little resemblance to the Ireland I knew in the future. Fintan's Highlands was a mountainous region that followed the contours of Ireland, but it was only a portion of a much larger country. Another difference was the mountain peaks, which routinely topped fourteen thousand feet and were jagged, as though recently formed

The Gaodhal Valley continued eastward from Fintan's Highlands for hundreds of miles. I estimated that several thousand square miles of that vast plain had been put to ranching. It was blanketed with cattle and sheep as far as the eye could see.

South of the mountains, countless hectares of forest stretched to the coastline, where several large ports were handling a brisk trade. Sailing ships cluttered the harbors and sea lanes.

From my perch in the heavens I saw villages and towns dispersed predominantly along the coast and in the central plains. Roads crisscrossed the lowlands, and traffic was surprisingly busy, considering the relatively juvenile civilization. Nary a knuckle-dragging cave dweller in sight.

The morning wore away until a gnawing in my stomach reminded me that I hadn't yet eaten. With great reluctance, I turned my thoughts to the friends I had left in that inaccessible mountain hollow. It seemed as though my cogitations were picked up by the dragon, for he changed course and headed northwest. Before long, we were over Fintan's Highlands and descending rapidly.

As we glided over the turbulence of Lough Fee, a whopping knucker formed a rather substantial shadow below the surface, and I was disturbed by how fast they could swim when under way. Not until then did I comprehend how narrowly I had escaped death in Kylemore Lough. A little further on, the wyvern slowed down and searched the water for something. He circled and dropped swiftly to the water, then stalled over a school of feeding fish to snatch a salmon with his talons. Clutching his dinner, he flew to shore and headed for a prominent crag in a secluded gully in the foothills.

The wyvern landed gently and lowered his head to the ground. I unhooked my clothing from the spines on the dragon's back, and stood up. I clambered along his shoulder and wing and leaped nimbly to the ground. It felt unnatural to be standing on firm ground once more. I would gladly have exchanged my obligations in both worlds for a lifetime of roaming with my dragon, but duty was clamoring to be fulfilled.

The dragon and I examined one another carefully. He sniffed me and studied me with soulful, golden eyes. I ran my hand along his smooth facial scales and blew gently into his nostrils the way my father used to bond with horses.

He used his outsized wings as a bat does, folding them until the joints touched the ground. Three finger-like claws grew out of the wing joints and he used those like hands, supporting his weight and pivoting on them when he needed to turn or move.

The dragon tore the salmon in half and dropped a chunk onto the ground at my feet. I looked at the fish in astonishment. So that his gesture might be abundantly clear, he shuffled back a few feet.

Without the slightest hesitation, I picked up the salmon and bit into it hungrily. The wyvern watched me devouring my meal and appeared to be satisfied. He wasn't a fastidious eater either, and it didn't take long to gulp his meal down.

"I wish there were salmon in the high lake where my friends are trapped," I said conversationally as I licked my fingers.

The wyvern cocked his head intelligently. He turned his gaze toward the mountain peak in question.

I laughed and patted him on the neck. "You act as though you understand me."

The creature lowered his head and nosed the wyvern appliqué on my tunic. Without warning, he puffed out his chest and exhaled a great snort of hot breath, then flapped his wings and leaped into the air. I cowered in alarm. The downdraft swept the crag clean and caused trees to bend and sway. Within seconds he was a mere dot in the sky. I squinted after him and sighed regretfully. Although I had established a close connection with the wyvern, I had no way of communicating with him. What I had experienced was a once-in-an-epoch occurrence, and one I would remember for the rest of my days.

I took stock of my surroundings. Closing my eyes so I could concentrate on my hearing, I listened for trouble. There was none on the wind, so I relaxed and took a deep breath, my face absorbing the sun. The air was redolent of pine, dead leaves, moss, and rich earth. I could also smell the ocean and seaweed on the breeze.

Satisfied that all was well, I washed my hands and face in a puddle of rainwater and leisurely rebraided my hair. It had come undone during my flight and I couldn't walk into Tubber until I tucked it away. I undid my parachute buckles and unfolded the heavy, woolen cloak that Kitti had made for me. I donned the cloak and pulled up the roomy hood. Then, slinging the parachute pack over my shoulder, I bounded off the crag.

Chapter 24

It was dusk by the time I reached the outskirts of the lakeside village of Tubber. I concealed myself within a copse at the edge of a small farm, less than a mile from the fortified village, or rath.

The farmyard dogs barked incessantly at my position, but were too afraid to approach. I reeked of draconsfeura, which explained their fear. They couldn't tell the farmer and his wife that a dragon was hiding in the woods nearby, but their terror was obvious, so the unmilked cows were locked up, flocks were cooped, and a sizeable brood of children was shuttered inside the sturdy farmhouse for the night. The dogs retreated behind the stone building, whence their trembling growls steadily emanated.

When the noise from the village told me that the last of the boatmen had settled down for the night, I emerged from the trees and trotted across the meadows toward the sturdy walls encircling Tubber. A powerful, running leap enabled me to hurdle the spiked stockade in a single, fluid motion, and I dropped silently to the ground on the other side.

I paused in the shadows, waiting for somebody to sound the alarm, but not even the dogs of Tubber were alert. A steady rain was falling and all souls had sought shelter on that cold night. The wind from Lough Fee was blowing my scent away from the village and back up into the hills.

As fortune would have it, the blacksmith's forge was very close to my ingress point. A light glowed through a frosted pane of glass, and the steady ringing of hammer on anvil honed me in. Like all the other buildings in the village, the smithy was of stone and oak construction. An ample, slate-roofed awning sheltered a hitching rail and a pair of sturdy doors, which were shut. I would have to cross open ground to reach those doors, and I would be very exposed, so I opted to go around the back.

When I sidled around to the rear of the smithy, a dog somewhere caught my scent. Instead of barking, though, the poor thing just whined. *Dragons have a bad name in these parts,* I thought.

A door at the back opened easily and I slipped inside. Standing still until my eyes adjusted to the gloom, I found myself in some kind of storage room. Dozens of tools were arranged neatly on one wall. This blacksmith was obviously very particular about his stuff. The tools were clean and oiled, and arranged according to type. I chose an iron spike and dropped it into my empty sheath. Then I pulled a short-handled pitchfork from its clamp on the wall.

Thus armed, I tiptoed down a short, dark corridor toward the forge's flickering light. The sound of the hammer assured me that the blacksmith was hard at work. Ahead, a half-open door beckoned. I crept forward and peeked through the jamb. Sweat gleamed on a heavily muscled forearm and a hand gripping tongs. The other arm rose and fell rhythmically, and sparks showered with each ringing note.

I studied him carefully, attempting to judge his book by the cover. I was not impressed. The image he presented made me doubt his mental acuity. He wasn't dressed like any blacksmith should be. I imagined he should have been covered from head to toe in protective leather, due to the dangers involved in handling molten metal, yet this fella looked like he was selling ice cream at the beach.

Dirty, leather, half-length pants exposed bulky calves and hairy shins to the vagaries of the splashing iron. He was wearing the flimsiest of sandals on his feet. And the… the *thing* he wore over his upper torso was hilarious! It was a sort of hooded cowl that covered his head and shoulders but laid bare his midriff.

What kind of twit dresses like that?

I noticed that he had a six-pack—well-defined abdominal muscles that would have been the envy of Coach Griffin's goons back in Galway. The cowl was held in place by leather straps that crisscrossed a very muscular and extremely hairy chest. The same blond hair also forested his legs and arms.

The hood obscured his features. Obviously, he cared about protecting his face from wayward sparks. I groaned inwardly, knowing I would be dealing with one of those egotistical, body-builder types, just like the MMA crowd back home.

A cat appeared out of nowhere and rubbed against my ankles, purring loudly. I flinched and then looked down at it with annoyance.

The twit's cat.

I pushed it away with my foot and it sat down with its back to me—for all the world as though it had been insulted—and began washing itself.

I'm going to have to rethink this, I said to myself. *There's got to be a better option than this idiot.*

I backed away from the doorway—and crunched the cat's tail. That stupid cat yowled as though I had tried to kill it. The caterwauling was horrendous and I must have jumped three inches into the air. I flashed a look at the forge... but the blacksmith was no longer there.

Where had he gone? More to the point, why had he run? Was he expecting a calamity, or was he just easily spooked? I had to act fast to stop the twit from raising an alarm. Since speed was now more important than secrecy, I swung wide the door and entered the shadowy forge in a crouching run, looking all around.

Suddenly, from behind a massive ceiling support, the hooded blacksmith lurched toward me, sword first. *Jeepers!* It was obviously 'act first, think later' with this guy! I pulled my head back just in time and the sword zinged past my nose. I hooked the sword with my pitchfork and flicked it up into the rafters. The reverberating *twang* told us both that the blade had buried itself deep in wood. *Buried to the hilt,* I thought smugly. *Not even Muscle Man here will be able to remove that.*

But Muscle Man did not stay around to congratulate me. He disappeared again with disconcerting speed behind the oaken column, and I skulked around it after him. *How can such a big man move so silently?*

Unexpectedly, I was grabbed from behind, spun

around, and slammed up against the post. A thick forearm pressed a dagger blade against my throat while a similar arm pounded my pitchfork hand against the solid oak. I gurgled my outrage while the fine bones on the back of my hand screamed with pain. I had no choice but to drop the pitchfork.

Now I was really ticked off. I tried kneeing him and stomping on his feet, but he blocked my legs with his own hairy tree limbs and pinned me bodily to the post. I couldn't believe this guy's beginner's luck. I had misjudged him, underestimated him, and my disdain for him had allowed him to get too close. I thought of Primrose Prendergast, but refrained. After all, this was Aoibh's grandson, the fellow who was supposed to help me rescue the old ladies. I couldn't hurt him, much as I wanted to. For once in my life, I was going to have to show restraint. I was actually going to have to be nice to this cretin.

My left hand was still free, so I ripped the blacksmith's hood off and saw the knee-knockingly handsome Cathal the Smith for the first time. Tough as I was, the look in his gorgeous blue eyes weakened me temporarily. I hated that it did. I hated that he was gorgeous. I firmly resolved *not* to become yet another sucker in what must have been a long line of moon-eyed admirers of this fashion-challenged, self-absorbed twit. I proceeded to pull savagely on his long, golden locks.

Cathal gritted his teeth, released my right hand, and pulled off *my* hood so that he could see my face. He froze when our eyes met, and his eyes went soft. I took advantage of this to grab the spike from my belt and shove the point of it against his bare belly.

Having reached this impasse, we stared at each

other, breathing heavily, and liking what we saw. You couldn't tell from his eyes that he was a twit and a cretin.

Cathal seemed to be mesmerized. *He must not get out much,* I thought. His eyes took in every detail of my face. My hair had come loose in the struggle and now covered my ears. A few tendrils hung over my face and I tried to blow them out of the way. This made him smile. I found myself blushing under his scrutiny and I was furious at my own betrayal. I pushed the spike into his bellybutton pretty hard, and he winced.

"Get off me, you twit, or I'll gut you," I gagged, breathing hoarsely because of the dagger at my throat.

"I might survive my wound, but you would never survive yours," was his reply. Did his voice *have* to sound so deep and rich? Everything about this guy threatened my independence and sanity. I shifted the spike and thrust it against his crotch.

"How about now?" I asked through my clenched jaw, but this also seemed to amuse the twit.

"That would be a fate worse than death," he said playfully, and jiggled one eyebrow.

"Then lower your weapon and step away from me," I gurgled because of the blade pressing against my windpipe.

Cathal's admiration slowly transformed into regret. He spoke solemnly. "First, I must see your ears."

"Why?"

"You sneak into my forge at night, you kill my cat and ambush me…"

"I didn't kill your stupid cat! I stepped on its tail."

"You're awfully tall for a Human."

"And you're a bit shrimpy for a Fomorian!"

"I'm a Human!"

"That's debatable," I sneered caustically, using Bróna's line.

I pushed him away from me and slapped his blade down; yet my own weapon was still pointed at him, so he slapped it away. Then he changed his grip on the dagger and pointed it at my throat.

In exasperation, I slapped his blade arm away once again. Cathal reached for my hair with his other hand and I slapped it away. Then the twit slapped me on the face! I sucked in an angry breath and slapped him right back… as hard as I could. A red handprint was the satisfying result. But the blacksmith wasn't even irritated. He chortled in amusement and sheathed his dagger.

"Really?" I asked sarcastically. "Giants are on the march, people are dying… and *you* want to play patty-cake?"

"Why don't you just show me your ears, Elf?!" he blustered.

Riled by his tone, I shoved him away from me and yelled, "No!" (Yes, I was being unreasonable, but it was his fault.)

For answer, he wrapped his huge hand around my throat and pushed me back against the post, then reached with the other hand to brush my hair back. Oh, but he didn't know when to quit. I'd had enough of this guy pushing me around, so I decided to get down to business. I kneed him in the groin. He sagged forward and groaned in pain and I headbutted his nose. He yelped and jerked away and grabbed his nose, and I finished him off with a few, quick, Primrose Prendergast moves.

Cathal's bulk slammed onto the ground. I followed through and knelt on his chest and held the spike against his throat—but he was out cold. I waited for him to move, but he started snoring quietly.

Hesitantly, gently even (although I had just knocked him unconscious, so being gentle now made absolutely no sense), I brushed the hair away from his ear. He wasn't an Elf, although I already knew that. I gazed in awe at his sleeping face and my anger subsided considerably. His nose was bleeding heavily. I began to feel guilty for having treated him so roughly. He didn't look like a bad person while he was sleeping. But a snort from him snapped me out of my contemplative mood and I slapped his face without meaning to.

I grabbed the straps of his garment and shook him, and slapped him several more times (not the slightest bit gently, I might add). "Hey! Wake up!"

I spied a bucketful of water nearby and heaved its contents onto Cathal's face. The shock of it awakened him—sputtering and disoriented. He sat up, feeling his nose and head gingerly.

I sat on the upturned bucket—unconsciously tucking a stray hair behind one ear—and folded my arms. Cathal noticed my ear and smiled. He had found out what he needed to know.

"And now, if you're finished playing games..." I said with scathing condescension.

As his memory returned, Cathal became all business. "You said something about Giants on the march?"

Chapter 25

Sunlight speckled the forest glade where thirty young men had gathered to hear Cathal the Smith. They may have been listening to Cathal, but they were drilling me with suspicious looks. I stood beside the blacksmith and kept my mouth shut while he tried to sell them on the idea of charging into the midst of a hornet's nest of angry Giants.

At six foot six I was taller than most of the men there. Only Cathal shared my eye level. My hair was tied back, deliberately exposing my ears to allay any fears the villagers might have. I had also scrubbed the dragon scent off me, since Cathal was not shy about telling me how badly I stank. For my part, I felt obliged to reward his honesty by giving him constructive fashion advice. I convinced him to dress like a nice young barbarian rather than a twit. He saw no logic in accepting my advice until I pointed out that his grandmother's life depended upon his adherence to my strict standards, since I would not allow myself to be seen in the company of a walking fashion violation. He grumbled a lot, but raised his standards in the end. The lure of adventure was too powerful.

"This is the day we've been training for," enthused Cathal. "Our people have waited several lifetimes for an opportunity like this."

Niall of the Boats stepped forward, scowling blackly. "It'd be madness to get involved," he growled. "No matter whose side we take in this, our villages will be razed and our families slaughtered."

A lot of voices agreed with him. Another man spoke up. "What have the God People promised us if we take their side?"

"Well, nothing yet," admitted Cathal. "They don't even know about the Fomorian attacks. But this is our chance to turn things to our advantage. Don't you see?"

"Why don't you leave well enough alone, Cathal?" said Niall. "Tell this girl to take her troubles elsewhere."

"Those are *our* people up there on that mountain!" argued Cathal, his patience wearing thin.

"They're old," said Niall dismissively. "They don't have long to live anyway."

I gasped at his callousness, but it was nothing to Cathal's reaction. Cathal's frustration spilled over and he punched Niall on the jaw. Niall returned the blow and they went at it until the crowd surged forward and pulled them apart. Cathal shrugged off their restraining hands. Niall wiped blood from his lip and jabbed his finger in my direction, hissing angrily.

"I warn you, Cathal the Smith!" said Niall. "Stay far away from this girl and her madness. Don't bring death and destruction down upon us—or you'll pay!" He spat on the ground and strode away. The others followed until only young Fergus was left.

Cathal and I were distraught. Without their help,

we couldn't possibly mount a rescue effort. We would have to find another way.

"Bah! They're just small men," interjected Fergus. "You're wasting your time on them."

Cathal contemplated Fergus thoughtfully for a moment, and then turned to me. "He's right. We must talk to the clan leaders. This whole thing is bigger than us. Perhaps we can bring our case before High King Iarann."

"Is he an Elf?"

"No, he's the Human king, descended directly from Partholon himself. He's in hiding, of course, but he's been organizing and planning the overthrow of the Elves for several decades."

"How can we get to him?"

"We can't go directly to him. His location is secret. We'd have to convene the chieftains first, and petition them to bring our case before the king."

"We don't have time to cut through all that red tape," I argued. "Whatever course of action we choose, it must be the one that delivers the quickest results. Your grandmother is trapped up there with twenty others, and they only have enough food for a week."

"Well, they'll have to eat the donkeys. I can't clear the Giants out of Scucca Pass by myself."

"What about Farra?" asked Fergus.

Both he and Cathal looked at me hopefully.

"Who's Farra?" I asked.

"Your dragon," said Fergus.

"We call him that because he's always watching," said Cathal.

"Why don't you fly to Tara on him?" said Fergus eagerly. "You'd get there in no time."

"How did you know about my dragon?" I asked in amazement.

"We saw you yesterday," said Cathal. "You flattened my field of fighters." He said this with a broad grin, and a dimple danced in one cheek.

Once again, I was annoyed at the man for the way my breath caught when he smiled at me. I simply could not afford to become attached to anyone in this world. I was determined to return to Galway and I refused to let anything get in the way.

"Farra's not mine," I said a little bit snippily. "He's a free spirit. I doubt if he'd let me ride him again."

"How did you get on him the first time?" asked Cathal.

There was no way I was going to let this man know how I had blundered from catastrophe to fiasco, and had fallen onto the dragon, rather than taming it with some sort of miraculous power.

"That," I said, "is a secret. If I revealed it to you, you'd have to forfeit your miserable life."

Cathal guffawed in great amusement and my traitorous heart lurched again.

"So, what do we do first?" asked Fergus. "Rally the clans, warn the Elves, or save the old women from the Giants?"

Cathal and I answered simultaneously. He said, "Rally the clans" and I said, "Warn the Elves."

Then we looked at each other, paused, and spoke again—in unison this time. "Save the old women."

"But to do so, we'll need help," said Cathal.

"The Humans won't help, so we'll have to get the Elves," I said.

With one accord, we gathered up our weapons

and shouldered into the packs we had prepared the night before. Cathal noticed that Fergus was preparing as well.

"You're staying home, Fergus."

"No, I'm not!" retorted the teen. "You'll need my help. Two people never saved Danaan Land alone."

Cathal and I laughed at that.

"Oh, and three have?" I asked in amusement.

Cathal clapped a hand on Fergus's shoulder and smiled appreciatively. "Ah, Fergus, if only I had a thousand like you! But you can't come. You'll only slow us down."

The boy winced at that remark and tears filled his eyes. I fully sympathized with him and spoke to Cathal in his defense. "Why can't he go to Tully Cross and rally the clans?"

"Because his father would say that I put him up to it, and his mother would kill me stone dead. That's why. Besides, he's only a boy."

He noticed how crestfallen Fergus had become, and spoke to him in a gentler tone. "I, myself, have never been farther than Leenaun. There are untold dangers out there, and I would never forgive myself if anything happened to you."

He grabbed Fergus's homemade sword and cast it aside. Then he spoke forcefully. "You're staying here, and that's that. Right, Fergus?"

Fergus hung his head and nodded silently. Yet on his face a grin and a plan were hatching unbeknownst to us. He pretended to mope whilst Cathal and I hit the trail. When we turned to wave goodbye, he just pouted at us. As soon as we were out of sight, he checked his weapons, slung his pack over his shoulder, and cut across country toward the southern village of Inch.

Also unbeknownst to us, the great wyvern watched with great interest from his lofty aerie as Cathal and I ran eastward at an easy lope across the lazy plains.

Chapter 26

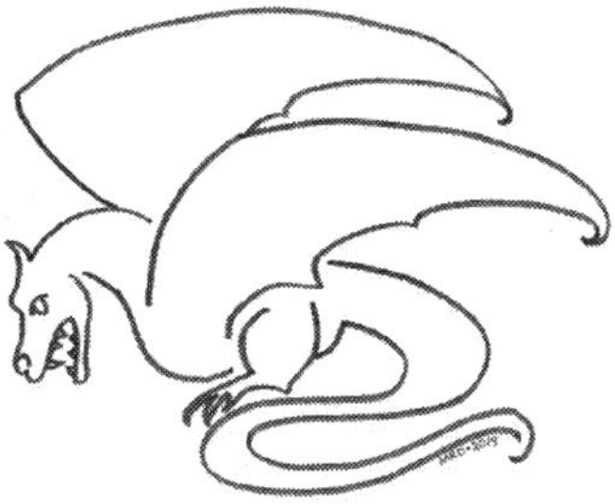

Nighttime found us in the northern foothills of Aranafalla Mountain. We had covered a good thirty miles since morning. The going was slower than we wished, but we had decided to avoid the roads and travel through the uncharted woods, not wanting our quest to become known. The town of Erriff was another day's journey ahead of us, at which point we would turn south, then east, on the road to Cong. Once safely past the Elven stronghold of Cong, it was a straight shot across the central plateau to the city of Tara.

We startled a drift of wild pigs in the early afternoon and I killed one with the bow that Cathal had given me from his stash back in Tubber. I was thrilled by my lucky shot and Cathal didn't hide his delight in my skill. I liked that about him—he didn't hold back his praise.

We made camp in a hollow that was hidden by overhanging trees. That far away from civilization, we were not afraid of attracting Human or Elf attention to ourselves, so we built a moderate-sized fire to deter wolves, knowing that the smell of pork roasting on a spit would be unbearably tempting.

We arranged to take turns on guard duty through the night. Cathal offered to take the first watch, just as soon as we had eaten. We sat by the fire, our stomachs growling and mouths watering while the pig sizzled over the flames. By this time, we had settled into a comfortable acceptance of one another.

"This is way too much food for two people," I said, very proud of my kill.

"And this is only a small pig," he said.

"It seems pretty big to me," I said, more than a little miffed.

He knew he had dinged my pride and he chuckled. "I'm glad we didn't run into a full-sized boar. We would have needed ten spearmen to take him down. No," he continued, settling himself against his pack and pulling a blanket around his shoulders, "this pig was perfect."

Somewhat mollified, I quizzed him. "How big do they get?"

"I once saw a sow that was twice the size of a horse."

"Holy cow!" I exclaimed.

"Imagine something that big coming at you."

"I had no idea. Animals don't grow very large where… ahh… on the crustal section that my tribe is drifting on."

"I thought I detected an accent," he said, his curiosity roused.

"Yeah, I'm from Ninevah," I lied.

"Really?" He was excited, but I didn't want him to start asking questions.

"We have lions and bears," I said hurriedly, "but

no wild pigs. Are pigs as dangerous as lions?"

"They're very aggressive," he said, "but not as mean as dire wolves. Dire wolves are clever hunters. What brought you to Danaan Land?"

"I just… ahh… dropped in for a visit. I'm not staying long. As soon as my… ah… transportation is arranged, I'll be heading back."

"How do you know my grandmother?"

"I'm a distant relative of Bróna," I answered. It wouldn't do to tell him everything. He might be captured and tortured, and spill his guts to the Elves.

I was no stranger to falsehoods; they helped me survive. I relied upon lies to hide my Traveller background or to keep people at arm's length, but telling lies to Cathal seemed wrong and I didn't know why. I found myself trying to scale down the magnificent whoppers I was used to. What was it about him that made me want to tell the truth? Yet Bróna had not foreseen this fork in the road, so she hadn't briefed me on Cathal. I didn't know him and was reluctant to reveal my true identity, so lies would have to cover for me. I changed the subject.

"It's a long road to Tara," I said. "How long will it take us?"

"There's an Elven colony at Cong," he answered. "We should go there first."

"I thought we had agreed to avoid Cong. Bróna told me the Elves of Cong want Ampherat's throne for themselves."

"Yeah, they do," he said with a mischievous grin, "but they also breed the fastest horses in Danaan Land—and that might shorten the road a bit." He laughed and my heart did its thing again.

"The Elves at Cong wouldn't give us horses to help the king," I argued with a frown, not understanding what was so funny about the horses of Cong.

His dimple danced and his eyes twinkled. I didn't know how much more of this I could take.

"We might have to borrow them," he said.

"Borrow?"

"Just to shorten the road."

Then I understood his grin. I burst out laughing and he joined in heartily. Our companionable laughter warmed the hollow.

Chapter 27

We reached the northern tip of Lough Trasna on the evening of our third day from Tubber. Since it was late, and Cathal said the town gates would soon be shutting for the night, we decided to camp in the woods and await the new day. After our supper of cold pork sandwiches, I climbed a low hill to survey the valley. As a student, I had visited Cong several times to join an archaeological dig in that most ancient of places, but the Cong that greeted my eyes on a cold November day in the Year of Adam 3046, was vastly different from the one I had known in the distant future.

The Cong I once knew was situated between two lakes—Lough Mask to the north and Lough Corrib to the south. Here, however, there was only one lake, which Cathal called Lough Trasna. Trasna stretched for twenty-five miles or more along the eastern flank of the Aranafalla Range. The lake was about five miles wide, and beyond it an unbroken forest spread in all directions to the horizon.

That night, we slept without a fire for the first time

since starting out; our proximity to civilization meant we ran the risk of attracting attention. Two Humans roughing it alone in the wilderness was unheard of in a time when savage beasts abounded, yet we had to shun all company, Human or otherwise, because of our long hair and numerous illegal weapons and the fact that our quest favored Elves. We would have been unable to strike up a conversation with anyone, and that would have appeared suspicious as well. Neither did we need a fire to ward off wolves, because dire wolves rarely hunted this close to population centers.

The next day was beautiful… sunny and dry. A lot of people took advantage of the weather, and the roads were busy with farmers and fisher folk heading to town to buy and sell. Cathal and I blended in with a group and passed through the sentry gate without suspicion. We kept our hoods up to hide our hair, but most of the people wore hoods and caps to ward off the autumnal nip in the air, so nobody paid any attention to us.

I was dressed in my leggings and tunic, which was what men wore in those days, so Cathal showed me how to walk like a man. He said I swung my hips too much, and that I should swing from the shoulders instead. I added a slouch to my walk to make me look shorter. And I fastened the buttons on my cloak to hide the fancy appliqué on my tunic.

The town was only a mile in diameter, which isn't very large by modern standards, but Cathal said it was the third largest population center in all of Danaan Land, after Tara and Javan. It housed the Western Battalion of the High Elven Army and the mansion of the regional governor, Under-Lord Seustra.

This was Cathal's first time in a big town and he was suitably impressed. I didn't have the heart to describe the size of Galway, the City of Tribes, in the Year of Our Lord 2015.

Our mission was to spy out the stables and paddocks where the horses were kept. We planned on returning at night to steal two. We would be miles away before anyone noticed. That was the plan. We hadn't worked out the details yet, but we were confident of success. We discovered during our casual stroll around Cong that none of the horses were guarded. Cathal ventured to guess that this was because the penalty for horse theft was death, and no Human in his or her right mind would steal an Elven horse. While that did not instill much confidence in me, I knew I could easily handle the wimpy-looking security detail guarding the Under-Lord's mansion. The few soldiers we saw patrolling the town looked lazy and unmotivated. I suggested we should take two horses each so we could switch mounts on the fly and thus extend our getaway flight by having fresh horses to ride when the first ones began to tire. Cathal loved that idea and said I was a genius, and I didn't tell him I'd only thought of it because of all the Western novels I'd read as a child. I used to plan perfect getaways in my mind while waiting for my chance to escape the foster care system.

When Cathal and I had ironed out all the details of the horse theft and getaway, my thoughts turned toward food supplies. I stopped short on the crowded footpath and was jostled by other pedestrians as I confronted Cathal.

"What harm would it be," I said, "if we bought some extra bread and vegetables?"

"What's wrong with you?" Cathal asked in surprise. He looked around nervously and tried to force me to continue walking, but I shook off his grip.

"You know we can't talk to anyone," he hissed through clenched teeth. "We have to keep to ourselves and not attract the slightest bit of attention."

I was very sensitive about my fixation on food and his comment rubbed me the wrong way. "Who died and made *you* boss?" I snapped angrily.

"We've already discussed this," he snapped back. "We're going to buy at farmhouses along the road. Not here in Elf Central."

"Well, I'm going to get some bread and apples," I said. I spun on my heels and jogged down a busy alley which led to the bustling Market Square.

Cathal gritted his teeth and suppressed a retort, then looked nervously both ways on the busy street. Half a block away, an Elven policeman was watching, eyes squinting in a frown. Cathal pretended to be checking for a gap in traffic, then strolled across the street. Before entering the alley, another surreptitious glance up the street confirmed his dread—the officer was confabbing with another, and both were looking in Cathal's direction. Not surprisingly, either. We were both much taller than the average Human—closer to Elf height—yet we wore peasant attire. Elves were of the upper class, and always dressed accordingly; therefore, we presented a visual incongruity. We still were hooded, even though the morning had warmed up and most people were now bare headed; plus we carried suspicious bundles. Cathal mentally berated himself for having stopped to argue with me and thus making us stand out in the flow of pedestrian activity. We had drawn unwanted attention.

When Cathal caught up with me, I was standing in front of a fruit vendor's stall, picking out some delicious-smelling apples. He glared at me, but I refused to look at him.

"We've been spotted," he muttered. "I'll get the bread, then we leave."

I ignored his warning, assuming it to be a lie designed to hurry me. People always project their own thoughts and intentions onto others, and I stupidly made that faulty assumption based upon my own lying nature. Therefore, I resisted Cathal's urgency and deliberately took my time. I also forgot to act like the man I was pretending to be. The apple vendor's forehead puckered in vexation at my detailed examination of the fruit—a man wouldn't have cared a whit about the condition of the apples.

Cathal ambled across the aisle to a bread stall and pointed to some round loaves. When the baker asked him how many, Cathal held up two fingers.

Suddenly, a ragged boy of seven or eight grabbed a sticky bun from one of the baskets on display and made a dash for it, but was caught by the seriously overweight baker. The baker's nine chins wobbled as he shook the urchin with uncalled-for brutality. The boy whimpered in terror and dropped the bun. Cathal backed away from the pair.

I instinctively moved toward them, meaning to help the lad, but Cathal anticipated my impulse. He caught and restrained me, and shook his head in warning. "Come on, let's get out of here."

I nodded and turned away, although it killed me

to turn my back on the victim of a bully. I could hear the boy's screams as the baker started beating him. I leaned against the fruit stall and began hyperventilating.

Cathal grabbed me by the shoulders. "What's wrong with you?" he whispered with genuine concern.

My breath heaved as I tried to gain control over memories of a little girl of seven, crouching under a similar stall in a crowded marketplace, eating rotten fruit she'd found on the ground, being dragged out by the angry fruit merchant and hauled off by a monstrous policeman to a place where they served three meals a day along with prejudice and disrespect.

"Ashling!" Cathal's whisper brought me back to the present. "Let's go. We can't get involved here. The lad would be doomed with or without us, and we have other lives to save."

I hung my head and heaved for air. Cathal lifted my chin and his urgency stilled. Tears flowed down my face, which was all twisted in a knot that resembled my stomach.

"I was that little boy, once upon a time," I whispered raggedly. I steeled myself against my ingrained response to the boy's pleas for help. "Nobody stood up for me, either. I hate walking away from bullies. But you're right. I have already put our mission at risk, and we have the lives of twenty-one women to think about."

I could not risk the mission. If we were arrested or killed, nobody would care about the old ladies under siege in the mountains, and they would die, plain and simple. So, I turned my back on the little boy and shut out his plaintive cries and the obnoxious shouts of the bully baker. My phobia about hunger had brought us to the edge of calamity. If Cathal had not stopped me, I would have charged in and risked the lives of many friends for the sake of a total stranger. I dropped the bag of apples onto the stall as though they were on fire.

Cathal studied me the way an electrician examines a wiring schematic, and finally understood why I was wired the way I was. I couldn't bear the compassion in his gentle eyes. Who was this man to probe my soul like this? He was weighing the value of me and I felt woefully lacking and off kilter.

Then the blacksmith of Tubber reached an irrefutable decision. "Every life has value," he said.

He strode to the bread stall and wrested the baker's stick away, and something swelled and cracked deep inside of me. For Cathal wasn't just saving that wretched boy from cruelty and tyranny—he was saving the little girl I once was. By refusing to turn a blind eye to this injustice, he was telling me that *I* mattered; that he would have saved me if he had been there; that he would never turn his back on *me*. His actions and words transcended time to redeem the soul of a little girl who was scared and alone and constantly hungry.

Cathal and the baker stood close together with the boy squirming between them, firmly in the grasp of the fat man.

"Stay out of it, bucko!" warned the burly baker.

"Let him go," suggested Cathal quietly, "and I'll pay for the bun he stole."

"And who'll pay for the bread he stole yesterday?" demanded the bully. "And the day before that? No, this lad is a scourge to the decent merchants of Cong, and he'll get his comeuppance."

"I can't let you beat him to death," said Cathal in a

quiet, respectful tone. "Come now, how much does he owe you?"

"Money won't change his habits, bucko," said the baker. "Either I take it out of his hide right now or he does hard labor in the quarry to satisfy the law."

A throng of curious onlookers gathered. This—and the baker's blustering voice—drew the attention of two Elven police officers on horseback. They pushed their horses through the assemblage and stopped beside the trio.

Off to the side and still unnoticed, I unbuttoned my long cloak for quick access to my hidden sword.

"What is it now, Baker?" demanded one of the officers.

With a sadistic grin at Cathal, the baker thrust the boy forward. "I caught this lad stealing from my stall, Officer."

The ragamuffin screamed in fear and struggled violently. One of his thrashing hands grabbed Cathal's hood and yanked it off, and all those assembled gasped at the sight of Cathal's long hair.

The boy escaped from the baker's unnerved fingers and darted away through the crowd.

The reaction of the Elven policemen was immediate and panic-stricken. They commenced to blow their whistles to call reinforcements. The crowd dispersed into the warren of side streets, not wanting to be associated with this new criminal and the rebellion that his long hair implied.

Cathal tried to run, but the baker grabbed his cloak and would not let go. Cathal dragged the baker's four-hundred-pound bulk for a few feet, but it was obvious the man's nerve had returned in force after letting the slip of a waif break free.

"I've got him!" yelled the baker loudly. "I've caught the rebel!"

In short order, a dozen mounted policemen charged into the market place and advanced in a bristling ring of nocked arrows and drawn swords. I threw off my cloak and ran to Cathal's side, then punched the baker so hard that he somersaulted over his bread stall and came to a sickening, neck-cracking halt against a stone wall.

Cathal and I stood back-to-back, our swords swishing dangerously as the circle tightened about us.

"Well, well. A pair of rebels," sneered the Elven officer. "Take them alive. We'll question them about the insurgency."

Knowing that things could get bloody, and not wanting to put Cathal in harm's way, I pulled out the beautiful pendant that Séú had given me and held it up on its gold chain for all to see. "We are on a mission from the House of Elasippus to King Ampherat," I boldly claimed. "Here is our token. You are bound to give us safe passage."

The Elves were taken aback. "How come you by that trinket?" demanded the officer.

Cathal sheathed his sword in an impatient manner. "Take us to your chieftain," he demanded arrogantly, "for we will not suffer to dally with an underling."

I looked at him in astonishment. There was more to this blacksmith than met the eye. I backed his play and sheathed my own sword. "Make haste," I commanded. "It is bad enough that you've exposed our secret mission without also stirring revolt amongst the Human populace."

The police officers obviously didn't know what to do next, but they lowered their weapons, clearly no longer wishing to harm either of us. They indicated that we should walk in front of them, and escorted us to the impressive house of the Elven governor Seustra, Under-Lord of the Western Midlands.

Chapter 28

The two-story, granite-block mansion sat on a hill that bulged upwards from the center of the Elf Quarter. The modest homes of Cong's privileged citizens were lavish compared to the simple hovels on the outskirts of town where the Humans were housed.

A high wall enclosed the governor's house, stables, barracks, and several outbuildings, and all traffic was made to pass through a pair of wrought-iron gates and past a sentry box.

Seustra's audience room was palatial, surpassing the finest estates in Ireland in my time. It was oval in shape. The floor was polished Connemara marble. Twelve fluted columns encircled the large chamber, soaring skyward and fanning out to support the ornate ceiling. Between the columns and the outer wall was a walkway paved with plush carpets. Gold-trimmed crown molding was everywhere. Elaborate murals on the ceiling—easily outshining Michelangelo's work in the Sistine Chapel—depicted the twelve constellations and recounted the story of how Lucifer's legions subjugated the planet. Delicately wrought metal filigree, evoking patterned lace, encased an array of windows that ringed the audience room. The effect was light, airy, and cathedral-like.

The center of the room was dominated by a crescent-shaped desk of Connemara marble and a high-backed chair of mahogany and gold, upholstered in forest-green velvet.

Uniformed guards, armed with lavishly ornamented swords and sheaths, stood at attention between the marble pillars girding the room. I marked each Elf's position and attitude as I strode with Cathal into the center of the audience room and halted before Seustra's desk.

That was where the beauty ended, as far as I was concerned. Although bedecked with opulent clothing and extravagant jewelry, Under-Lord Seustra was fat and slovenly and reeked of wine. The governor was not as tall as the average, seven-foot Elf and his heavy jowls, sagging eyelids, and drooping belly enhanced the impression of a skeletal structure that was daily succumbing to gravity.

We halted in front of his desk and waited for him to speak. He studied us with obvious hatred, which appeared to me to be tinged with a goodly amount of fear. We had been disarmed, and our hair was exposed as evidence of our criminality. Our hands were not bound, however, which indicated that the Elves were not expecting trouble from us. That is, they were unaware of the amount of trouble we were capable of, and assumed they could handle any puny efforts to escape. I had not witnessed Cathal's fighting skills (other than our brief skirmish in the forge the night we met), yet I just knew he would account adequately for himself in battle. He moved with the grace and controlled power of a tiger, and handled his weapons as an extension of himself. His gentle demeanor did not stem from weakness but rather from self-assurance. I knew he would charge Hell with me if I but gave the word. He was afraid of nothing. No doubt he would lecture me after the attack on Hell, and rebuke my foolhardy and impetuous nature, but he would be there with me through the thick of it.

Cathal was outwardly calm, but I knew how desperate his situation was. A young male Human, with long hair and armed like a bandit, could expect no mercy from his Elven overlords. He was lucky he hadn't been killed on the spot and strung up in Market Square to serve as an example to other would-be dissenters. It was the token of Elasippus which had stayed the Elves' vengeance, but that brief respite was rapidly drawing to a close.

I wondered if I had enough strength in me to postpone the proscribed punishment. Was I fated to die here in Cong, and my bones to be unearthed by clueless NUI archaeology students, eons from now?

Seustra fingered Séú's delicate gold pendant with a chubby hand and peered suspiciously at us through narrowed eyes. When he supposed that our terrors had been toyed with enough, the governor spoke. His voice was startlingly thin and reedy coming from such a corpulent rostrum.

"As you know," he squeaked, "the Elven colony at Cong is famed for our horses. As such, our respect for the horse lords of Elasippus is immense."

Cathal and I nodded, but remained silent.

"I will not hesitate to put my men at your

command," Seustra continued, "yet I must know more about your mission to King Ampherat."

"Sir, we are not at liberty to disclose the details," I said.

If he found out about Séú he would use her to gain the throne for himself. I had formulated a network of lies to use as our cover story—the only problem was, I wasn't qualified to meddle in Terran politics. The little I had learned at the Refuge was simply not enough. I was ignorant of the rules which governed interplay between the various species in this world. I had composed lies which were successful in easing my way through Earth's societal warren, but my fibs failed pathetically on Terra. The Lucifer Laws did not benefit Humans; Elves were all-powerful; and racial hatreds ran deeper than the pits of Hell.

Seustra glowered from one to the other of his prisoners. "I find it strange beyond measure that an elevated member of my race should entrust matters of any importance to a Human."

"The House of Elasippus is ushering in a new age of brotherly love and interspecies cooperation," I lied glibly.

Cathal looked at me, surprised by this information—and Seustra noticed. Seustra's repugnant appearance had not impressed me, yet the fat Elf was not as green as he was cabbage-looking. There was no way a Human could out-fox an Elf—they were part Angel, after all—but nobody had explained that to me. I was arrogant in my ignorance, as always, and consistently rushed headlong into situations where even Angels feared to tread; yet this foolhardiness often caused others to give way before me, wondering if my self-confidence perhaps stemmed from a royal mandate.

"Hmm," was all Seustra said. He stood up and paced back and forth behind the desk, swinging the gold pendant in circles. Then he stopped and faced us, and deliberately slipped the pendant into his breast pocket

"I'd like that back, please," I ordered haughtily.

"I'm sure you would," said Seustra in an oily voice. Then he struck like a snake: "And so would its *rightful* owner."

I was instantly angered by his insinuations. *Did he* really *just accuse me of stealing it?* Cathal nudged me in warning, but I paid no heed.

"That necklace was given to me by Séú of Elasippus!" I blurted out, incensed.

"Ah-ha!" exclaimed Seustra. "The daughter of the great lord himself!"

Cathal's shoulders slumped ever so slightly, and that reproval stung me more than a thousand words ever could. I bit my stupid lip so hard that it bled.

"What word from the lovely Princess Séú?" crooned the governor. Then his demeanor became menacing and he shouted, "Or did you rob her dead body?"

Cathal turned to watch the sentries, sensing a trap. Seustra nodded to his bodyguards and we were quickly surrounded.

"You will remain as my prisoners until this tale is rightly told," Seustra informed us. "Already my emissaries are speeding their way to your village of Tully Cross—" Cathal and I looked at one another in desperation. "—which will be razed to the ground should your story have even the slightest trace of falsehood," finished the Under-Lord triumphantly.

My lie was supposed to have protected our identities, but instead I had jeopardized the lives of hundreds of innocent civilians with my fabrications!

Desperate and ever impetuous, without any plan or thought of consequences, I rent the air with my heart-stopping war cry.

The Elves were petrified with shock. Even Cathal was momentarily paralyzed by the sound.

I used that split instant of immobility to unleash my fury upon the encircling soldiers. In just a few seconds, four guards died at the end of a requisitioned sword, and I threw Cathal a weapon.

Seustra started screaming for help.

Cathal and I rotated back-to-back within the circle of guards, inflicting damage wherever the opportunity presented itself. In no time at all, the inexperienced soldiers were dead on the cold marble. Cathal ran to the door and I made a dash for the squealing governor.

I held Seustra at swordpoint and retrieved the gold pendant from his pocket, then forced him to cross the room to where Cathal was listening at the door.

"The clans must be warned!" was Cathal's first thought.

"It's too late for that," I said, and jabbed Seustra with the tip of my sword to get him to stop whining.

"What have we done?" asked Cathal with great remorse.

I felt guilty enough for both of us, and was ready with an alibi. "If we told them where you are really from, your village wouldn't stand a chance. At least Tully Cross can field several hundred fighting men."

Seustra laughed raucously. "I sent a *thousand* of my best soldiers to that measly little village! Your clansmen will be roasting on spits before another rotation of the sun."

In a boiling rage, Cathal tried to transfix Seustra with his newly acquired sword, but I prevented him.

"Kill him later," I advised. "We need him to shield us if we are to get out of this place alive."

Seustra gulped in fear. His pale face was gleaming with sweat.

Cathal opened the door and peered out quickly. When he pulled his head back inside, he looked puzzled. "Where are all the guards?"

I looked at Seustra, whose face reddened fiercely.

Realization dawned upon me and I laughed without humor. "He sent them all to Tully Cross!" I concluded correctly.

Chapter 29

Seustra's household Elves were preoccupied with blockading the manor's front door when we ventured from the audience room. Something outside had driven them into a panic. While Cathal held Seustra to a code of silence at swordpoint, I rounded up Seustra's underlings like sheep and locked them into a row of prison cells in the rear of the building.

Outside, a horde of Humans surrounded the governor's mansion, demanding to know why the army had been marched to the west in full battle dress.

We brought Seustra out to explain things to the unruly mob. At Seustra's request, the sentries at the gate threw down their weapons and allowed Cathal to take them prisoner. By that time, the crowd had simmered down and Seustra's thin voice could be heard over the rumblings of discontent.

Reciting the speech we had prepared for him, the Under-Lord announced, "Good people of Cong! It is my great pleasure to announce…" He hesitated and I prompted him with the sword I had appropriated. "…that I have been taken captive by leaders of the

Human rebellion. My army has been sent to rape and pillage innocent villages—" He gulped as the rabble murmured angrily. "—and Cong is wide open for the taking."

The people of Cong looked at one another in amazement, but nobody made a move. Cathal opened the gates wide and addressed the people in his powerful voice.

"My name is Cathal the Smith, from the village of Tubber. The Western Battalion has been lured away and Cong is staffed by only a handful of God People. Get your children to safety. The rest of you, go to your homes and retrieve your weapons."

The mob started to shuffle and somebody ventured a cheer, but Cathal was not finished so he waved for silence.

"Spare the noncombatants and treat all prisoners humanely. We will not sink to the same level of depravity as the Elves. Anyone caught committing atrocities will answer to me, personally."

The men in the front of the crowd raised their fists and hollered their agreement. The rebel clarion call of "Abú!" was picked up by the throng and carried throughout the streets as both men and women rushed to participate in the long-awaited battle for freedom.

The Elves were subdued and the town was secured by nightfall with surprisingly little bloodshed. The superior race had been totally unprepared, having been lulled by generations of security. With their army gone, they surrendered without a fight.

The descendants of Adam and Eve were so brainwashed by centuries of subjugation that they found it difficult to play their new role of overlord, and this restrained many of them from taking revenge; however, being only Human, there were more than a few who gloried in the opportunity to repay the God People for their cruelty. There were also some incidents of looting and vandalism in the backlash of unaccustomed freedom. Cathal tried to make the victors understand that they were destroying what was now their own property. His wisdom prevailed, thanks in great part to the group of young men who had attached themselves to him as lieutenants.

When things were under control and the fighting and looting had petered out, Cathal came looking for me with his band of brothers in tow. They found me in Seustra's stables, saddling a pair of dapple-grey geldings. Our gear had been taken from us that morning when we had been arrested, and I had been unable to locate it, but a search of the mansion unearthed a gratifying amount of new 'stuff'. I found a change of clothes, an Elven cloak, an oilskin sheet, a bow and quiver of arrows, two swords and a dagger—and a larder full of food. With the exception of the weapons, which I carried on my person, I packed my supplies into leather duffle bags and tied them to the spare horse.

Cathal was flushed with success, but his face fell when he saw what I was doing. "Where are you going?" he asked.

"Tara."

"Without me?"

I tightened the cinch and tucked up the loose strap before answering. "You have to stay here," I pointed out.

"We started a war and somebody has to lead it."

"I can't lead them," he protested. "You and I are on a quest and I won't abandon it… or you."

Cathal's lieutenants looked dismayed, but he didn't notice their reaction.

"Cathal," I said gently. "We have to roll with the changing tides. If you don't continue this uprising, it will peter out. You must gather an army and march them to the coast. Seustra's soldiers must be stopped."

He looked crestfallen at first, but it didn't take him long to realize that I was right. He sighed and nodded.

"Besides," I teased. "You have never been on a horse before. You'd only slow me down." We smiled at each other as Cathal learned what it was like to be on the receiving end of that comment.

A world of unspoken words passed between us. I could tell he wanted to travel with me to protect me and share in my adventures… and maybe more. Or was I merely projecting my own desires onto him?

"Do you have enough food?" he quipped slyly.

Indicating the laden sacks on the other horse, I grinned and said, "If not, I will buy from farmhouses along the way."

That night, three thousand armed and cheering Humans crammed into the town square to hear Cathal speak. Flaming torches were ensconced all about and the mood was euphoric. At the outskirts of the assemblage a few brazen men and women sat astride magnificent, prancing, snorting horses. A majority of the horses had been ridden west by the Elven army and only a small herd remained.

Cathal addressed the townspeople from the top of a hay wagon. His voice was strong and his words convincing. "People of Cong! You have liberated your town with the strength of your arms!" He had to pause until the roar of approval diminished. "Now I ask you to follow me to Tully Cross, to punish Seustra's army for the atrocities they are committing *at this very moment!*" The horde cheered lustily. "Word has been sent to every town and village across the land. The insurgency has begun—right here in mighty Cong!"

Thunderous cheers threatened to shake the town apart. Cathal shouldered a heavy pack, hefted a spear, and led his enthusiastic army out of town on foot. Behind them, a convoy of thirty horses and half that many wagons, recruited to haul the supplies needed to sustain their campaign, trundled over the resounding cobblestones. All told, their number equaled that of the Western Battalion they were pursuing.

At that very moment, I was bent over the back of one of the fast horses I had 'borrowed' from Under-Lord Seustra. We were tearing up the sod along a dark country road some miles from Cong. I galloped through a sleeping village, shouting the rallying cry at the top of my lungs.

"The Rising has begun! Cong has fallen!"

As I thundered by, mud from my horses' hooves splattered a stone road marker pointing the way to TARA→25 LEAGUES. Cathal had explained to me that a league was how far a laden oxcart could travel in one *dódhéagú*, or twelfth. Their days were divided into twelve fragments instead of twenty-four, so one *dódhéagú* was equivalent to two hours. Cathal gave the length of Lough Fee as an example of distance, saying that it was three leagues from end to end. This was something I could visually calculate, since I had seen it from the air, and from that I estimated that a league was probably close to six miles. Therefore, the trip to Tara would take me about three days, but only if I could push the horses to cover fifty miles per day.

This was the fifth day since my leap from the hanging valley. Their food would be half gone by now. Three or four more days to Tara, one day to convince the king to organize a rescue party, then nine or ten days back to Maumseachtain… barring unforeseen delays. Then we would have to battle the Giants in Scucca Pass. After that, there was still the landslide to surmount.

I prayed fervently that Bróna would be able to ration the food for at least three more weeks. I pushed the horses harder than I should have. I knew I must not fail.

Behind me, dogs rushed out to the road, barking frenziedly, and lights began to come on in all the houses.

Chapter 30

After putting some distance between me and Cong, I got off the main road and set up camp within the crumbling walls of a ruined and roofless building.

The next morning, I ate a large breakfast from Seustra's stores and hit the road while it was still early. The road was atop an esker which ran in a straight line from east to west across the heavily forested central valley of Fintan's Highlands. The low ridge was like an oasis in that sea of trees and proved to be a natural pathway through the wilderness. Not only was travel easier, but we were also safe from the wild animals that preferred to lurk in the dark forests. The top of the esker was broad enough to drive a wagon on, and a rutted track indicated that wagons did indeed use it on a regular basis.

The road looked to be well maintained. In some places, it was edged by low stone walls. There were even sheltered benches at intervals for travelers to rest upon, and a water pump every ten miles. On the approach to one of the small villages along the route, a sign announced that I was traveling on Esker Riada. *Wow! No way!* I had read about the famous *Slí Mhór* that traversed Ireland in millennia past; the Great Road that facilitated the movement of troops in wartime and commerce during the remainder of the year. I was *living* history! Living, breathing, and shaping it.

I opened up the throttle and made excellent time. Every ten miles I stopped and pumped gallons of cold, clear water for the horses. I switched mounts at each rest stop and was thrilled by my progress. I covered about sixty miles that day. Because of the lateness of the year, fellow travelers were few and far between.

Two days later I ran into trouble.

One of the horses came up lame. I picked out and examined its hooves… nothing. I felt along each leg… and found a problem. The off foreleg was radiating heat from knee to fetlock. It wasn't swollen, but that heat screamed infection. I transferred the supplies to his back and rode the other horse for a spell. Our pace was slowed to a walk, but within an hour the poor creature could barely put any weight on that leg. Now I could see the swelling and I knew for certain he couldn't go any further. There was no option but to cut him loose and hope he could survive on his own, although there wasn't much chance of that. I simply could not stop and wait until he got better. One horse's life was not worth more than a Human's, and I had twenty-one Humans depending on me. I unsaddled the gelding and left all his tack on the ground between the roots of a rowan tree.

Now I had another problem: I had to abandon most of my supplies. I decided to change out of my cumbersome woolens and put on the lightweight Elven clothing I had found in Seustra's manor. I wrapped my

Kitti-made clothes in the oilcloth and stashed them underneath a cairn of rocks, vowing to retrieve them on my return. I dumped most of the food. Leaving the food behind was tough on me, an orphan who had known hunger and insecurity, but by far the hardest thing I have ever done was listen to that sick horse whinnying pitifully, calling us back to him as we galloped out of sight. He tried to limp after us, but his pain was excruciating. When I looked back one last time I saw that he had given up and was standing, trembling with effort and pain, with his muzzle sagging to the ground.

Desperation and remorse drove me onward. I kept seeing my father's eyes reproaching me about the horse I had left behind. I argued with him inside my head until I was convinced he saw things my way and agreed that my mission was of paramount importance.

By the time my internal struggle was over, the horse I was riding was lathered and breathing heavily. I pulled him up in alarm, and my guilt was compounded. I unpacked and unsaddled him and rubbed him down with some grass. We rested, and I let him roll and graze before heading out again at a slower pace. I knew I had to alternate between cantering and walking if this horse was to make it all the way to Tara.

While we progressed across the vast midsection of Fintan's Highlands, I had nothing to do but think. In the future, Tara would be close to the east coast of Ireland, but my flight with Farra had shown me that Danaan Land continued past the hill city of Tara for hundreds of miles. Cathal had informed me that Tara was the easternmost outpost of Fintan's Highlands. According to the map he had drawn in the dirt, Fintan's Highlands was roughly the same shape as the Ireland of my time.

I didn't understand why there was more land surrounding Ireland in the past. It was as if Ireland and Great Britain were joined together, forming one complete land mass. I supposed it was possible. Perhaps the two sections had yet to split apart as part of the expansion of Pangeaden. I made a mental note to warn my friends to stay away from the great valley that separated Fintan's Highlands from the Peleg Hills in the east. If I was right, Gaodhal Valley was slated to become the Irish Sea! I felt a twinge of guilt. Shouldn't I stay and make sure that the lowlands were evacuated? But, no, that was not my problem. Anyway, it had already taken place before I was born. It was meant to happen. And I was meant to return home. I had a university degree and the potential of a prestigious career awaiting me in the twenty-first century *Anno Domini*.

Who would listen to me anyway? I was a nobody on Terra, as insignificant as I had been on Earth.

On my fourth day from Cong the land ahead of me started to slope gradually upwards to where low hills were outlined against the horizon. Thousands of acres of lush grassland skirted the base of the hills. That would be the Plains of Meath. Cathal had described it, and I knew that somewhere in those distant hills was the fabled city of Tara. I only had five or six leagues left. Now that my destination was in sight, my spirits lifted considerably.

On a high point overlooking the Plains of Meath a group of Elven horsemen was focused on the tall figure approaching, her red hair billowing as she cantered along the esker. The force of one hundred Royal Guardsmen halted on this lookout spot on The Great Road and awaited the approach of the well-dressed she-Elf. The fact that she was traveling without an escort did not bode well, following upon the heels of the king's missing bride and amidst rumors of rebellion fomenting in the outlying districts.

When I reached the group of Royal Guardsmen at the rest site, I fished out Séú's amulet and told them I had news of the princess that was meant for King Ampherat alone. I kept my ears covered under the silken hood of the beautiful Elven cloak and adopted an air of entitlement and birthright, which was strange territory for me, a waif without either birth certificate or tribe. They didn't doubt me, not even when I insisted upon talking to them in Shelta. I had saved them a long, arduous trip to the coast. They had set out for news of Séú and I had brought it to them. The whole group turned back and escorted me to Tara.

The journey to Tara took one more day. I arrived at King Ampherat's palace exactly ten days after leaving the old ladies to get help.

Time was running out.

Chapter 31

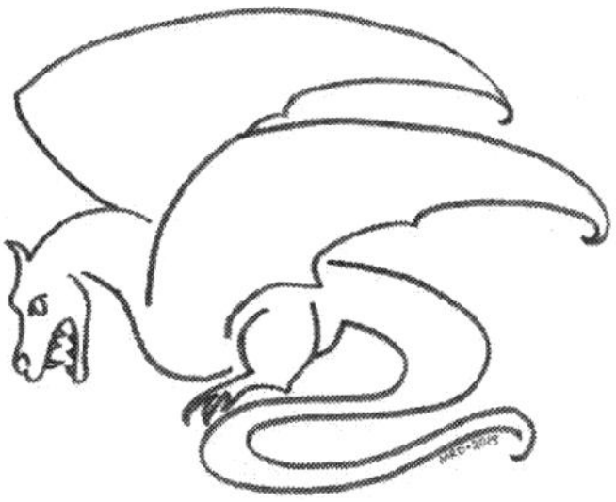

I was ushered into King Ampherat's throne room immediately upon arrival. Seustra's mansion had caught my breath, but the palace at Tara was exponentially more magnificent.

King Ampherat was haughty, haggard, and lean, with bright eyes, cruel lips, and years of hard living behind him. I formed an instant dislike for him.

Ampherat had summoned his chief advisors to hear what I had to say about his betrothed. The court's proceedings were conducted in the Elven tongue, and to my horror, that was how I was introduced to the king. I removed my hood as a sign of respect, and curtsied slowly and gracefully, but was at a loss as to how to respond to the questions which were posed to me in rapid-fire succession.

What should I do? My cover would be blown when it was discovered that I only spoke the Human tongue. The soldiers who had accompanied me to Tara hadn't cared. They had treated me with respect, but had not spoken to me after our first encounter, assuming me to be nobility and above their class; but that charade would never hold up to Ampherat's scrutiny. If I revealed to him that I was not an Elf but a Human, the Elves would revile me for impersonating a lady of their race and I could be put to death before I had a chance to ask for help. But if I continued the pretense and told him about Séú, and he *then* found me out in a lie, he might dismiss my entire story as a rebel plot. What a quandary!

What was I willing to risk in order to save my friends who were under siege on Maumseachtain? I didn't owe them anything, did I? The Giants would have attacked them whether I had crashed into this world or not, and they would have died without my intervention. Was that why I must continue this rescue effort—because I had intervened in something that wasn't my business in the first place? Did that somehow compel me to finish what I had helped set into motion? My driving desire was to return to the future as soon as possible; I had pressing matters to set right. I must prove that I belonged in respectable society, that my parents and I had been wrongfully shunned, and that I could become successful under my own steam, without anybody's help or handouts.

As I debated with myself, a new truth began to emerge; a growing certainty that I would never respect myself if I abandoned my friends in their darkest hour.

Telling Ampherat the truth was no guarantee that my life would be spared, and yet I had entertained that possibility from the moment I decided to go for help. The truth was I was an anomaly in this world; I broke all the rules; I was a threat to the status quo. The irrefutable summation was that these Elves would not allow me to live. There was no hope for me—I accepted this calmly—but I could still save my friends. That thought gave me direction, and peace about my choice.

"Your Majesty," I said in my thick Human brogue, "Princess Séú of Elasippus trusted me with her amulet and bade me bring news of her dire circumstances."

Ampherat signaled a sergeant-at-arms to take the necklace from me. One glance was all he needed to know it was real.

"What are my lady's circumstances?" Ampherat asked in Shelta. "And why are you speaking the language of dogs in the presence of a king?"

There was a hefty silence during which I decided to ignore the latter question and address the former. "The princess was attacked by Fomorians and her entire entourage was killed. She took refuge in my home, but we were forced to flee before the Giants. Séú is under siege in a small mountain valley, with little food and no hope of escape. She sent me to you for help."

Ampherat scowled fiercely at me. He repeated his last question as though he hadn't heard a word I'd said. His voice was bubbling with rage. "Why do you address me like a dog?!" he roared.

There was a worried silence amongst the courtiers. I took a deep breath and drew back the hair on either side of my head so that my ears were exposed. The courtiers gasped and shouted angry comments. The king glared hotly at me and a thick, blue vein bulged on his forehead.

"I am not an Elf," I said with resignation. "I never intended to deceive you otherwise."

"Arrest her!" shouted Ampherat in a fury.

I was surrounded by guards, and manacles were placed around my wrists, yet I was not led away. I tilted my chin proudly and remained calm.

The exquisitely dressed Elven courtiers were disgusted by me, and murmured disdainfully to one another behind elegant hands.

"Your tale is a fanciful one," continued Ampherat with reluctance, "and yet the fact remains that my betrothed is overdue. How is it that you were able to escape the siege?"

I hesitated before answering. I could not compound my sins by admitting I was able to fly. "I... I slipped away while the Giants weren't looking."

"And why, pray tell, would a noblewoman of Atlantis entrust a Human with such an important errand?" he asked scornfully.

What had he just said?

"Tír na nÓg is Atlantis?" I asked in astoundment.

The king and his courtiers were puzzled by my response; an inhabitant of this world should have known the two were one and the same. I hastily tried to recover what slippery footing I had.

"She is holding my... ah... my mother hostage to ensure that I follow her commands. I was forbidden to contact any Humans due to the... ah... hostilities between our two races. The princess bade me ride directly to Tara, and I have done so." Okay, so maybe a little lying was necessary.

The king considered my explanation carefully and conversed with his advisors in Elven. When he addressed me once more, he had lost much of his anger.

"This token is indeed proof that the princess is under extreme duress—or dead," he pronounced. "She would not willingly part with her family's amulet. We have heard rumors of Fomorians sailing in great numbers from their island domains, and of unrest amongst our Human subjects. Undoubtedly, there is evil afoot. We shall investigate the truth of the matter."

"I will lead you to her as soon as I get a meal and a fresh horse," I said eagerly.

Ampherat was disdainful of this suggestion, and frowned irritably. "You? No. You will give my aides directions to this mountain valley. It will take a week to assemble my army and prepare for a campaign—"

"But that's too long!" I interrupted. "They may starve or be overrun before then."

Ampherat was angered by the audacity of my aberrant interruption. His knuckles turned white on the burgundy-seamed marble of the throne's armrest. "You have played your part," he said coldly. "You will remain in Tara until your story is verified."

"Your Majesty," I objected, fighting to control my temper, "it would be best if I went with you."

He waved his hand dismissively. "A battlefield is no place for a woman. You will remain a prisoner until your words prove true." He delivered his final words with a menacing growl: "And then you will answer for your multiple violations of the patrician restrictions."

A battlefield is no place for a woman? Huh! There are Fomorians in Hell who know better. I clamped my lips together. My eyes simmered with anger. But I had been granted more time to plot my escape, so I held my peace.

Chapter 32

Three days after the Battle of Cong, Cathal arrived in the grassy expanse of Partholon's Meadows at the head of seventeen hundred Humans. Rebel fighters from villages along the way had swollen their ranks during the push to the coast.

The walled town of Tully Cross was under heavy assault from Seustra's forces. The Elves were encamped a mile from Tully Cross and had set up roadblocks on all roads out of the area. The bridge outside of town had been demolished.

Two lines of Elven archers were showering the besieged town with a continuous hail of arrows. A trebuchet was busy lobbing flaming projectiles into the town's thickly populated center, and two more were under construction. Many buildings in the small town were burning. Smoke rose in a dense pall over Partholon's Meadows and drifted inland on the sea breeze.

With the bridge out of commission, escape to the north was blocked by the river and forest, so the Elves were concentrating their attack from the south.

Cathal led his army through the southern woods, avoiding the road, and thus it was that they sneaked up on the Elves' bivouac from the far side of the valley and overran it. Without pausing for breath, Cathal urged his men onward through the tall grass of the plain. In complete silence, the Human warriors spread out and encircled the enemy troops laying siege to Tully Cross. At a prearranged signal from Cathal, the Human force attacked the Elves from behind.

Hundreds of Elves were killed before their leaders were aware of the second front. The trebuchets were knocked out of commission. As the noise and disturbance from the rear of their ranks increased, the Elves progressively became aware of the danger. Half of them turned to face the unexpected assault.

Cathal looked toward the town for a response, but the gates remained firmly shut and not a head peeked above the parapet, so Cathal raised the rebel yell. "Abú!" he roared. "Tully Cross, Abú!"

The men around him took up the cry and the Elves on the front line were gradually made aware of the second battlefront. In dribs and drabs, they turned to meet the challenge. The Elves were disoriented long enough for Cathal's men to push them back within range of the archers on the walls. Watchers on the ramparts sprang to their posts, and a fusillade of arrows streaked overhead. A deafening cheer preceded the gates of Tully Cross being flung open. Six hundred armed men raced onto the field to engage the outnumbered Elves in hand-to-hand combat. Trapped between two armies and pressed hard by superior numbers, the Elves were forced to surrender.

The Humans had won. Such a thing had never,

ever, occurred in the history of gods and men.

After the battle, when the prisoners had been secured and sentries had been posted on all routes into the plain, Cathal strode in triumph through the gates of Tully Cross with his band of lieutenants. The victorious fighters were greeted by Chieftain Killian of Conmacna and his twelve sub-chiefs.

"Cathal the Smith, Savior of Tully Cross!" hailed Killian, the highest-ranking Human in the entire district. He gripped Cathal's arm and thumped him on the shoulder, grinning from ear to ear.

"And Liberator of Cong!" added Sub-Chief Talty of Cong, who had accompanied Cathal's campaign since the first minutes of the uprising.

Amidst all the backslapping, Cathal noticed Niall of the Boats standing with the warriors from Tubber. Cathal greeted his pals and pumped Niall's hand in delight.

"Niall, it has begun!" he crowed. "We may see a Human on the throne in Tara before the week's end."

"We have much to talk of, young Smith," said Killian. "The council awaits your report."

Cathal and Niall were led to the Town Hall amidst euphoric celebration and joy. The town was bursting with civilian refugees. Cathal was hailed by many people he knew, and returned their greetings. He spoke to Niall with a question in his words. "I see faces here from every village in Conmacna."

"Yeah," responded his friend. "After you left, young Fergus scuttled off to stir things up."

"*Fergus* rallied the clans?" asked Cathal in astonishment.

"The chiefs had already gathered to discuss the Fomorian problem. Fergus told them Ashling's story, so Chief Killian sent for me."

"The rally cry went out just in time," added Killian. "Seustra's horde burned every rath and crannóg between here and Cong."

"We saw that, and feared the worst," said Cathal.

"Where's that redhead Niall told me about?" asked Killian with a grin.

"She rode to Tara to alert the Elven king," Cathal told him without thinking.

All those within earshot were dismayed at this news.

"What?!" yelped Killian. "She's warning him of our uprising? Why didn't you stop her?"

"Well, because she had to tell him about the princess," said Cathal, only just realizing how bad this sounded to the others.

"What care *we* about the life of a she-Elf?" cried Killian in outrage. "You fool! This rebellion was over before it ever started."

The men who had just been singing Cathal's praises were now angry and accusing.

"I told you we should have stayed out of her affair," growled Niall.

"Some of our own people are with the princess!" argued Cathal.

"Those old women chose to isolate themselves from the world. We owe them nothing," countered Niall heartlessly.

"You've signed our death warrant in Elven blood

outside these gates," grated Killian.

Cathal scanned the hard faces around him and threw caution to the wind. His response was challenging and proud. "I've left my signature in Cong as well."

"Ampherat will crush us," proclaimed Niall morosely.

"And your girlfriend is leading him right to us," accused Sub-Chief Talty.

"She also promised to rally the clans between Seóla and Breaga," offered Cathal, hoping to assuage their animosity by allaying their fears.

"You forced us to show our hand before we were ready," said Talty.

"You were ready enough to take over Cong!" argued Cathal. "Besides, this thing with Ampherat is none of our business. He's coming to deal with the Fomorians in Scucca Pass."

"They're not just in Scucca Pass anymore," Killian informed him. "Thousands have put ashore in the last few days. They're all camped out on the Moytura Plain."

Cathal's face lit up as realization dawned. "They're waiting for the God People to take the bait!" he announced with great excitement. "Don't you see? They *knew* Ampherat would come for his bride!" His colleagues frowned at Cathal impatiently, not following his line of reasoning and almost ready to lynch him. The blacksmith continued in a rush. "Just as the Tuatha Dé once overthrew our people—on the very same spot—so now the Fomorians seek to conquer. The Elves and Giants will clash at Moytura, and after they've annihilated each other on the battlefield, *we* can attack whoever's left standing! If we play this right, we will be lords of our own land once again."

The chiefs looked at one another thoughtfully as the implication of Cathal's analysis struck them.

"We'll have to send runners all over Danaan Land," admitted Killian grudgingly. "This may indeed be our chance."

Chapter 33

I was locked up in a small room at the back of the palace, on the third floor; a maintenance closet whose only source of light was a tiny grating at ceiling level. Shelves of cleaning supplies lined the walls. Barrels of mops and brooms and a stack of metal buckets stood in one corner. I was given a straw mattress to sleep on. A woman named Saoirse came to feed me twice a day. She was a kindly soul and managed to secure a change of clothes and some personal hygiene products for me.

I suspected that I was shoved into a closet and not a dungeon for two reasons: the first was that the dungeons were probably already jam-packed with insurgents, and the second was that I posed a low flight risk since they saw me as a helpless, dull-witted female of the lowest class. I was no stranger to that kind of discrimination and sexism. It would appear that here were two more qualities shared by both men and Elves. I therefore resolved to be a model prisoner, exemplifying their assumptions so as to allay suspicions and increase my opportunities for escape. In a garrison city the size of

Tara, with thousands of soldiers on high alert, I would not get far if I attempted a brazen run, even at night. I resolved to gather as much intelligence as I could, and wait until the opportune moment to make my break.

There were no toilet facilities in my cell, so I used one of the empty buckets. Every other day I was allowed to carry my bucket to a pit toilet that was built into the stone wall of the palace. The toilet was in a curtained alcove at the end of a long corridor. There I would empty the bucket, under guard the entire time. The two Elves who were assigned to guard me on my trips to the potty epitomized the generic brand of Elf which made up the bulk of Ampherat's army recruits. They were arrogant and small-minded, as are all racists. They hated the demeaning chore of guarding a rebel Human, and their faces and attitudes showed it plainly. They couldn't bear to touch me, and gagged at the contents of my bucket.

I rummaged through the supplies in the small room and made a note of anything I could use in my upcoming escape. I manufactured a pair of nunchucks out of two short lengths of broomstick joined together by a chain handle from one of the buckets, using a nail to drill holes in the wood and hemp twine to secure the parts. With a pumice stone normally used for scrubbing stone floors, I shaved the tip of another broom handle down to a sharp point and stored this spear upside-down in the barrel, ready for use whenever needed.

My search of the room also uncovered a clay jar of yellow sulphur powder. I couldn't read the label, but one nostril-burning whiff provided instant identification. Back at the Refuge, Bróna used sulphur to staunch blood flow whenever anyone got cut. It also had uses as a bleaching agent and a disinfectant—plus one other purpose that I knew of. My discovery of the sulphur germinated the seeds of a plan that I carefully cultivated throughout my short captivity.

The next time I was due to go to the toilet closet, I placed the full bucket inside an empty one. The guards questioned me suspiciously about this and ordered me to separate the buckets so they could look inside. I explained that the toilet bucket had sprung a leak and the second bucket was to prevent the drips from soiling the floor. Well! That made them jump back. They took my word for it and never examined the second bucket again.

The pit toilet ran the entire height of the castle wall, serving all the floors. The refuse all fell to the base of the castle wall, where it was shoveled daily by a servant and buried outside the grounds. There was an opening at the top, under the roof, to vent the methane gas that built up inside the chimney-like shaft. Because of this aperture at the top, the shaft had become home to thousands of bats, whose droppings clung to the walls in a thick layer of guano.

Each time I emptied my bucket, I would draw the curtain for privacy. My guards never questioned this. Then I would separate the buckets and scrape some of the guano into the extra bucket. Once the potty bucket was emptied, I would fit it over the guano bucket and nobody was the wiser. I cached all the guano in a pigskin sack I found on one of the shelves in my cell. By the end of ten days, I had enough.

I struck up a conspiratorial friendship with Saoirse, the woman who brought me my meals. My two guards forbade us to discuss the movements of the army as it prepared for the upcoming campaign against the Fomorians, so I would ask for news of the cattle herds.

She caught on immediately, and fed me information about the size of the king's herd, the number of prize bulls, the number of cows being brought in to bolster the herd, the number and types of cow bells in stock, etcetera. The Elf guards were quite bored by these mundane agricultural reports, but by this method I learned about the weapons the army possessed, and also that Ampherat had called up a force of ten thousand soldiers. This number staggered me. Why would Ampherat mobilize his entire army for a small rescue operation? But Saoirse explained that this was to offset a serious plague of hoof-and-mouth disease rumored to be spreading across the land from some distant islands. From that, I knew the Fomorians were invading in great numbers.

The guards were agog with excitement one day when King Nuada of the Peleg Hills arrived in Tara with a contingent of several thousand soldiers led by the famous warrior champion, Lugh. I could hardly believe my ears when I overheard them talking about this mythical character from the past. How I wished I had paid more attention to those 'fairytales' that peppered Ireland's earliest documents; those infuriating supernatural tales that I wrongly had blamed for muddying the historical account and painting our ancestors as gullible morons. My guards animatedly compared Lugh's merits and past victories much as sports fans would someday discuss boxing greats like Muhammad Ali. Apparently, a contest between Lugh and the Fomorian chief, Balor of the Evil Eye, had long been anticipated, and my two guardians had placed hefty bets on the upcoming battle.

Having learned a valuable lesson from Seustra's mistake in Cong, I waited impatiently for the city to be emptied of soldiers before attempting my escape.

Ten days after my arrest, I hammered at the door of my cell and demanded to know why my breakfast had not yet arrived. The guards laughed at my misfortune.

"One threat from the Giants and—poof!—all our servants disappear from the city," said the one I had nicknamed Laurel.

"You Humans are a stupid and cowardly race," said 'Hardy'. "You cannot survive without our protection."

"You may not get any food today," snickered Laurel.

"If Fomorians are approaching the city, then why aren't you on sentry duty?" I asked.

"This city is impenetrable," said Laurel in disdain.

"The king marched out this morning to wipe that scourge from the face of Terra," said Hardy. "The cow who serves your food took advantage of this and ran to the hills."

Laurel sniggered. "But she will be herded up with the rest of the beasts when the army returns," he said. "Everyone who deserted Tara will be executed for treason."

"How many have gone?" I asked.

"Everybody," answered Hardy. "Even the elderly and young. The city is deserted."

I smiled broadly, though they could not see me through the heavy door. "Will you at least allow me to empty my bucket?" I asked plaintively.

My answer was the sound of a key turning in the lock. Laurel's hand was still on the door knob when I pulled him into the room. I knocked him senseless and tossed him aside so I could deal with his partner. Hardy's expression was classic. He was completely unprepared for me to be as strong and capable as I was. I knocked him out too, but not before breaking one of his arms and his nose. I regretted having to be so violent, but he did try to kill me with his sword. I removed the key and closed the door in case anyone walked by while I was trussing and gagging the two guards. Then I retrieved my bags of guano and sulphur, disarmed Laurel and Hardy, and threw their weapons into a third pigskin sack. I didn't need my broomstick spear, so I left it in the barrel with the mops.

I stripped the skinny Elf and donned his uniform, then belted a sword around my waist. My hair hung loose below the helmet just like any other Elf, which added to the disguise.

I made sure to lock the door behind me and throw the key down the potty shaft on my way out.

Chapter 34

Under the guise of complaining about how much walking she had to do as part of her work, Saoirse had managed to convey to me the layout of the palace. I knew she had to trudge up one hundred and nineteen steps on the back stairs to get to my cell from the kitchen, that the stairs were thirty-five paces down the corridor to the right, and that the kitchen garden was enclosed by high walls with no exit, and therefore was never guarded.

The back stairs were empty and I gained the kitchen unaccosted.

I walked into the kitchen as though I owned it, but was stopped by a sour-faced she-Elf who ordered me to do something. She spoke in Elven, so I hadn't a clue what she was saying. There were only two Humans working in the kitchen, compared to the twenty or so that normally staffed it. I ignored the Elf and made a beeline for the back door, and this infuriated her. She charged across the kitchen and blocked my exit. Without a word, I swung my nunchucks and clobbered her across the temple. She dropped like a stone. The kitchen helpers raised their heads and looked at me for the first time. I lifted my helmet and showed them my rounded ears, at which they smiled in delight.

"You be that gal prisoner Saoirse be goin' on about," said the fat cook.

"That's right," I said. "Can you tell me why all the Humans have fled the city?"

"They've gone to join the rebellion," whispered the scullery maid. "Them that's not able to fight have run to the hills so's they can't be held hostage by the God People."

"Them what can run, that is," amended the cook.

The two old women giggled like children.

"Has the rebellion started, then?" I asked.

"Oh yes!" said the cook brightly. "Everyone was called to the west, to Cong, where it all started."

I smiled to hear that Cathal had followed through on what we had begun and that our efforts had not been in vain.

"Well, thank you for your hospitality," I said, "but I think I'll be going now. I'll certainly miss your cooking, dear ladies."

They laughed in delight.

"Saoirse told me to give you the best, not the scraps as most prisoners do get," beamed the cook.

"You'll be needin' a bite of food for your journey, no doubt," said the maid, and she bustled off to fill a flour sack with dried meat, bread, and other essentials.

They told me what streets would offer the least amount of resistance to me in my escape, and I thanked them and took my leave.

Scaling the garden wall was a simple matter of parkouring from the winter cold frame to the shed roof, and onto the wall. I waved to the cook and the maid from the top of this edifice before dropping to the lane on the other side and trotting off in the direction of the Shepherds Gate.

Because of the wholesale elopement of Humans, this gate was guarded, although normally it was not. Three saddled horses were tied to a hitching post beside the sentry box and I strode confidently toward them. Two sentries stepped out of their hut and asked me where I was going. At least, I assumed that's what they wanted to know. I was dressed like one of their own number, so their guard was down. I shook my head and pretended to be unable to hear them, all the while walking swiftly forward. Before they could repeat their question, I dropped the sacks onto the ground and whipped the nunchucks from my belt. In a matter of seconds both the sentries were sleeping soundly, and I dragged them back into their hut.

I decided to take all three of the horses with me rather than leaving convenient mounts for any pursuers. Plus, I would be able to go farther without stopping if I had three horses to switch out. I lashed the sacks onto the spare horses and rode the third through the gate, leading the other two.

Nobody accosted me as I cantered down the dirt road that led away from Tara.

Chapter 35

By switching horses on the run I did not have to stop for one hundred miles.

The good weather had ended sometime during my captivity in the broom closet. Ampherat's troops had churned up the mud and the Great Road was a quagmire, so I chose to travel along the base of the esker. In some places, the forest nudged right up against the incline and I had to maneuver around trees and shrubs, but the going was good otherwise.

Having had a good, long rest in Tara, my energy sustained me through a day and night of arduous travel. As dawn lightened the horizon, I arrived at a limestone plateau littered with dolmens. It was an Elven graveyard. No Elf would bother me here. This place was an incarnation of their worst fears. The dolmens represented doorways to the Underworld, through which the souls of Elves passed after death.

I chose one of the slab-sided sepulchers to camp under, and slid wearily from the saddle. The rain was pelting down and there was no shelter for the horses, so I picketed them near a patch of scrub grass and left them to their own devices. I didn't bother to unsaddle them, figuring they wouldn't want to roll or lie down on the rocky ground, and that the saddles would provide some warmth for them.

I stowed my supplies under one of the stone monuments and set about gathering some wood. I tried to light a fire beneath the dolmen's arch, but everything was soaking wet and I quickly abandoned that idea. After eating some of the food I had brought, I settled down to an uncomfortable sleep in a sitting position against the smooth rock face. It was bitingly cold, but at least I had shelter from the driving rain.

A scream of terror jolted me awake sometime later. I darted out from under the overhanging slab with Laurel and Hardy's swords in hand. All three horses were plunging and rearing against the picket line. Ferocious snarling blended with the horses' squeals. In the pouring rain and grey light of morning I could vaguely make out the shapes of dogs the size of cows, biting and tearing at the horses. One of the horses went down and was quickly torn apart.

I breathed the name of this new terror. "Dire wolves!"

My first thought was for the horses. I dashed out and slashed the picket line to free them, and then the wolves were upon me. Although I gave my weapons no pause or rest, the wolves were swift and sly, circling and darting until my arms and legs were bleeding from numerous gashes. There were six or seven of the beasts, by my reckoning. My sword accounted for only two before I was forced against the dolmen, holding another three of the slobbering, evil-looking creatures at bay. Tall as I was, these beasts were shoulder level. Snarling ridges along their muzzles pulled back their lips to expose razor-sharp fangs—a terrifying experience face-to-face.

Now that they had me cornered, they held back… waiting.

A deep growl sounded over my head. Up on the sloping roof, a fourth wolf was preparing to pounce. My mind raced ahead and urged its lagging tenement to keep up, but slow motion ruled my movements and I knew I could not reposition my swords in time.

At the very instant my death fell from above, the familiar screeching of an angry wyvern cut through the wolves' snarling. The dire wolf was plucked out of the air above me and its body ripped in two. Farra landed amongst the wolves and scattered them in a great rage of teeth, talons, and tail.

I sank against the dolmen, breathing heavily, dazed by my close escape, while Farra dismembered my attackers.

I could not express my gratitude in words. The young dragon shuffled toward me on his wings and breathed into my face in quiet reunion. I smiled and caressed his scaly face, whispering unintelligible sounds of endearment that came from a part of me I thought had died when I lost my parents. A gravelly rumbling rose from deep inside the wyvern's chest. He was telling me he was glad to have found me again.

I leaned my face tiredly against his and started humming. Then the humming became words and I began singing our flight song.

Through the tunnels of time I have traveled
Back to The Beginning, I'm told...

Farra turned around and offered me his back. He wanted me to fly with him again!

"Wait a minute," I said.

I wiped my swords and re-sheathed them, then ducked under the dolmen to retrieve the sacks. I opened the neck of one and withdrew a handful of sulphur. My gashes were bleeding freely, particularly a deep puncture wound on my left calf. The sulphur burned like crazy when I rubbed it on. I packed the yellow powder into the tooth marks on my calf until I nearly passed out from the pain. Sitting there, waiting for the weakness and nausea to subside, I could hear Farra munching on something outside the shelter.

Once again, I was forced to leave my food behind, even though the ladies in the cirque would sorely need some right about then. With my friends in mind, I stuffed the packet of dried meat under my shirt. I tore a few mouthfuls of bread off a loaf and discarded the rest. I abhorred the waste, yet I would not be able to carry it and hold onto Farra's back at the same time.

I looped the drawstrings of the sulphur and guano bags through my belt and snugged it tight. With that done, I exited the dolmen and climbed carefully aboard the young wyvern. After I had settled between his wings and hooked my clothing to his dorsal spikes, I patted him and said wearily, "Let's go, Farra."

As Farra launched skyward I tensed against my various aches and pains.

Chapter 36

How beautiful the land looked from the air! My heart swelled with the pride and possessiveness of belonging to such a gorgeous place. Trees covered the rolling hills like rumpled green velvet. Diamond lakes glittered from inaccessible hiding places within the deep forests. Majestic mountain splendor reflected the sky in Technicolor shades of purple, orange, pink, and blue.

An acute yearning stirred inside me; an elusive, unnamed desire that struggled for expression. My soul fought and burned at my core. I felt driven to run, leap, dance, and dare all with invincibility. I couldn't pinpoint the source of my exhilaration. It was as though a voice was calling out to me with an urgent message that I couldn't grasp, and it eluded me, leaving me longing for resolution; and I knew I would search my whole life to satisfy the yearning and quell the thirst.

The northwestern mountain ranges of Fintan's Highlands circumscribed a hundred-square-mile area of open tableland known as the Moytura Plain. Towering peaks scattered the heavy clouds that were drenching the midlands we had just left behind, and Farra and I had a clear view of this wide and soggy plain as we flew high above. Below us, ten thousand Elves and half as many Giants were battling for supremacy over Danaan Land—my future Ireland. I remembered from my history studies that two major battles had been fought here. The first was when the Human colony of Firbolgs had been overthrown by the Tuatha Dé Danaan in Southern Moytura. The second was a brutal battle between the Tuatha Dé and the Fomorians—and it was undoubtedly that very war which was unfolding before my disbelieving eyes. I was witnessing a spectacle that historians of the future would banish to the realm of fantasy and the supernatural.

I urged Farra to circle once or twice while I focused my enhanced vision on the combatants in the field. It looked like a Grimm scene from an age gone by. That familiar dream state crept over me, threatening to short circuit my ability to process and react to information. I blinked hard and shook my head several times.

"I don't see any Humans in the fight," I said. "Keep going, Farra."

It was while we were heading south toward Lough Fee that movement on the roads and in the hills and river valleys around Moytura began to attract our attention. Farra flew lower to investigate. It was Humans! Traveling in groups of scores, hundreds, and thousands, Humans were gathering from all over Danaan Land to… What exactly were they doing? Didn't they know they were heading toward annihilation if they engaged both the Elves and Giants at the same time? What was Cathal thinking? They should let the two armies battle it out and then… But, of course! That's exactly what that wily blacksmith was planning! I knew it as surely as I knew how brilliantly he had led the uprising in Cong. I whooped aloud in delight and Farra responded with a shriek of his own.

Chapter 37

The Human encampment in the foothills of the Sheeffry Range was bustling with activity. Old-growth trees crowded a tule-and-cattail-edged lake in the secluded valley that had been chosen as their headquarters. The majority of tents were pitched in a clearing by the lake, with other facilities being erected between the trees on an as-needed basis. Fighting men and women arrived in a steady stream and were shown where to bivouac. Several blacksmiths had set up a temporary forge and were mending weapons and constructing everything from tent pegs to candle holders. A farrier was busy examining horses and trimming hooves. An armorer disbursed swords and spears from a long tent. A length of heavy canvas converted one side of the clearing into a makeshift mess tent, under which several cooks were sweating over kettles and cookfires.

Near the central cluster of officers' tents, scores of horses were tied to picket ropes strung between the trees. Cathal was cleaning out the hooves of a saddled horse when Farra's distant scream jerked every head skyward.

One of the rebel soldiers pointed at the sky and

cried a warning. "A dragon!"

A second man was quick to point out that there wasn't any danger. "Ah, don't worry," said he. "It's just a wyvern."

"How can you tell from this distance?" asked the first man.

"Note the huge wingspan in proportion to the body," was the knowledgeable reply. "It's two-legged, not four."

"Big fella, isn't he?" the first man acknowledged with relief.

The men and women resumed their preparations for the upcoming battle. Cathal, however, continued to squint at the large wyvern circling amongst the multi-textured storm clouds hundreds of feet above him, its scales gleaming brightly in the sunshine.

After a brief internal debate, Cathal sprang aboard the horse and trotted along a trail that approximately paralleled the wyvern's flight path.

Niall happened to exit a tent at that moment and saw Cathal disappearing into the trees. He beckoned to the thirty warriors from Tubber who were sitting around a campfire. They instantly and without question got to their feet, gathered their weapons, and followed Niall to the picket line, where they mounted some of the captured Elven horses and rode out in pursuit of Cathal.

Back at the bivouac, Sub-Chief Talty frowned as he watched the warriors leaving. He had not seen Cathal depart. "Just where do they think they're going?" he wondered quietly.

The other young men of his group—who had sworn allegiance to Cathal during the Battle of Cong—looked at one another, then around at the busy camp, and began unobtrusively gathering weapons and food enough for a journey. They, too, took horses from the picket line and rode casually after the boys from Tubber.

Chapter 38

At long last, after an absence of three weeks, I found myself maneuvering to land near the campsite in the hanging valley on Maumseachtain. Farra's hundred-foot wingspan ruffled the grass and lake surface and stirred the trees as he hovered over the tiny cirque, descending slowly for a careful landing. The horses and donkeys bolted in fear to the farthest corner of the valley.

The setting sun cast a dazzling halo around Farra as he touched down, and his scales and wings shimmered with reflected golden light.

I searched fearfully for signs of life and was hugely relieved to see most of the women from the Refuge out and about, taking advantage of the weak winter sunshine.

They did not seem to be frightened at all by Farra. My first thought was they were too frail to run away from him, but then they actually ran toward us! They approached the wyvern cheerfully and even expectantly. I couldn't understand it at all. I wondered if perhaps they were insane from hunger, or blinded by intestinal parasites because of eating the horses. However, despite the fears and guilt that had driven me while I was away, they all appeared to be strong and well fed, and none the worse for wear. My eyes darted to the donkeys and horses, but just a glance proved they were all accounted for. How had the women been able to thrive on their starvation diet?

I saw Séú emerging from one of the tents. She was only using a walking stick for support, and was barely limping. Her eyes fell upon the wyvern, which shone like gold in the sun, and she slowed to a halt. A look of uncertainty crossed her features.

Farra bent his head close to the ground and the women caught sight of me for the first time. They responded with amazement and incredible happiness, and broke into a mad dash toward us. But Séú crumpled to the ground in abject fear and watched me dismount with terror in her eyes.

My reunion with the old ladies was joyful and I found myself crying as I hugged each one in turn. They were all chattering at once and their smiles outdid the sun for brightness. Bróna noticed the torn clothes, and blood on my arms and legs, and examined my wolf bites with great concern.

"Ladies! Ladies! Order please!" she called. "We must get Ashling to the tents. She is injured." And to me she said in the rambling fashion she adopted when emotions ran high, "I must tend to these cuts. You used sulphur. Good. We don't have to worry about infection. Dear girl, you have an uncanny ability to amaze and astound me. You flew away on one bird and back again on another. We weren't sure if… Well, Aoibh never doubted. She never doubted at all." She was sniffling and wiping her eyes and nose on her sleeve while talking.

I looked around for Séú. When I saw the Elf on the ground I assumed she had collapsed due to her injured leg, and I ran to her, but Séú reached up with an outstretched hand to block me from coming nearer. Now the old ladies saw Séú's condition and the fear upon her face, and they ran to help her, exhibiting a great affection that had not been there when last I was amongst them.

Aoibh knelt beside Séú in great agitation. "What ails you, child of God?" asked the kind-hearted woman.

All the women displayed great concern. And to my own dismay, my Elf friend started to sob brokenly, as though all the pressures and pain of the previous weeks could no longer be contained. I tried to get closer, but she whimpered and shook her head at me, and scooted backwards away from me. This apparent rejection affected me terribly. What had I done to cause her such loathing?

When she got her emotions under control and was able to speak, she pointed shakily at me.

"You…" she quavered.

"Séú, what is it, my friend?" I asked, distraught to see her so stricken.

"It has long been foretold by the gods that your arrival on Terra heralds the destruction of my race," she said.

I gaped at my friend in disbelief before laughing in merriment. Now it was I who could not speak, and tears once again filled my eyes, but they were tears of laughter. "Don't be ridiculous!" I gasped through my hilarity.

Séú shook her head, positive she was right. My laughter faded.

Many hands helped Séú to her feet, and she addressed me with unfathomable sadness. "'When a Daughter of Cain rides a golden dragon across the heavens, the Island of Immortals will sink beneath the waves forever'," she quoted.

Time spun and circled around behind me, then slapped me upside the head. I heard the old Traveller woman from Tall Peadar's Winter Camp prophesying over me, seeing me for who I really was through the millennia that separated us.

I stared in mute horror, unable to contradict Séú or refute the prophecy. A chill of doom crept up my spine as the many disparate details and puzzle pieces began to consolidate into a single image.

Bróna clucked like a mother hen. "Well now. Look at the two of you—acting as though somebody just stepped on your graves. It's merely an old wives' tale."

I shuddered. "It's not an old wives' tale, Bróna. Atlantis *is* going to be destroyed. The entire continent will sink without a trace." I gulped. "Thousands of years from now, Tír na nÓg will be nothing more than a children's fairytale."

A paralysis of shock gripped us all. Our lives appeared to be at the precipice of eternity.

Séú was the first to gather her senses. "I must warn my father!" she cried. "Ashling, get me off this mountain!" Her command did not entertain the possibility that I might be unable to achieve that herculean task.

That's when I recalled my plan. I undid my belt and held up the pigskin sacks for all to see.

"What have you got there?" asked Cáit.

"I'm going to blast that landslide into the middle

of next week," I proclaimed.

"How will you do that?" asked Kitti.

"We're going to make gunpowder," I explained. "I learned the recipe during an extra-credit assignment at NUI. God bless Professor Carlyle!"

The old ladies echoed me with a heartfelt chorus of "God bless Professor Carlyle!"

"I knew you would think of something," gushed Aoibh.

I gave orders for the preparation and each one set about her given task.

While they were thus occupied and I was having my wounds cleansed and bandaged, Séú limped toward Farra, who had been listening to our conversation. They gazed solemnly at one another. The gentle dragon stretched his neck until his face was inches from the Elf's. She reached out and hesitantly touched the tip of his muzzle.

"Mighty Dragon," she said. "You brought salmon every day to keep us from starving, but I fear your generosity was wasted on me."

The mighty beast rumbled deep inside his chest.

"My days on Terra are numbered," concluded Séú fatalistically.

Chapter 39

Cathal galloped into Scucca Pass with his cadre of thirty-seven warriors. Hacking and stabbing and shouting their rebel yell, they rode into the midst of twenty Giants who were guarding the Notch.

The battle very quickly became one sided. Despite the initial success of their surprise attack, the men and horses proved to be no match for the tremendous strength of the Fomorians. Their valiant effort was doomed to the annals of lost causes.

Warrior after warrior was crushed until only a small knot of men remained. Cathal and Niall found themselves fighting desperately side by side, when the mingled shrieks of Human and dragon rent the air.

Farra seemed impossibly large within the confines of the narrow pass as he plummeted from the peaks and plowed through the ranks of Giants. The wyvern wheeled and came to earth, facing the Giants and snarling ferociously.

The Giants regrouped and advanced upon the wyvern. The Human warriors fell back.

Farra lowered his head and I leaped to the ground.

The wound on my calf burst open when I landed, but the pain only served to provide impetus. I drew my sword and once again gave voice to my battle cry, challenging my enemies to take me on. The battle fury was upon me.

When the Fomorians saw me dismount from the dragon, they were petrified with fear and superstition. Some exclaimed in their own tongue, and this was later translated to me by Niall of the Boats, who traded regularly with the Giants and spoke their language.

"A wench on a dragon! The prophecy has come to pass!" screamed one.

"The end of the world is nigh!" shouted a second.

At that, the Giants wheeled and fled, dropping swords and spears and discarding heavy armor as they ran.

The ten or so men who remained alive looked at me with awe. Cathal was dumbfounded.

As I limped toward them, most of the men knelt and bowed their heads in humility and respect. I glanced at them in surprise as I approached Cathal. I assumed they were bowing to Farra.

"Giants who fight and run away, live to fight another day," I joked, grinning at Cathal. I hoped my face wasn't showing how glad I was to see him again.

Cathal glowered at me. I wasn't expecting this from him. I cocked my head.

"What were you waiting for?" he yelled angrily. "You must have reached the mountain at least three days ago! Why didn't you deal with the Giants then?"

I was astounded at his venom. "What is your problem?" I responded angrily, stung that he was treating me this way.

"Look around you! Twenty-five of my men are

dead because of you!" he shouted. "If you had taken care of these Giants before now, the pass would have been clear and no one would have died."

"I was making blasting powder! That takes time." I was angry and defensive. The gunpowder had taken three days to prepare.

"Will your magic powder bring my friends back to life?" he raged.

"No, of course not."

"Then I don't give a devil's damn about it or any of your excuses."

Cathal grimly turned to the task of checking the bodies of his comrades. Among the dead was Sub-Chief Talty. Niall of the Boats helped Cathal while the other survivors tended to each other's wounds.

Cathal's rebuff knocked the wind out of my sails. Was he right? Had I mixed up my priorities? Yet how could I have known he was going to attack the Giants in the pass? It was grossly unfair of him. My resentment grew the more I contemplated it.

I stood to one side, torn between staying and helping, or coming back another time to set the charges. I busied myself with untying the panniers of explosives on Farra's back and stacking them against the cliff wall.

The remaining warriors laid their fallen brethren in a row and arranged the bodies respectfully. None of us had any coins, so Cathal cut gold pieces from the harnesses of the Elven horses. The gold was to pay the Gate Keeper on the soul's journey into the Heavenlies. The slain fighters were sent to the afterlife with gold over their eyes (our eyes being the portals through which the soul migrates after death), arms folded across their chests, and swords gripped in hand for the journey ahead. Then we all gathered around to pray for the safe passage of the souls.

Every one of those tough, bloodstained fighters shed tears for the fallen. I stood with them, sharing their loss but unable to express it. Farra blew gently on the corpses as though administering a warrior's final blessing, and the survivors were greatly affected by the dragon's tribute. It was truly fitting that the selfless sacrifice of their comrades should be honored by a dragon's breath. We covered the long grave with rocks until the cairn was three feet high.

After the ceremony, I told Farra to get away from the pass in case he got hurt. He understood me perfectly and disappeared in a hurricane of wing strokes.

Next, I explained how the gunpowder should work. Cathal and his friends helped me decide where best to set the charges, and then clambered around the rockslide and placed the explosives while I led the horses to safety. My leg was sore and I was glad not to have to do strenuous acrobatics.

Finally, I lit the fuse I had made out of twine soaked in oil, and we watched in awe from a safe distance as a series of explosions blasted rocks, debris, and thick smoke to the heavens.

All manner of flying creatures took to the air in a tumult of terror.

The next morning, the old ladies finally emerged from their mountain prison. I went first, leading the horses of Elasippus through the recently cleared Notch.

Landslide debris littered the floor of the pass.

Many trees had been crushed or broken under blackened boulders, and the fallen warriors of Tubber and Cong had been granted a permanent resting site under the displaced rocks.

Cathal descended next, leading a horse ridden by Séú. Behind them, Niall and the other warriors assisted the old women and their donkeys.

I mounted the very horse Finoula had ridden on our night flight weeks earlier, and watched jealously as Cathal paid extravagant attention to the beautiful Elf.

Once out of the gully, the men helped the old ladies onto the horses that had been ridden the previous day by the warriors who died in the Battle of Scucca Pass.

Séú rode forward to join me.

"How's your leg holding up?" I asked with concern.

"It is healing fast. Bróna knows the secret arts. How about yours?"

My calf wound was a source of concern for me. Bróna had cleaned it out and stitched it shut the day of my return (all without anesthetic, but I don't want to talk about it), then wrapped it with a clean bandage, but this morning it was swollen and throbbing, probably due to all my activity the previous day. I didn't tell anyone about the inflammation, because there were too many things to do. I knew Bróna would insist on rest, but the volcanoes on Atlantis wouldn't wait for me to heal. Also, the temperature had dropped below freezing the night before and I knew the ladies could not remain in that icebox valley another day.

Regardless of the pain, I pushed on, allowing the wound to split open and ooze freely. The bandage was soaked with pus underneath my loose, Elven trousers. At least the infection was coming out, but it hurt like blazes.

So, I shrugged and lied. "Doing well."

"Can you handle the journey?"

"Absolutely."

I looked for Cathal without meaning to and was surprised to find that he was already watching me. Our eyes locked for an instant, and sparks flew, but then he looked away. He still blamed me for the deaths of his comrades the day before. Regret for what could have been gnawed at my gut. I was leaving, never to return. Cathal was being relegated to history and I was embarking on a journey to Atlantis, where I would somehow find a portal to take me back to my world.

"Come on, Ashling. Let us be off," said Séú impatiently.

We waved a final goodbye, then wheeled our mounts and galloped away.

The warriors and old women watched silently, long after we were out of sight, reluctant and sad at the parting.

"We ought to get going," hinted Niall.

"Kylemore isn't going anywhere, young man," said Bróna with a lot more gentleness than she would have exhibited a few weeks earlier.

Finally, with heavy hearts, they turned and rode the other way, heading home. Cathal fought with his horse, which wanted to follow its companions. He remained behind and his horse pawed impatiently.

Niall turned back to speak with his friend. "Aren't you coming?"

"No."

"But she's your grandmother, not mine."

"She no longer needs me. I'd be better put to use

in Moytura."

"Our families should be our priority, not the High King and his crown."

"Will you take care of my family?"

"You know I will. I'll take your sister and her children to the Refuge when I bring my own family."

"And my mother?"

"Oh, if you insist." Niall grinned at Cathal. "I'll even rescue your crazy cat."

"She's a great ratter."

"I never knew that about your mother." Niall's eyes glinted with humor and his lips curled slightly at the corners. Cathal shook his head in aggravation.

"What tools should I save from your forge?" asked Niall.

"Leave them. They can always be replaced."

"Do you really think there's going to be a disaster?"

Cathal shrugged. "We can't afford to treat the warning lightly. There have been too many signs and wonders."

"Ashling's story is beyond believable."

Cathal lifted his chin defiantly. "Prodigious events have been set in motion because of her."

"Most of our friends are dead," reminded Niall sourly, "and things have only just begun."

"Hope is not dead." Cathal shifted in the saddle and tightened the slack in his horse's reins.

"Why throw your effort after foolishness?" Niall was angry. "War is a king's occupation. Nobody will sing the deeds of the faceless thousands when we have gone the way of death."

"It's the thousands of nameless faces who give the

king his crown, and his reason to fight," said Cathal. "I'll do whatever is required to wrest our home from the gods. No matter that my efforts will be unsung when the stories are recorded."

Niall recognized the determination on his friend's face and nodded in understanding. "Go, then," he joked. "We have men's work to do rebuilding the Refuge, and you'd only get in the way."

That made Cathal smile faintly. The friends clasped arms in farewell and spurred their mounts in opposite directions without another word.

Chapter 40

Séú and I galloped northward from Lough Fee. Urgency lent us speed. We had to get to the harbor of Leenaun where—Niall had assured us—we would have no trouble finding a ship to take us to Atlantis.

We halted our horses in amazement when we crested a hilltop overlooking the Killary Inlet. The bristling masts of hundreds of Fomorian galleys and Elven caravels cluttered the long harbor. There should have been voices, shouts, carts, people unloading cargo and haggling, and all the crazy activity those ships should have produced; yet the town and docks of Leenaun were eerily silent. The townspeople had fled when the first of the Fomorian ships had started arriving, both to avoid the depredations of the Giants and to be absent when the two powerful races clashed, which they knew to be inevitable.

Séú suddenly jabbed her finger and exclaimed excitedly, "That is my father's flagship!"

She spurred her horse down the hill and I followed.

Our horses' hooves clattered loudly on the cobblestones as we pulled up beside the flagship of the Elasippus fleet which was moored at the docks in Leenaun. Hungry seagulls wheeled and screeched hopefully above us. The air was rank with the odor of rotting things. Lines and hardware slapped noisily aboard the abandoned ships.

"Ahoy, the *Wave Crester*!" Séú shouted in Elven.

After a longer-than-expected wait, a sailor popped his head over the gunwale and gawked at Séú. They conversed in their own language.

"It's the princess!" he said to no one in particular.

"Tell my father I am here!" Séú commanded.

"The king marches to war with the Fomorians to avenge the deaths of his children," reported the sailor, pointing inland.

"Ready our fastest ship," she decided swiftly. "I sail for home on the next tide."

"As you wish, Your Highness."

He disappeared to do her bidding and Séú turned to me. "My father is on his way to Moytura to battle the Giants," she said. "You must go to him and warn him not to return to Atlantis." Her eyes begged me to comply.

"No. I'm going with you." I argued. "Don't go changing the plans at this late hour. You promised to purchase my access to Mount Olympus. If I can't get through the portals before the cataclysm, I'll never be able to return to my world."

"I must go ahead to start the evacuations," she said urgently. "I cannot delay. You can follow in another ship, but you *must* warn my father first." She paused as her voice broke with emotion. "I beg of you," she pleaded. "If you do not warn him, he will return to Elasippus, and all his soldiers with him."

I jutted out my chin and shook my head stubbornly. I had already given enough for these people and their problems. I refused to jeopardize my personal agenda any longer.

"Nope," I said. "If the volcanoes erupt before I get there, I'll be stuck here forever."

"When I left home, the mountains showed nary a smoke or rumble," urged Séú. "You have more than enough time."

I shook my head firmly. "Don't ask me to do this, Séú."

"Ten thousand lives are in your hands."

My internal struggle must have been evident. My horse pranced and fought the reins nervously, sensing its rider's turmoil. Séú awaited my decision with bated breath. I sawed on the reins and quieted my horse. Atlantis was definitely going to be destroyed, yet what if I could save ten thousand Elves who would otherwise be killed? Because of their tainted Angel blood, Elves could not go to Heaven when they died. They enjoyed longevity on Earth and were immune to disease, but when they died, their souls were doomed to spend eternity in Hades.

After staring at the cobblestones and shaking my head quite a few times, I sighed in resignation. "What if your father won't listen to me?"

Séú smiled with gratitude and relief. We reached across our horses' necks and hugged fiercely, as a premonition draped us with foreboding.

"Fly to him on Farra's back and he will believe you," she advised. "You and Farra are the fulfillment of a very ancient prophecy. Your arrival was meant to signal our doom, but perhaps you were also destined to be the instrument of salvation. An early warning from us will save hundreds of thousands of souls from damnation."

"Be off, then!" I commanded. "Time and tides wait for no man."

"But perhaps they will wait for a woman," Séú amended wisely.

I laughed and wheeled my horse and cantered off without a backward look.

As my horse dashed through the empty streets of Leenaun and out into the countryside, tears glimmered in my eyes and threatened to spill over. I wiped them away angrily. I had a strong feeling I would never see Séú again, and part of me hurt to think of that. Despite my resolve to remain aloof from the people of this world, I had allowed her to get past my defenses and become my friend. Once I realized this, the blast shield around my heart was lowered and I finally allowed myself to grieve for the ladies of the Refuge as well. I would never see any of them again, and I had not let them know how much they had come to mean to me. I hadn't known it myself.

I cried uncontrollably for the first time since my parents died, and the horse galloped toward the mountains without any guidance from me.

When I reached Farra's favorite crag in the Maumseachtain foothills, I unsaddled the horse and set it free. It began to graze nearby, but I knew it would eventually make its way back to the docks at Dún Aengus, where it had disembarked with the rest of its herd. Or perhaps it would return to the Refuge. I could not allow myself to worry for it. It may or may not be molested by wolves, but I could not put the life of one horse ahead of thousands of Elves. How often in this world would I be called upon to make such difficult choices, the significance of which caused my previous worries to pale? I would much rather stew about the SUSI Review Board and my university debt than be forced to make these life-or-death decisions.

I tilted my face to the clouds and called for Farra.

Chapter 41

Meanwhile, King Ampherat's Elves held the field at the Battle of Moytura Plain, but their number was reduced to two thousand, including their wounded.

The plain was littered with frost-coated bodies, and swarms of carrion eaters were already busy at work. There were ravens, rats, crows, pterodactyls, wolves, foxes, and even a small, four-legged dragon. At night, a slew of other creatures would slink out of the dark forests and marshes to feast on what was left over after the diurnal scavengers. It wouldn't be long before the battlefield was cleansed.

The Elven leaders gathered in King Ampherat's tent and consulted together while the field was scoured for wounded. Injured Elves were carried on stretchers to medical tents for treatment. Among them was King Nuada, whose right hand had been chopped off above the wrist.

Most of those who were physically uninjured sat amongst the dead of both armies in a stupor of horror and exhaustion. The finality of death always filled Elves with dark dread. It was devastating to lose friends and brothers one had known for hundreds of years. The knowledge that death had propelled their loved ones into a bottomless pit where they would suffer agonizing torment for eternity, inevitably caused excruciating psychological torture to the survivors. The reason the gods and their offspring were so jealous of Humans was because only Humans have the choice of entering Heaven after death.

Of the five-thousand-strong army of Fomorians, only three hundred or so were still alive. These were lined up on their knees and executed. The wounded were dispatched with identical ruthlessness. They neither asked for nor received quarter from their ancient enemies. Dead Giants shared the same fate as Elves, although a separate pit awaited them, but either Giants were not as cognizant as their cousins, or the prospect of exchanging life on Terra for an eternity in Hades was not abhorrent to them.

A trumpet call split the air and the Elves halted their gruesome labors to see what had caused the strident notes. A Human army of a thousand score emerged from the forest line that rimmed the bloody plain, and tightened in an inevasible noose around the Elves.

King Ampherat saw in one sweeping glance that his forces could never hope to defeat this new army, following so closely upon their recent exertions. Ampherat's bloodshot eyes registered defeat. His bodyguards summoned what little energy they had left to surround their king, but he wearily ordered them to stand down. They reluctantly lowered their weapons.

"Resistance is futile, brethren," he said. "The Sons of Cain have the field."

The surviving Elves were disarmed, herded into a tight group, and ordered to sit on the ground. Those in the first-aid tents were placed under guard. Ampherat was dragged forth and made to kneel before High King Iarann of the Humans, whose force had emerged victorious over both the Elves and the Giants without so much as lifting a bow.

Iarann was a robust man in his sixties, whose grey hair and beard were no disguise for the eye twinkle that betrayed his vigor. He was descended directly from Partholon via the male line and thus claimed the right to rule the Humans of the land. His people revered him for his wisdom. He had always exhibited restraint and tolerance in his dealings with the Elven usurpers of his ancestor's Island of Destiny; yet on this day, forbearance was not a term that would describe the harsh penalty he meted out to his rival on behalf of the Humans of Danaan Land. The Humans considered the punishment to be just and well-deserved, although having suffered centuries of enslavement and injustice under Ampherat's long reign, a few thought Iarann too lenient for not proscribing instant death to every Elf in the land.

"These are the terms of your surrender," pronounced the High King in a strong, resonant voice. "You have ten days to gather your families and personal possessions, after which you will sail from these shores, never to return. From now unto eternity, no hole in the ground will be big enough to hide the race of the Túatha Dé Dannan."

Ampherat sat back on his heels in defeat. He glared around at the pressing numbers of gloating Sons and Daughters of Cain, whose dream of this day had been passed on to them along with their genetic codes.

They had been rocked in the cradle to songs of liberty and freedom, and the taste of it was intoxicating to their souls.

Unexpectedly, at the very moment Iarann finished pronouncing his judgment, the ground began to rumble and tremor. Both Humans and Elves were startled. Alarmed cries of "Terrashake!" broke forth amongst the Humans. The Elven prisoners interpreted the event as a sign of the gods' anger and began smiling at one another. The shaking and rumbling continued unabated and grew in intensity and volume.

At the same time, a commotion and outcry from the outer ranks of the Human army flashed inward to the center of the circle where the key players were positioned.

Chieftain Killian of Conmacna pushed through the soldiers and rode swiftly up to High King Iarann. His horse was jittery and fought the reins, backing and spinning and nearly trampling some Humans who leaped away and slapped the horse in annoyance.

"The God People have arrived from over the sea and are moving to flank us!" Killian announced fretfully.

Iarann immediately put his sword to Ampherat's throat.

The chieftain's alarming news spread fast, causing the circle of Humans to turn around and face outward. There was a lot of jostling and grumbling until the news was picked up and spread, and soon the entire army had completed an about-face to deal with their approaching foe.

The Elves from Atlantis thundered onto the Moytura Plain from the west and encircled the Human army at a gallop. It was their pounding hooves that had caused the ground to shake. This was the force that had come to avenge the noble sons of Elasippus.

The two armies faced each other across a No Man's Land of churned earth, forming a ring within a ring. Ockto's disciplined army numbered fifteen thousand, while the rag-tag Humans numbered about twenty-one thousand. In terms of size, strength, skill, experience, and equipment, the Humans were vastly outnumbered. The two thousand Elves held prisoner by the Humans began to stir and stand. They did not immediately commit to a course of action, being restrained by uncertainty, exhaustion, lack of weapons, and fear for their king's life, but they eyed their captors with evil intent. Their Human guards were decidedly unnerved to be caught in this unenviable place; the first to be killed should their prisoners decide to throw in their lot with their Atlantean counterparts.

King Iarann forced Ampherat to his feet and marched him through the throng of Humans until they were standing on the outer edge of the ring, directly across from King Ockto of Elasippus. Iarann's challenge rang across the open ground between the two forces.

"Stay your troops, foreigner!" commanded the Human monarch. "We hold a goodly number of your race at the point of the sword, including your deposed kinsman, Ampherat of Everlasting Shame." His words dripped with hatred and the edge of his blade pressed keenly against the throat of his royal hostage until blood began to trickle.

"Ampherat is no kinsman of mine," growled King Ockto savagely. His eyes were lit from within by the fires of insanity. "Do with him what you will. I am here to satisfy my blood lust. I care not who jumps in front of my sword!"

King Ampherat was shocked, but wisely held his tongue. His discomfort under Iarann's sword was very apparent and he did not want to irritate his captor any further.

King Ockto raised his sword overhead and opened his mouth to scream the order to charge, but was cut off short when his soldiers started to shove and press him from behind. He turned to see his army scattering in terror from a huge wyvern bracing to land on No Man's Land. Horses were plunging out of control and knocking one another over.

A stray burst of sunshine slanted though the clouds and spotlighted the great reptile, setting Farra's scales on fire. A haze of bright sunlight outlined the creature and turned him to gold as he settled on the ground, feet first, with wings outspread.

Moans of anguish replaced the hum of war as thousands of Atlanteans saw something that was obscured from their king's eyes. The Elves on the outskirts of the field at first rushed away from the embodiment of their doom; then their military training overcame their fears and they halted to watch what their leaders would do. Many Elves closest to No Man's Land were tossed off their bucking horses. Many dropped their weapons and surged through the seething mass in an attempt to flee the coming calamity, but most did not know which way to turn and chose to prostrate themselves before Farra in hopes of placating disaster.

Ockto was dismayed at the weakness and confusion displayed by his troops. He looked around in consternation as his hardened soldiers dropped to their knees with a clatter of armor and weapons. The enraged king began whacking those nearest him with the flat side of his blade. "On your feet!" he roared with fury. "What is this wasting disease that assails my troops?"

Ockto's portly general, Phonecius, his eyes bulging, croaked out a response to his king. "Fear, my Lord."

General Phonecius sank to his knees and bowed his head in the direction of Farra, and Ockto began kicking him in a blindness of anger and frustration. He emitted an animal squeal of rage, clearly under the grips of madness.

That's when I saw Séú's father for the first time. I understood the tremendous loss he had suffered with the deaths of his sons and nephews at the hands of the Fomorians, and I was glad I had decided to come to Moytura and give him some good news—the news that Séú had survived. The rest of my news was not good, I admit, but my report about his daughter should help soften the blow.

"King Ockto?" I raised my voice so that it would carry to his ears above the din of the multitude. My voice sounded rich and strong; not commanding, but not brooking argument either. The surrounding Elves were on their knees—no doubt because of the prophecy. The Human soldiers were gap-mouthed with amazement.

Ockto shaded his eyes and squinted against the sun's glare. The sun was directly behind me and I must have been just a silhouette to the king. Reading my mind, Farra raised his wings until they met behind me, effectively blocking the sun, and I was now visible to the puzzled king.

I remained on Farra's back, prevented by my injured leg from leaping to the ground in front of the assembled kings and chieftains. Up there, on the back of the dragon, I spoke with the confidence of an equal. I had everybody's undivided attention.

"Your Majesty," I began. "I have been sent by Princess Séú to tell you she is alive and well. She sent me to warn you that Atlantis is soon to be destroyed. You and your army must remain in Danaan Land until the danger has passed."

A variety of emotions tumbled across Ockto's countenance. "Séú is alive?" he cried out. "Oh, thank the Lords of Olympus! And what of my sons?"

"The news you heard of them is true," I said with genuine sympathy. "They fell under the swords of the Fomorians. No finer warriors have I ever met."

But Ockto was once again plunged into his state of grief, distraught with madness. He began pulling on his hair and weaving from side to side as though trying to avoid the truth that was aimed directly at his heart. I felt very sorry for him, but also was deeply concerned that this man was in charge of the destinies of so many when clearly his sanity had flown. I continued to speak, hoping to ease his fears.

"Séú has returned to Elasippus to begin the evacuation of your people."

Ockto's eyes stared and his mouth fell open. A new pain contorted his features as he processed this information. "Séú has gone back?" he asked rhetorically. "Then all whom I love in this world are over the sea… soon to be underneath it." He was reasoning to himself aloud. "I must be with them!" Wild of demeanor, the once-mighty king of Elasippus screamed at his second-in-command: "General Phonecius—back to the ships! Back to the ships!"

The cry was taken up by the Atlantean Elves and the army thundered from the battlefield, drowning out my protests. Every one of Ockto's men had family in Atlantis, and their only thoughts were to return to their homeland to save the women and children they had left behind. When the thunder, and shouting, and shaking ground had finally stilled, the Humans were left standing in confused silence while their Elven prisoners of war looked stricken.

Oh, dear God in Heaven, I thought. *Now what am I to do?* I had failed Séú! I would arrive in Atlantis with her father and all his soldiers, when I was supposed to save their lives by convincing them to stay in Danaan Land. Séú would be furious! There was no way on Terra she would help me find a way onto Mount Olympus, and from thence home, unless I could save her father. And yet, there might still be time; we could not know when the destruction of Atlantis would occur. If I had time to climb Mount Olympus, there most assuredly would be enough time for the king to evacuate the island. And perhaps the evacuation would leave the portals unguarded! Or else I could merge with the panicked populace during the mass evacuation should they choose to escape their doom through the portals as they had done in the days of Noah.

I squeezed Farra gently with my knees and he beat his massive wings and rose majestically into the air. The downdraft caused the soldiers to duck and cover. We circled once or twice to gain height, and then zoomed into the sunset.

The assembled Humans burst into a tumultuous roar of cheering, and clashed swords upon shields in appreciation of our contribution to their supremacy on that day of fluctuating outcomes.

Cathal the Smith alone was silent amidst the uproar, staring after me with furrowed brows. He shook off the embrace of an excited warrior and pushed through the horde to where King Iarann was standing. He had to shout to be heard above the din.

"Your Majesty!" yelled Cathal. "When Tír na nÓg is destroyed, massive tidal waves will engulf our coast. You need to order our people to head to high ground."

"Who told you that?" asked Iarann.

"The girl on the dragon," answered Cathal, jabbing a finger in the direction I had taken.

Iarann Ua Partholon studied Cathal with great interest. "What's your name, boy?" asked the king.

Cathal realized he was speaking to the highest-ranking Human in Danaan Land, possibly on the entire planet, and he gulped at his audacity. He also realized that his name needed a bit of an adjustment if he was to sound authoritative.

"Cathal of Tubber," he announced boldly.

"Ah," said the king with a twinkle. "I have heard of you. Very well, Cathal of Tubber. As my newest general, you will oversee the civilian evacuations and report directly to me."

The High King turned and rapped out orders to his other generals, but Cathal did not hear. He was in a daze and his surroundings appeared to be a swirling blur. He could not believe his good fortune, or the swiftness of his elevation to such a position of responsibility. He vowed to be worthy of the High King's trust.

Chapter 42

By the shores of Kylemore Lough, the cattle and sheep were found clustered around the barn when their owners returned, and the reunion was very touching. Most of these animals were pets. Several sheep were missing, but the majority of the flock and herd was alive and well, looking a little the worst for neglect. The cleanup after the Giants did not take as long as anyone had expected. The stables and most of the workshops were intact, and the fire damage to the main residence and barn was minimal due to the quenching rains. The warriors from Tubber and Cong only needed a few days to restore the buildings to a livable condition before taking their leave of the grateful ladies, with promises to return in haste with their families in order to avoid the calamity I had warned them of.

A light mist drizzled over the area one day while the women of the Refuge were going about their daily chores. Aoibh tapped Bróna's arm and pointed to the path by the lake, where a long line of refugees trudged with handcarts and wagons and livestock. Niall of the Boats marched in front of the diaspora, carrying a young boy on his shoulders and prodding a lumbering ox ahead of a high-sided wagon filled with children.

Bróna took a deep breath, knowing they stood on the threshold of a new adventure. "Sisters," she said. "Here are the first of the refugees from the coast. Let us go down to the gate and welcome them."

The women looked at one another with nervous excitement. After five decades of isolation, their world was about to explode with people and change. They followed their leader to throw open the gates, giggling at the strangeness and delight of being restored to a place of importance amongst their own race.

Chapter 43

The journey from Moytura took King Ockto's force two days. He quartered his troops in the abandoned houses of Leenaun while they scoured the town for supplies for the trip home. Most of the warehouses along the wharf had been emptied, but one was found to contain pallets of corn stacked to the roof. Ockto's soldiers were unused to manual labor, and it took them longer than necessary to transfer the corn to the ships' holds.

Unable to convince Ockto to take me to Elasippus, and treated as an object of horror by his minions, I holed up in a cottage outside of town for three days, vying with the Elves for food, eating too much, and nursing my worsening leg. I paid a daily visit to the wharf to petition the king, but he was ensconced aboard his flagship and I was repeatedly denied access.

In the interim, General Cathal of Tubber sent riders to all points along the coast, warning people to flee to higher ground in advance of the devastation to come. He and his men executed their task so well that a weight lifted from my soul upon hearing of their work.

In the early light of the fifth day since the Human victory at Moytura, I sat on a bollard at the end of a long pier watching the last of the Elven fleet sail with the ebbing tide. The town of Leenaun reposed hauntingly still. The beauty of the majestic caravels riding on the morning tide caught my breath. The sailcloth on hundreds of masts spanked in the offshore breeze, displaying the assortment of pastel hues that represented the different clans of Elasippus, much like a flock of multicolored flamingos taking flight in the fresh sunlight.

Scores of Fomorian vessels remained abandoned at anchor in the harbor, dark and hulking and forlorn, awaiting feral masters whose warlike tendencies had earned them permanent rest on this foreign shore.

My throbbing leg caused the reflections on the water to dance and weave in exaggerated patterns. I was feverish, and knew I must get back to the Refuge right away so my adopted mothers could lance the wound on my calf and drain the infection. I was tired beyond measure. I contemplated the long walk ahead of me. Perhaps I could call Farra down to pick me up? I hadn't seen him in all the time I had been in Leenaun. The Elves spoke darkly of him, and I believe he picked up their thoughts on whatever extra-sensory wavelength he used. Naturally enough, he avoided Leenaun while the God People were thronging its streets.

A clattering of hooves on cobblestones caused me to turn. My heart and stomach tried to swap places. It was Cathal and several of his men. I had thought never to see him again and yet here he was! He rode right up to me and reined in. His men halted a respectful distance behind to allow for a private conversation.

There was a new strength and confidence in

Cathal's deportment, it seemed to me, and he looked devastatingly handsome in his new clothes. Obviously, somebody else had dressed him. I had wondered who would be his fashion advisor once I was gone, and it was clear that I had already been replaced.

Why was I thinking like this? There had never been anything between us except the mission. I had never been anything more to him than a prodigious means to a political end.

I waited for Cathal to speak first. My cup was too full of disappointment to be interested in starting a conversation with him. We had not parted on friendly terms and I didn't know him well enough to know if he was inclined to hold grudges. Not that the deaths of twenty-five of your closest friends is a minor thing to begrudge. I couldn't blame him, really. Ever since I had appeared on his scene there had been nothing but bloodshed and upheaval.

Cathal studied me quietly for a long moment while these tumultuous thoughts stabbed through my feverish brain. I imagined him dissecting me with his mind. A faint smile hovered over his features and I lifted my chin defiantly in response. He restrained one of his heart-stopping grins and I clenched my teeth.

"You were supposed to go with them," he said.

Did I detect a hint of hope in his voice?

He swung down from his horse to stand beside me. I turned back toward the ocean to avoid the closeness. The flags of the hindmost caravels were dipping below the horizon.

"They said I would bring them bad luck," I said, biting back the regret and despair.

Cathal's face brightened, giving lie to his next

words. "But you must go with them in order to return to your world." There were no secrets between us now. He had learned the true story around the campfire during our last night on Maumseachtain.

I sighed in resignation. "I'll have to find another way."

"Your family must be very worried about you."

What family? I thought. The only family I ever had was taken away from me by a drunk driver when I was just a little girl, and I was left to toss about on the cruel waves of life, struggling against tremendous adversity to make a name for myself and thus ensure that my Mammy and Daddy would be proud of me and that people would regret the whims of Fate that had struck down the parents of such a successful person. My heart ached inside my chest.

And now I was separated from my second family, the ladies at the Refuge, who loved me like a daughter. I grew calm as new thoughts began to fill the void of my despair.

"I don't have a family," I told Cathal thoughtfully, as I began sorting out my situation realistically for the first time. "I was orphaned as a child and grew up a ward of the state."

"Then you have a husband or lover waiting for you?" he asked.

I gazed seaward and shook my head. "I have no one," I said without rancor.

Cathal sighed with relief. "Don't worry," he said softly. "I'll find a way to get you home."

I looked at him again. "I'm sorry I let you down in Scucca Pass."

He knit his eyebrows for an instant and then

raised them in understanding. "Oh," he said shamefacedly. "I was wrong to blame you for that, Ashling. It wasn't your fault."

"Well, I didn't plan it very well," I admitted. "I should have chased the Giants away first and then…"

Cathal cut me off. "You were injured. You had to get started on the blasting powder. I understand all that now. I was angry and pumped up with adrenaline, and lashed out at you because… because…" he ended lamely and shrugged his shoulders. Then he added softly, "Because *I* had failed my men."

He had the grace to blush, and the strength to name his weakness, and the courage to admit his love for his brothers-in-arms—and I loved him for that. The emotions I was dealing with were threatening to overwhelm me. I was fighting a fever and had no experience with affairs of the heart, so I forced it all back inside and tried to lock it up.

"You didn't fail them, Cathal. You chose to do a noble deed and they chose to follow you."

He nodded, and I could tell he was comforted by my words. After a short pause, he spoke again. "Look, why don't you come back with us to the Refuge until this storm has passed? I'll rebuild your wings and we can wait for the next Dragon Wind. It appears every so often and is almost predictable—"

A shout from one of Cathal's men interrupted him. "Look at the water!" There was fear in the man's voice.

The water level against the quay wall was dropping abnormally fast. I knew immediately what was happening, and fear temporarily suspended my heartbeat. It jarred to life again with an erratic clamor that shook me and filled my ears.

"Run!" I screamed. "The tidal wave is coming!"

The ground suddenly heaved and shuddered beneath our feet and the horses reared in panic. The sound of a distant explosion reached our ears from far over the waters, followed by an endless series of muffled blasts that assured us that somewhere—beyond our vision but not our hearing—a tragedy of epic proportions was unfolding.

Cathal pulled his horse's head down and swung into the saddle. He offered me his hand and pulled me up behind him. Why, at this most needful of times, had my great strength left me? I should have been able to run as swiftly as the fastest horse, and yet I was burdening the horse that should be taking Cathal to safety.

"Hell-for-leather to Maumturk, lads!" he shouted.

I wrapped my arms around his waist and clung tightly to him. My teeth rattled violently inside my mouth as we jolted over the uneven streets of Leenaun and out into the open countryside. My leg screamed with fire.

"We won't make it, riding double," I gasped. The words were knocked out of me at every stride and I almost got my tongue bitten off for my trouble.

"I'm not leaving you behind," he said firmly. He clutched my hands with one of his, as though holding me in place.

The ground was shaking continuously from the eruptions on Atlantis. *It must be indescribable there,* I thought. *I hope and pray that Séú got away in time.*

Behind us, the water drained steadily out of Killary Harbor and receded from the inlet, exposing the debris of centuries on the muddy bottom. The inlet emptied completely along its twenty-five-mile length. All along the western seaboard the scene was duplicated as the Atlantic Ocean pulled away from the land. Rivers were sucked dry and even a few inland lakes emptied.

On the outskirts of Leenaun we raced past some stragglers with a cart that was piled high with possessions. It was a rich merchant and his wife, along with their children and servants.

"Leave your things!" shouted Cathal. "Flee for your lives! The wave is coming!"

The horses galloped toward the nearing mountain, but ours was gradually outpaced because of the double load it carried. Cathal drove it unmercifully, yet the other soldiers pulled far ahead.

Like a bolt from the blue, Farra swooped out of the sky. He hovered above us as he did when fishing in Lough Fee, and I yelled at Cathal to kick free of the stirrups. Farra snatched both Cathal and I off the horse like salmon in his talons, and lifted us high above the danger zone. The huge dragon was amazingly gentle. He held us firmly, yet we never felt uncomfortably squeezed, in the same way he could carry a salmon without mashing it to smithereens. His feet must have been extremely sensitive to touch.

The horse we had recently vacated raced desperately to catch up with its pals, who had already reached the base of Maumturk.

"Ashling! Look!" urged Cathal.

Far out on the Atlantic a towering wall of water was hurtling toward the coast, preceded by a roaring noise which built in intensity as the killer wave neared. The horizon was darkened by an epic cloud of smoke and ash hurtling into the stratosphere.

Below us, the trees were bouncing due to the constant terrashakes. Landslides triggered by the geologic upheavals caused cliffs to shear away and mountainsides to crumble. Rocks and boulders rolled down the slopes and a great pall of dust filled the air.

Thousands of wyverns, pterosaurs, and lesser creatures of the air rose from the landscape *en masse*, creating a deafening cacophony as they fled inland with Farra, Cathal, and me.

Farra hovered over the lush grass of a meadow on the western side of Maumturk Mountain and dropped me and Cathal gently before landing next to us. We turned to see what was happening on the valley floor two thousand feet below.

I leaned against Cathal, whose arms were tight around me, holding me up. Mute with horror, we clung to each other and watched as the destruction unfolded.

Trees and houses were blown away by hurricane-force winds that preceded the great wave.

Then the monster wave engulfed the coastal towns and surged into all the lowland valleys and plains. It was easily a thousand feet high. Fleeing herds of livestock and deer, and the family with their overloaded cart, all were swallowed up before our very eyes.

King Ockto's doomed fleet was swept back to shore with the tidal wave, tumbling helplessly in the maelstrom. Fifteen thousand Elves were being jettisoned to Hades at that very moment, and heartless as it sounds, all I could think about was that I could have been on one of those ships.

Maumseachtain was the first outpost of Fintan's Highlands to be struck by the wave, and the mountain was shaken to its core. The crumbling cliff in Scucca Pass collapsed and the pass was permanently blocked. The juggernaut wave inundated the network of caves that riddled the mountain, and the structural integrity of Maumseachtain was fatally compromised.

The tide surged inland, its unrelenting progress mitigated only when blocked or diverted by high ground. The imposing Elven fortress of Dún Aengus, atop a thousand-foot escarpment, was split in two when part of the cliff collapsed and crushed the prosperous seaport nestled at its base.

The Refuge was spared because of its altitude and the blockading mountains. The floodwaters rushed up the Kylemore River, causing the current to flow backward and the lake to spill over its boundaries, but the Refuge was saved from this secondary destruction by the high stone wall surrounding it.

Further south and east, the wave raced unhindered through the central valley that was named after Gaodhal Glas. As the Atlantic Ocean rushed in to divide Fintan's Highlands from the Peleg Hills, billions of trees were uprooted and entombed in mud. The water was blocked at the northern tip of Gaodhal Valley by the Giants Step, an escarpment of basalt pillars which withstood the destructive wave and ultimately became a land bridge connecting the two halves of Danaan Land. This geological upthrust was later renamed the Giants Causeway. Danaan Land was split into two sections that closely resembled the Ireland and Great Britain I was familiar with in the future.

The midlands of Fintan's Highlands suffered a

similar fate, although the trees there were not buried, due to the hills that strained out the mud and debris of Atlantis. The felled trees were piled high and left to decompose in a shallow lake, and this was the beginning of Ireland's central boglands.

The coastline was rearranged. Lowlands were flooded and became the new Continental Shelf. Mountains became islands. Rivers were rerouted and eventually eroded new channels for themselves. Many towns and villages buried in the disaster would later be relocated and rebuilt by survivors, and named in honor of their lost hometowns.

The great continent of Atlantis was obliterated and its rubble was blasted skyward or washed onto foreign shores. The bulk of the debris was deposited on the floor of the Atlantic Ocean, which raised the sea level around the globe an average of two hundred feet. All along the coasts of Europe, Africa, and North and South America—river mouths, harbors, and shipping lanes were rendered impassable by the detritus of Atlantis.

Fishermen were prohibited from venturing far from land because of trolling sea monsters that had been churned up from the ocean floor. Sailors were afraid to challenge open waters because the ocean continued to roil and eddy for many months as a whole continent subsided into its sub-marine crypt. Fears developed into superstition. Rumors spread that the world dropped off into nothingness over the horizon. Nothing but death and destruction awaited the foolhardy seafarer.

The Atlantic Ocean became a vast graveyard in one day and night of earthquakes and explosions, when millions of Atlanteans were overtaken by their preappointed watery doom. No right-minded citizen of the world would tread over the gravesite of the gods, and thus the central Atlantic was shunned for more than a millennium. Global travel and trade were impossible for decades, so people on the various continents were isolated from one another and gradually forgot about each other's existence.

The wave hit Maumturk so hard that the mountain shuddered and we were knocked off our feet. Farra took flight, screeching in terror. The crest of the wave struck just below our vantage point and we were washed about in a violent pool that swirled over the lip of the meadow and tried to drag us off our perch. Mud and fish and a flopping, snapping shark, plus seaweed and rocks and pieces of ships were flung all over us. We had difficulty standing up in the knee-deep water.

The wave didn't turn and flow back to sea immediately; it kept forcing its way inland. The entire Atlantic Ocean was trying to relocate, being pushed to its farthest reaches by the sinking of a continent. The water churned and eddied, eating into the mountainside; and we could feel the meadow floor shifting beneath us. Cathal grabbed my arm and we half crawled, half stumbled out of the meadow, which was crumbling and separating from the bulk of the mountain. Wide rifts appeared in the distressed soil and we leaped over them to reach stable ground.

A harrowing, gurgling, sucking noise accompanied the wave when it eventually rushed back out to sea again, dragging trees, hills, and whole villages with it.

As the water withdrew from the labyrinth of caverns inside Maumseachtain, it sucked tons of rock with it. Then the peak caved in and the upper portion of the mountain collapsed. The hanging valley and the Notch were erased. The mountain was hewn in half, and its wreckage raised the level of the plains at its base.

Cathal and I watched impotently as the entire valley below us was buried under four hundred feet of mud, splintered forests, and the fragments of a destroyed civilization. There was no more Tubber, no more Leenaun, and no more Killary Inlet. The landscape had been changed utterly, forever.

And far out at sea, another wave was building.

With Cathal supporting me, we turned away from all we had not wanted to witness, and headed further inland. We hit upon a trail that led east and followed it with as much speed as I could muster. All that running, leaping, and scrambling had caused my leg wound to split open, and the pain was tremendous, yet it is astonishing how the instinct for self-preservation can demote formally vital aspects of one's life to second place. I skip-hopped beside Cathal until we were safe, and then sank to the ground in agony. Cathal urged me to get up and keep going. I leaned on him and he half dragged me.

The sky darkened. The apocalyptic cloud from afar had finally made landfall, and ash and pumice fell around us. The air was thick and difficult to breath. The strong smell of sulphur burned our throats. We tore cloth from our cloaks and fashioned bandanas to cover our nostrils and mouths. The sun glowed red behind the grey and brown sky. Every creature blessed with locomotion was fleeing from the coast in a desperate, dumb rush; the rabbit bounding next to the wolf, temporarily united in fleeing from this mutual enemy.

A short time later we ran across Cathal's men, who had caught and held our horse and had agreed to wait for us on the road as long as there was a chance of our survival.

Cathal mounted the horse and I was lifted up behind him, and we turned our faces to the east. Our surroundings complemented my surreal, fever-induced hallucinations. The only thing that kept me going was Cathal's anchoring presence. I clung to him like a limpet, and when I ultimately passed out, he tied me to him.

Chapter 44

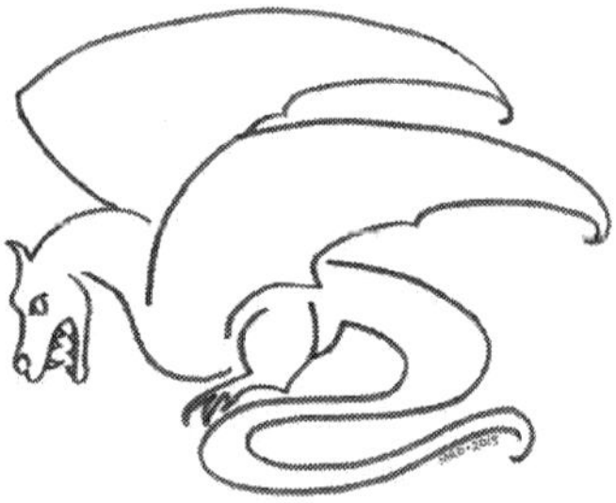

At the other side of Maumturk we were greeted by a wide, muddy lake where once the crossroads town of Pella had been the central hub of a large area of farmland. Because of my illness and the lateness of the day, Cathal decided to board at an inn in the foothills.

The inn was teeming with refugees and their baggage. We arrived in the middle of a riot over food and berths. The appearance of the High King's famous general and six soldiers on horseback made quite an impression on the unruly mob. The aggression dissipated and the people turned to Cathal for leadership. The innkeeper pleaded with him to solve the dispute over limited lodgings. There wasn't enough food to feed the refugees and the inn only had ten beds. Our arrival bumped the number of guests up to ninety-eight, not including the innkeeper and his wife and three sons. Nobody recognized me as the flaming-haired beauty on the dragon, because I was a far cry from *that* Ashling. I was bedraggled, bleary, incoherent, and plastered with ashes.

"First things first," said Cathal. "I must get medical attention for my injured friend."

Many eager hands lifted me off the horse and I was carried inside. Cathal hopped up onto a stone wall and spoke to the gathering.

"Fellow Humans," he began. "We have just lived through a calamitous disaster. Our homes have been swept away. The very heavens are set against us. Yet we have survived. We have been chosen to carry on for those who have died. I, for one, am determined to elevate the race of Adam by my actions in these dark days. We each have unique talents and skills which have been ordained since the Beginning to be brought to such a time and place as we find ourselves in now.

"Many of you are freshly arrived from the Battle of Moytura. I see many familiar faces. As you know, our race has succeeded in defeating the God People and the Giants. We have banished our enemies and reclaimed our beloved Island of Destiny." Raucous cheers greeted this statement. Cathal's voice sobered. "However, we did not win because of our strength, or overwhelming numbers, or skill at arms. We won because of superior wit, excellent timing, and the fulfillment of an ancient prophecy."

The crowd fell silent, desperate for hope and clinging to every word. He paused and searched the devastated faces. "Children of Adam, rejoice! The age of the gods has ended!" The people roared their approval. "What our Heavenly Father sought to destroy during the Great Deluge of Sixteen Forty-Six has finally come to pass. The inheritance of Humans has once again come full circle." Cathal's voice brimmed with confidence. "Now, let us show them all what we are made of."

I wasn't conscious for that rousing speech, but the words were set to music and are still sung around the campfires and hearths of our people to this day.

Cathal established priorities for our little band: care for the injured, erect shelters, ration the food, corral and protect the livestock, form hunting parties, gather information, list our assets, and begin building a boat.

I was given a bed indoors with the injured and the elderly. It was my great fortune that one of the refugees was a shepherdess from the region who knew a lot about doctoring animals. She knew right away what was needed to reduce my fever and heal my leg. The process hurt so much that I'd rather not talk about it. Suffice it to say that the shepherdess squeezed out all the infection and doused my wolf bites with whiskey, although I don't remember anything past the first cut and my last scream. Cathal and five other men had to hold me down until I fainted and stopped struggling. The innkeeper's wife told me that Cathal continued to hold me in his arms long after the surgery was over and my fever had broken. Then our good hostess insisted that he go to the barn and get some sleep or else he would be no good to anyone.

Chapter 45

Cathal sent hunters and scouts in all directions to find food, look for survivors, and map out the traversable ground. Only two days after the tidal waves, our group had built a flat-bottomed boat to navigate the floodwaters. Two soldiers and two civilians rafted off with orders to find a way to Cong, report to King Iarann, and get information from other parts of the country. Cathal's men tried to convince him that he should report to Iarann in person, but he refused to leave my side.

The tremors stopped twenty-four hours after the first major terrashake. Soot and ashes fell even more thickly, and birds dropped dead from the sky in distressing numbers. Children were muffled against the foul air and sent out to gather the suffocated birds, and our group processed and preserved the meat to stave off the starving time that was sure to come.

The only clean water came from a well, and Cathal built a roof and walls around it to keep out the cloying, clogging ash.

After five days, when the sky failed to clear and

days blurred into nights, indistinguishable from one another, a niggling memory worked its way to the forefront of my thoughts. I immediately sent for Cathal.

I was sitting up in bed in the room I shared with seven elderly women, and Cathal's entrance was greeted with giggles and winks. He looked great in his new outfit, which he had somehow found time to clean. I wondered for the second time why he was suddenly interested in his appearance.

I asked the women to give us a few minutes alone. After they had gone, Cathal closed the door and sat on a bed opposite mine.

"Don't you look fashionable?" I teased.

He plucked at his clothing self-consciously. "Appearance counts when you are a leader," he said. "I decided to clean my uniform since I represent the High King while I'm wearing it."

"Oh, it's your uniform!" I said. "I was wondering who was dressing you."

Cathal grinned ruefully. "Imagine my dismay when I learned there's a dress code in the king's army. No more fashion violations for me!"

"Thank God for that," I joked, pretending great relief.

"You can thank him yourself," he replied. "You're going to meet him in person."

"Who? God?"

"No—King Iarann," he said, laughing at my confusion. "A boat has arrived from Cong with a message for us to join the King's Counsel as soon as you are ready for travel." He was clearly proud and excited at being invited.

"Good," I responded soberly, "because I just

remembered something I once read. Tree ring samples from around the world recorded a serious climate disaster that occurred more than three thousand years before my time. There was a long period of no summer growth and failed harvests. Experts surmised there may have been little or no sunlight during that period. They guessed that a volcano erupted and dust covered the sun. It was probably caused by the destruction of Atlantis."

"Right," agreed Cathal, wondering where I was going with this.

"The scary thing is it lasted for *eighteen years*! No sunlight for almost two decades! All the crops failed and famine spread throughout the land. Cathal, we have to prepare the people to leave this country and emigrate farther south until it's safe to return."

He didn't answer right away, but looked at me with a troubled expression. "Is that what is written?" he asked finally. "Or is it just your worry about going hungry?"

"Hey! Why would I lie to you?"

"You've lied before," he answered, and my stubborn pride caved in. There we were, on the brink of extinction, and my habit of telling lies to survive threatened to spell the end of everyone I cared about.

"Okay, I admit I haven't always been truthful. I had to be careful about trusting strangers. But I have no more need for lies. The truth is already too fantastic to be believed."

He watched me steadfastly without speaking; judging me, it seemed. I was desperate for him to believe me, yet I knew I had a long row to hoe before I would regain his trust. I vowed I would weave no webs of deceit before this man ever again. His trust was too valuable to me.

"The only reason I remember this particular piece of information is *because* of my fear of going hungry. When I read about the famine I was horrified at the thought of all those people starving to death."

Cathal nodded, accepting this fact, and I continued to persuade him.

"My food fetish will stand us in good stead in preparing for what is to come. I know a lot about different methods of food preservation and long-term storage."

"What else did you read about our people after the disaster?"

"They were forced to flee southward. They wandered the Mediterranean for thirty years and returned under their new leader, Milidh."

At the mention of this name, Cathal's head jerked up and his eyes widened in recognition. He looked at me with astonishment, then got to his feet.

"I've heard that name," he said, and it was my turn to be surprised. "King Iarann's youngest son is that man. And one I would follow through the seven gates of Hades."

He strode to the door and I called out, "Wait! Where are you going?"

He turned and smiled, and his dimple danced. "I have to pack for a journey," he said.

"The people must start preserving food immediately," I advised. "We will have no more vegetables or fruit, and pretty soon the livestock will begin to starve for want of grass. The hay and animal feed will have to be rationed. Also, we need to build water filters out of charcoal. I can show you how."

"Something else Professor Carlyle taught you?" he asked.

"No. Something I learned from the Travelling People—my people."

"It would appear that we are soon to become Travelling People," he mused.

"And I will have come full circle." This revelation stirred my soul. I had wasted my life striving to distance myself from the stigma of being a Traveller, only to discover how integral that connection was to my sense of identity. I had adopted the *settled community's* shame, which was theirs alone to bear, and I had become lost and rootless. Now, for the first time since childhood, I experienced the security of belonging.

Cathal sat back down—on my bed this time. Something was troubling him.

"Look, I know your greatest desire is to return home to your people, and I want you to know it's my goal too. I'll get you home, come Hell or high water. This little disaster is taking up a lot of my time, but..." My laughter stopped him.

"'Little' disaster indeed!" I chortled.

"I've been thinking. What if you were to fly into the Dragon Wind on Farra's back—"

"I've been thinking a lot about home, too," I interrupted. Inexplicably, after fighting my attraction to Cathal for so long, I simply surrendered to it. I longed to see his dimple dance again, just for me.

Cathal's spirit was quenched. He looked away to hide his pain, and pretended interest in tracing the bright patterns on the quilt. "Oh. You have?" he asked in a desultory fashion. Then, feigning cheerfulness, he added, "Well, good!"

"It's not far away, after all," I told him.

He turned to scrutinize my expression. "You'll be leaving soon, then?"

"There's no need."

Hope battled realism on his countenance, but he said nothing.

I smiled into his eyes. "Home is where the heart is—" I said softly, splaying my fingers across his chest, "—and mine is right here."

Cathal's initial disbelief was chased away by sheer joy, and I laughed to see his emotions so unguarded. He took me into his massive arms and hugged me fiercely. Amazingly, that familiar claustrophobic fear was absent. Instead of panicking and struggling, I relaxed, and trusted, and melted into him. I buried my face in the curve of his muscular neck and smiled happily.

All this time I had been looking for a way to return home, and all this time 'home' was right where I had found it. It took a good man and the unconditional love of a group of elderly women to show me.

Chapter 46

As soon as I was well enough, I traveled with Cathal to Cong and gave counsel to the king, but I was impatient to learn the fate of my dear friends at the Refuge. I bid Cathal adieu on the edge of the forest, near the place we had camped prior to sparking that infectious uprising in Cong. Then I hiked and climbed through the mountains to the Kylemore Valley, accompanied by a small retinue of soldiers.

Our reunion was filled with all the emotion I had wrongly held in check in the past. All my life I had fought for myself alone, and had remained alone because of it. So much time and energy had been consumed blaming others and striving to reach the top of the heap just so I could prove to everyone that I didn't need anyone. But we were created to need one another, and so long as I denied myself this basic truth, my life had been incomplete.

I was a changed person and would not let the sun go down each day without letting my loved ones know how dear they were to me.

Several of the ladies had passed away prior to my

return. Maddy and Kitti had died of pulmonary failure due to the bad air, and one other had succumbed to old age and infirmity. I grieved deeply and violently for them; a rebound effect of having suppressed my love for so long.

Niall of the Boats was there, as was the surviving group of warriors from Tubber and Cong who had fought the Giants in Scucca Pass. Many had brought their families with them to escape the tidal waves. All were hale and hearty, and were crazed for news of the outside world.

I stayed with them long enough to inform them of the coming evacuation and to tell them how to prepare. Then the young men and women took axes and shovels, and together we blazed a trail through the wilderness to Cong.

Thousands of Humans and Elves in Danaan Land lost their lives when Atlantis sank beneath the waves, but many more Humans got to high ground and were saved thanks to my early warning. However, untold numbers succumbed to the poisoned air and polluted water in the months following the disaster. Carcasses bobbed on the floodwaters and diseases raged unabated. The widespread failure of crops produced a famine that would have finished us off had the High King not ordered that food be stockpiled. A mass-scale evacuation was organized before we became too weak to flee. We built wagons and wheeled conveyances in the interim. It was tough going for many months, but we eventually set out from Fintan's Highlands with a large remnant of Partholon's Colony.

Chapter 47

The rest is history. In the overall account of civilizations and nations, the lives of ordinary individuals do not feature prominently, and so I will shelve the stories of the individual players in order to recount the drama of our people as a nation.

We set out across the Giants Causeway to the Albany Hills—the future Scotland. Then we headed south to the Peleg Hills, the area that would someday be known as England. There we set up camp on the shore while we built barges to ferry us and our livestock and wagons across the channel separating us from the continent.

Our crossing was not uneventful. The rumors of sea monsters were discovered to be true to the word and letter. Our losses were minimal, however, because of the large body of fighting men and women with us.

Our pilgrimage took several years and we encountered many adventures along the way. We lost some of our group through natural attrition, but others were born to us and our numbers increased.

Bróna and the other women from the Refuge set

up a mobile school and passed on much of the knowledge and skills that were the privilege of Humans prior to the Lucifer Laws. We formed a tightknit military cadre, and every able-bodied adult was required to contribute to the defense of the group.

We trekked across what would one day be known as France and Spain, and eventually reached the warm Mediterranean. The inland sea was clear and blue and fragrant, and we knew we had finally reached a safe haven. The Jet Stream did not flow this far south, so the ashes and smoke circling the globe did not pollute this latitude.

The mud and debris of Atlantis plugged the entrance to the Mediterranean at the Pillars of Heracles (later renamed the Straits of Gibraltar) and no shipping could enter or leave for four years thereafter. Trade suffered, and the nations of the region grew hungry and restless, and waged wars upon one another to fill their larders and alleviate their boredom; but for the first time in millennia, Humans were forced to rely upon their own strength and skills, for the gods were chained up in the Underworld and no longer influenced the affairs of man. In the world of the living, dynasties fell, crowns changed hands, and new allegiances were forged in the absence of supernatural sponsorship. Humans also had to contend with the many sea monsters that had been disturbed from the depths of the Atlantic and washed into the Mediterranean before the Pillars of Heracles were sealed.

Our group, however, stuck to the land. We traveled by horseback and wagon, and roved like gypsies for many years, hiring ourselves out as mercenaries to the highest bidder. We amassed a small fortune as the outcome of our adventures. For thirty years, we explored the sunny Mediterranean, until King Iarann's crown was passed to his youngest son, Milidh.

King Milidh was possessed of an unquenchable yearning for the green grass of home, and so it was that we outfitted a fleet of ships and followed our hearts to the west—to our beloved Island of Destiny. The sea level had risen two hundred feet or more, and Fintan's Highlands—being elevated above the surrounding plains—was all that was left of our former home.

When we attempted to land, we were set upon by a force of Tuatha Dé Danaan who had sworn revenge for their defeat and humiliation on the Moytura Plain. Five of the sons of Milidh were killed in the Battle of Taillte on the Plains of Meath, although we were ultimately victorious. The surviving God People fled to the remote hills and took to living in caves and skulking at night to avoid contact with Humans. Many legends sprang up concerning them; wild rumors and superstitions about enchanted fairy folk living under the Irish hills.

We renamed our new home after Milidh's son, Ir, who accounted for himself famously and lost his life during the Battle of Taillte.

News filtered to us in bits and pieces that the Fomorian isles had been destroyed along with Atlantis. A few Giants survived; members of a raiding party who were out ravaging North American villages at the time of the cataclysm. Their depredations on that continent continued for some time, and encounters with the Giants worked their way into native lore. The palms-up greeting was adopted by Native Americans as a method of determining whether a stranger was friend or foe—five fingers were safe, six fingers meant death.

None escaped through the portals atop Mount

Olympus, because the massive eruptions caused a shift in the Earth's axis, which disturbed the planet's electromagnetic field and disrupted the quantum properties necessary for dimension traversal. The forcefield slowly realigned over time, and the portals reappeared in the sky above the spot where Mount Olympus used to be. That mysterious zone would someday be labeled the Bermuda Triangle.

Remnants of the angelic races did manage to survive the destruction of Atlantis. The offspring of the Uncommitted Angels continued a limited interaction with Humans. As successive generations of interbreeding thinned their Angel DNA, they were less inclined to hate Humans. Legends sprang up around many of them. They were the heroes of mythology, the demigods of renown. Fionn MacCumhail, Cuchulainn, Hercules, Perseus, Thor, and Achilles are some that come to mind.

Lucifer's Rebel Angels were darkly cursed and unable to sire anything of beauty or grace. Fortunately, most of the hybrids spawned by Lucifer and his ilk—giants, goblins, grendels, trolls, etc.—were sterile and their lines died out. As a child, I was exposed to those terrifying creatures in fairytale books, and my subsequent nightmares were no doubt fueled by deeply embedded racial memories. Having witnessed in person the scourge of Fallen Angels and their horrifying offspring, I praise God for the mass extinction that caused future generations of Humans to be blithely ignorant of a very real chapter in our history.

Cathal is outfitting an expedition to North America as I write this account. I have heard rumors that my friend Séú is part of an Elven colony that settled in the Nova Scotia region, and we shall attempt to find her.

We no longer wish to remain in Ir Land. The three surviving sons of Milidh are currently fighting tooth and nail with one another, because their wives quarreled about which of them should rule the most pleasant part of the country. Without a common enemy to unite us, we have fallen to bickering and fighting with one another. After all we have been through as a people, it sickens me to see how quickly our young ones have lost sight of the big picture.

Before we set sail, Cathal and I agreed that we should leave a written record of our adventures for posterity, for it is not likely that we shall return.

ASHLING

by MARY MACK™

ISBN-13: 978-0692761168
ISBN-10: 0692761160

About the Author

Photo by Martin Dunne

MARY MACK is a screenwriter, historian, editor, graphic designer, and homeschool teacher. She was born on a U.S. Air Force Base in England, spent her childhood in County Clare, Ireland, and currently lives and dreams in California's High Desert.

Mary has a career background in journalism, editing, desktop publishing, and computer graphics. Professional memberships include the International Screenwriters Association and the California Writers Club.

This novel is adapted from a feature film script which won Best Fantasy Screenplay in the 2015 Table Read My Screenplay Contest, out of nearly 1,000 entries worldwide.

72359351R00181

Made in the USA
Columbia, SC
16 June 2017

CL903932